W9-BRG-472

BISON
BOOKS

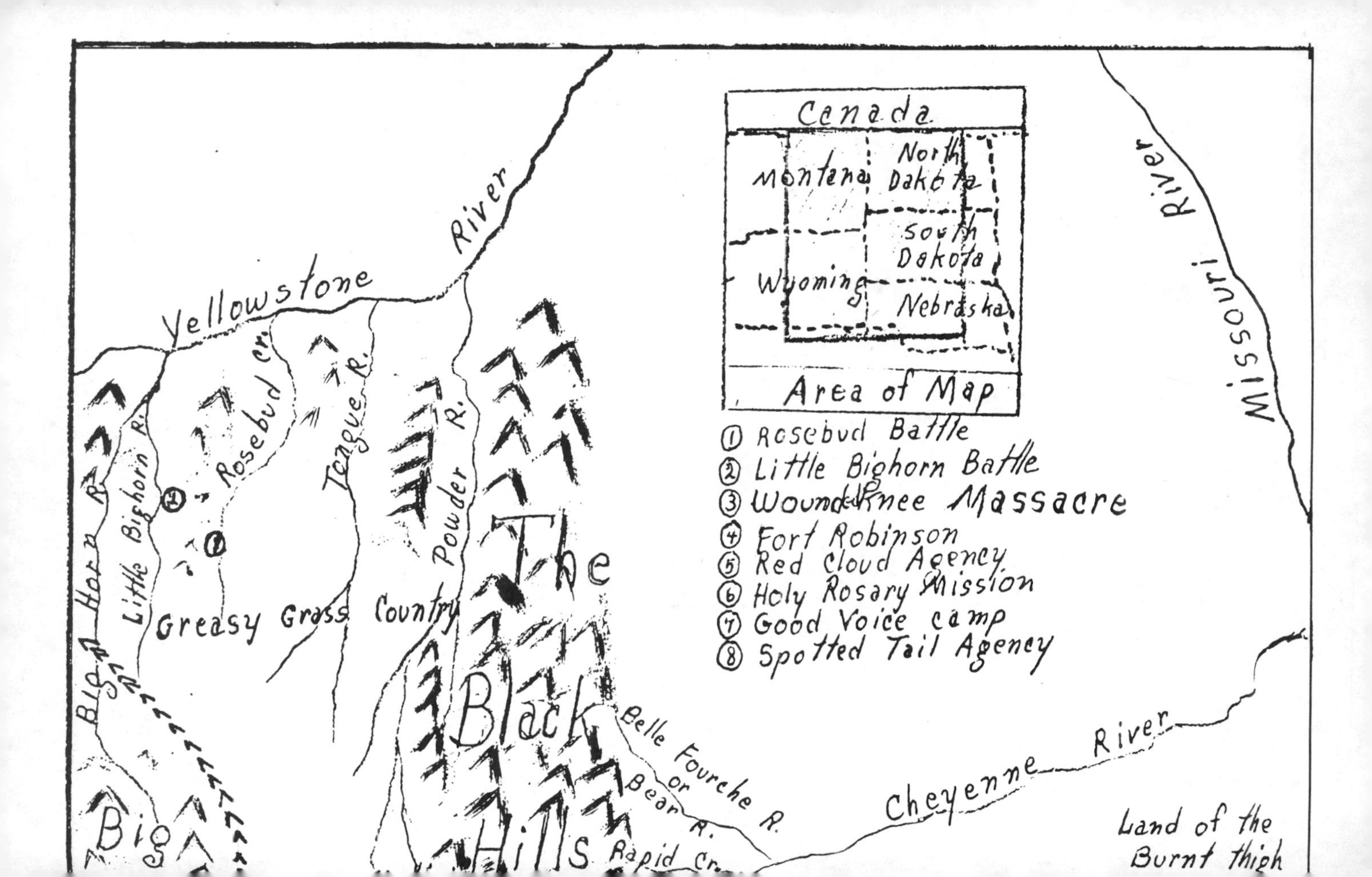

Yellowstone River
Missouri River
Canada
Montana
North Dakota
South Dakota
Wyoming
Nebraska
Area of Map
① Rosebud Battle
② Little Bighorn Battle
③ Wounded Knee Massacre
④ Fort Robinson
⑤ Red Cloud Agency
⑥ Holy Rosary Mission
⑦ Good Voice camp
⑧ Spotted Tail Agency
Big Horn R.
Little Bighorn R.
Rosebud Cr.
Tongue R.
Powder R.
Greasy Grass Country
The Black Hills
Belle Fourche R. or Bear R.
Rapid Cr.
Cheyenne River
Land of the Burnt thigh
Big

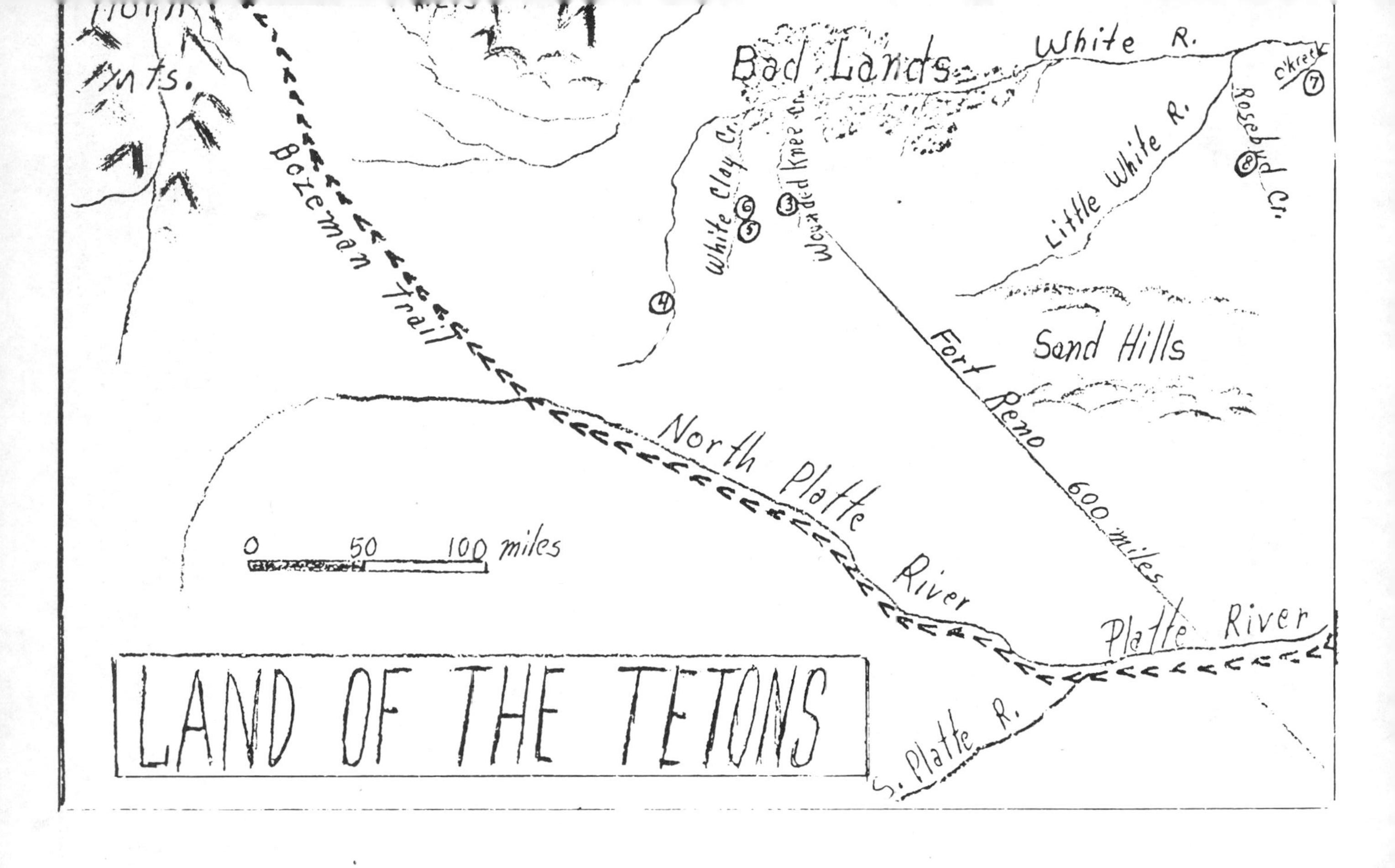

Mts.
Bozeman Trail
Bad Lands
White R.
O'kreek
7
White Clay Cr.
6
5
Wounded Knee Cr.
3
Little White R.
Rosebud Cr.
8
4
Sand Hills
Fort Reno 600 miles
North Platte River
Platte River
S. Platte R.
0 50 100 miles
LAND OF THE TETONS

Winter Count

Dallas Chief Eagle

INTRODUCTION TO THE BISON BOOKS EDITION BY

Chadwick Allen

UNIVERSITY OF NEBRASKA PRESS
LINCOLN AND LONDON

Manufactured in the United States of America

♾

First Nebraska paperback printing: 2003

Library of Congress Cataloging-in-Publication Data
Chief Eagle, D., 1925–
Winter count / by Dallas Chief Eagle; introduction to the Bison books edition by Chadwick Allen.
p. cm.
ISBN 0-8032-6432-1 (pbk.: alk. paper)
1. Teton Indians—Fiction. 2. Women pioneers—Fiction.
3. Indian captivities—Fiction. I. Title.
PS3553.H4755W56 2003
813′.54—dc21
2002043035

CHADWICK ALLEN

Introduction to the Bison Books Edition

His Heritage on Paper

In an Indian tent he was born.
In a crowded school he was alone.
In a modern world his legs would bend.
Only on canvas and paper he lives his heritage.
—Dallas Chief Eagle

It is now common practice in the fields of American Indian studies and American ethnic studies to refer to the late 1960s and the 1970s as a period of American Indian political and literary "renaissance." Indian activism gained significant media attention as early as 1964, when the National Indian Youth Council supported the fishing rights demonstrations of the Puyallup-Nisqually peoples and other Indian nations in the Pacific Northwest, and when a group of Sioux men living in San Francisco's Bay Area briefly occupied Alcatraz Island and claimed it as Indian land under provisions of the 1868 Treaty of Fort Laramie signed by the Sioux and Arapahos. By the early 1970s Indian activism was a pressing national concern. The urban-based American Indian Movement (AIM), which had formed in Minnesota in 1968, supported a second occupation of Alcatraz Island by the pan-tribal activist group Indians of All Tribes from 20 November 1969 until 11 June 1971. In 1972 AIM participated in The Trail of Broken Treaties, a cross-country caravan of activists who subsequently occupied the Bureau of Indian Affairs offices in Washington DC; and in 1973 AIM became involved in the occupation and armed standoff with local and federal forces at Wounded Knee, South Dakota, the event that has come to epitomize contemporary Indian activism.

On the literary front, 1964 saw the formation of the American Indian Historical Society and the launching of its journal, the *Indian Historian*, which developed into a substantial quarterly in 1967 and which, for the first time, made available to a broader public a distinctively Native perspective on American Indian history. Similarly, 1968 saw the emergence of the first national American Indian newspaper, *Akwesasne Notes*, published by the Mohawk Nation, which offered Native perspectives on current events. That year also saw the publication of *House Made of Dawn*, a powerful and aesthetically sophisticated novel by N. Scott Momaday (Kiowa) about an Indian veteran's difficult return to his pueblo home from World War II combat. Momaday's novel was awarded the Pulitzer Prize in 1969, the same year that Vine Deloria Jr. (Sioux) published *Custer Died for Your Sins: An Indian Manifesto*, the first in his series of humorous but hard-hitting critiques of federal Indian policies, of the work of anthropologists and missionaries, and of the dominant U.S. culture's on-again, off-again interest in Indians. Although a number of American Indians had published prior to the mid and late 1960s, these successes drew unprecedented popular and critical attention to Native writing and paved the way for other emerging Indian historians, journalists, creative writers, and social commentators.

Winter Count by Dallas Chief Eagle (Sioux) was written at the beginning of this time of so-called renaissance. First published in 1967, the novel has been out of print since 1968. Its unavailability has meant that it has fallen into relative obscurity within the expanding American Indian literary canon and that it has received little critical attention from scholars.[1] But *Winter Count* deserves the interest of readers and critics alike. It is one of a small number of novel-length works of fiction produced by an American Indian writer before the 1970s. And, unlike the numerous Indian works produced during the 1960s, 1970s, and early 1980s, most of which are set in contemporary times, *Winter Count* is a historical novel. Chief Eagle set his story during the fifteen turbulent years that preceded the infamous massacre of Sioux men, women, and children at Wounded Knee Creek in South Dakota on 29 December 1890. He thus re-imagines events that the dominant U.S. culture has preferred to forget or misremember and that many Sioux and other Indians continue to experience as profoundly painful: escalating conflicts with the U.S. cavalry, the negotiation and subsequent breaking of important treaties, the formation of the Sioux reservations, the difficult transition to reservation life, and the suppression of the Ghost Dance.

Moreover, Chief Eagle's account of those often violent years at the end of the nineteenth century is all the more compelling when placed in the context of its production in the mid 1960s. Although it is a historical novel, *Winter Count* is very much an artifact of the times in which it was written and first read. Chief Eagle's activism can be seen in his insistence on articulating a Native perspective on important events of American Indian history and of American history, even when that perspective is controversial. In an interview in the early 1970s, for instance, Chief Eagle reported that an eastern publishing house refused to bring his novel into print unless he agreed to alter his unflattering depiction of the 1876 death of General George Armstrong Custer at the Battle of the Little Bighorn. Following a Sioux account, Chief Eagle's characters argue that rather than fall bravely at the hands of an Indian combatant, "Yellow Hair" actually took his own life and thus died disgracefully. Chief Eagle was unwilling to revise his novel to make it more palatable to mainstream readers. Instead he retained the implication that Custer committed suicide and published *Winter Count* through a small company based in Colorado, with full understanding that pursuing that route would limit the size of his potential audience.[2] Furthermore, Chief Eagle prefaces his novel with a formal introduction in which he reviews the history of the "peace" treaties the Sioux signed in good faith in 1825, 1851, and 1868—only to see each successively violated by the U.S. government, the cavalry, and white settlers. Throughout the novel Chief Eagle maintains a consistent focus on this discrepancy in honor.

Chief Eagle's literary accomplishment can be seen in his grappling with the difficult question of how best to represent the American Indian past so that it will remain relevant to the American Indian present and to possible American Indian futures. In other words, he specifically addresses the needs of Sioux and broader pan-tribal audiences. His prose style, for instance, is restrained and carefully mimetic, especially when describing aspects of Sioux spirituality such as the Sun Dance or the vision quest. There is no sensationalism here, nor any pandering to audiences interested in Native mysticism or an exotic Other. Similarly, while his narrative tactics are largely inconspicuous, they are nonetheless innovative in their foregrounding of the textual artifacts of Indian historical memory. These include both written treaty documents that record the solemn promises made to the Sioux and their allies by the U.S. government "in perpetuity," and, as indicated by the novel's title, Plains Indian "winter counts," the pictographic calendars traditionally drawn on tanned buffalo, elk, or deer hides. Each year or "winter" is recorded on these remarkable calendars as a symbol that represents a significant event in the life of the community. Band historians used the calendars to supplement their memories of the oral tradition, and some extant Sioux calendars depict more than three hundred years of tribal history. Chief Eagle employs two types of traditional winter counts in his plot: a communal calendar kept on behalf of the entire band as an ongoing record of their collective history, and a personal calendar created first as an ongoing biography of the novel's protagonist, Turtleheart, and then continued by Turtleheart himself as an ongoing autobiography. Finally, although his techniques are often subtle, Chief Eagle articulates in his novel some contemporary arguments for American Indian cultural and political sovereignty. The prominent role Chief Eagle gives to his protagonist's personal winter count, in particular, invites a politically charged reading.

Chief Eagle, a Lakota born on the Rosebud Reservation in South Dakota in 1925, does not fit the popular image of the young, urban American Indian activist or writer who gained national attention in the 1960s and 1970s. Orphaned as a child, he was raised on the reservation by Lakota elders who did not teach him to speak English; he did not learn his second language until he began to attend mission schools. During World War II he served in the U.S. Marine Corps. After the war Chief Eagle returned home to finish high school and then attended several institutions of higher education in Chicago, Oklahoma, and Idaho, all the while working as a laborer. It was while he was working in a steel mill, already a man in his late thirties, that he began to write—and rewrite—*Winter Count*. His goal, as he stated in a 1973 interview, was to "write a book about the Sioux that would be culturally authentic and as historically accurate as he could make it."[3]

About the time *Winter Count* was published in 1967, Chief Eagle returned to South Dakota in order to help his people build a better future. He was made an honorary chief of the Teton (Western) Sioux through a special ceremony, and was thus entrusted with the spiritual role of unifying the diverse bands of the Tetons for common purpose. In the mid and late 1970s Chief Eagle worked as director of tourism for the Development Corporation of the United Sioux Tribes of South Dakota, and was involved in the Community Action Program, a development organization, for the Rosebud Sioux Tribe. Although he did not identify himself as an activist during this period, as a "traditionalist" and a veteran he supported Indian activism and viewed its ideals as a contemporary manifestation of the Sioux's warrior past. He visited Alcatraz Island during its second occupation, and welcomed members of AIM onto the reservation and offered them counsel when other Sioux leaders shunned these young men and women as "radicals." In addition Chief Eagle expressed his political activism by lecturing on college campuses about contemporary Indian issues and by campaigning for economic development on the reservations.

Chief Eagle was an accomplished painter as well as a writer and community leader. In the mid 1970s he also served as an interpreter and as a cultural consultant for the writer Thomas Mails as Mails researched his biography of the Lakota spiritual and civic leader Frank Fools Crow.[4] Chief Eagle died on the Rosebud Reservation in 1980.

The plot of *Winter Count* follows an accurate chronology from about 1875 until the Wounded Knee Massacre in December 1890, and the novel includes among its cast of characters well-known historical figures such as Crazy Horse, Sitting Bull, Gall, Dull Knife, and George Custer. That said, it is important to keep in mind that Chief Eagle deliberately produced a work of fiction rather than a conventional history, and that his narrative of the dispossession and subjugation of the Teton Sioux centers not on the lives of these historical figures but on the adventures and eventual destruction of the fictional warrior Turtleheart and his wife, Evensigh. Like their author these central characters are orphaned as infants and raised by the Sioux elders who adopted them. Their relationships to their families, to their band, to the Sioux Nation, and to the larger confederacies of Plains Indians are primarily cultural rather than biological. Moreover, Evensigh is not an Indian by blood, but a white woman who has become culturally Sioux through her upbringing; she is not a captive taken by force but rather an orphan rescued by a Sioux family. Her marriage to Turtleheart, which opens the novel, is an explicit argument about the power of culture to overcome racial differences and racial violence. It is also an implicit critique of dominant U.S. culture's long history of violent racism toward Indians.

Early in the novel the newlywed couple is ambushed by a

Santee Sioux working as a scout for white gold miners who have deserted the cavalry. These men brutally torture Turtleheart and kidnap Evensigh. Although Turtleheart survives and eventually rejoins his band, Evensigh, who assumes her husband is dead, submits to being sent away to live with a white family in St. Louis. Chief Eagle focuses primarily on the life of Turtleheart after this point, but employing the plot device of the separated lovers allows him to move back and forth between contemporary white and Indian worlds and to depict *both* of these worlds from a Sioux perspective.

During the four years the couple is apart Turtleheart undertakes the demanding ritual of the Sun Dance, fights alongside Crazy Horse and Sitting Bull in the Battle of the Little Bighorn, reluctantly agrees to settle on the reservation and to join the Indian police force, and pursues a personal vision through fasting and prayer. Meanwhile, Evensigh integrates into a loving white family, learns to speak and read English, and is pursued by a white suitor. She is unable to fully set aside her cultural past, however, and becomes increasingly alarmed by newspaper reports of escalating violence against Indians. Before agreeing to marry again she vows to return to the people who raised her—and to confirm that Turtleheart is in fact dead. She first visits the Cheyenne leader Gall and his people who have been incarcerated at Fort Reno, Oklahoma Territory. There she learns that Turtleheart still lives, and she makes a fateful decision to join the Cheyenne in their daring escape from prison and difficult flight north, pursued by the cavalry. Evensigh and Turtleheart eventually reunite, they live peaceably on the reservation for two years as they adjust to the labor of farming and to the imposition of Christianity, and they produce a son.

Chief Eagle does not end his novel with these scenes of Indian accommodation and adjustment. Instead, in the final pages he asks readers to bear witness as his model interracial couple is killed during the massacre at Wounded Knee. Their unprovoked murders can be read as a metaphor for the failure of the U.S. government to live up to its specific treaty promises to the Sioux, as well as a metaphor for the larger significance of this massacre—physical and symbolic—for all American Indian peoples.

Turtleheart and Evensigh's infant child, Little Sun, survives the massacre unharmed, and the novel's tone suggests that its author and his generation are descendants (figuratively, if not literally) of this mixed-blood survivor. Strikingly, Chief Eagle constructs the scene of Little Sun's survival so that Turtleheart, already shot and bleeding to death, takes his personal winter count, which is a combination biography and autobiography of his life as a Sioux, and forms it into a shield for Little Sun against the raging winter storm. Turtleheart is able to walk to the Christian mission and hand his son to the priest there before dying in the snow. The priest interprets this final act as a conversion to Christianity, but the detail that Little Sun has been wrapped in his father's winter count offers the possibility of other readings. Despite tragic loss and despite perhaps irreversible material and cultural changes, Turtleheart's Sioux memory, represented by the personal winter count, has been preserved and passed on to future Sioux generations. That Chief Eagle's novel exists at all suggests the fact of survival, and his historical narrative continues the tradition of Sioux winter counts by translating their pictographic form into the conventions of contemporary written literature. It is a survival and a literary accomplishment well worth our attention.

NOTES

I would like to thank Dallas Chief Eagle Jr. for supporting the republication of *Winter Count* and for providing biographical information about his father.

1. An exception is Charles R. Larson, who includes Chief Eagle's novel in his early study, *American Indian Fiction* (Albuquerque: University of New Mexico Press, 1978).

2. Larson, *American Indian Fiction*, 3. *Winter Count* was published in 1967 by the Dentan-Berkeland Printing Company, based in Colorado Springs. It was reprinted in 1968 by the Golden Bell Press in Denver, and by the Johnson Publishing Company in Boulder.

3. Brad Steiger, *Medicine Talk: A Guide to Walking in Balance and Surviving on the Earth Mother* (New York: Doubleday, 1975), 110.

4. Thomas E. Mails assisted by Dallas Chief Eagle, *Fools Crow* (Lincoln: University of Nebraska Press, 1979).

DEDICATED TO THE INDIANS

OF NORTH AMERICA

AND THEIR LEADERS

ACKNOWLEDGEMENTS

In the writing of this book, I am first of all indebted to my Grandparents and elder relatives. After I was orphaned at an early age, they raised me under the Sioux culture and taught me the Sioux language. It is to the Chief Eagle, Good Voice, Night Pipe and Holy families that I owe my depth of early native American background. For assistance with needed information, I am deeply indebted to hundreds of the tribal elders whom I interviewed over the past eighteen years. These were principally from the families of Black Feather, Bear, White Face, Black Horse, Kills in Sight, Crazy Bull, Red Cloud, Sitting Bull, Hollow Horn, Two Sticks, Moose Camp and Blue Thunder. Appreciation must also be given to the Blackrobes (Jesuit Missionaries), who patiently provided vital bits of information for this book; to Will Spindler and Bob Randle, the Pine Ridge and Rosebud Reservation Agencies, the Indian Records Department and the Congressional and Military Records Offices. Approximately sixty-five percent of WINTER COUNT uses Indian thoughts and language which has been interpreted into English. It is my hope that I have not failed my people too greatly in this, the telling of their story.

— D. CHIEF EAGLE

Table of Contents

INTRODUCTION

It was about the middle of the seventeenth century when the Chippewa Indians who lived near the shores of Lake Michigan, mentioned their "enemies to the west" to the French traders. It was after these conversations that the Frenchmen took the last part of the Chippewa word for enemy and spelled it in accordance with the French language. The result of this corruption was the word "Sioux".

The French-Canadian "Nadewessioux" was itself a corruption of the Algonquin word Nadowessay, meaning snake-like ones or enemies. This name has clung to the Sioux ever since. In their own language, the Sioux call themselves the Lakota or Dakota, meaning simply "Our People".

Books dealing with the Sioux are not uniform in their terminology. Some speak of the Sioux Nation as being divided into a number of tribes, while others state that the Sioux tribe was divided into many bands. The latter version is more in accordance with the Sioux beliefs, but as shown by historical and ethnological research, such a united nation or single tribe never existed.

The main Sioux Territory was included in the Louisiana Purchase of 1803. It was the following year that the now famous Lewis and Clark Expedition established the presence of eleven main bands of the Dakota and a few associates. These were parts of three main branches; the Dakota of the north (known as the eastern Sioux by others); the Lakota of the center; and the Lakota of the west.

Altogether their territory extended from the Mississippi River on the east to the Rocky Mountains on the west. North and south it covered the area from the Canadian border down to central Kansas. An area roughly 800 miles long and 600 miles wide, it was virtually bisected by the Missouri River. United States Government figures show that this tract of land contained 191,000,000 acres with a total population of around 45,000 people.

In the book WINTER COUNT, we are concerned with the Sioux of the west who were known as the Tetonwan or simply the Teton Sioux. This segment consisted of seven bands who collectively recognized the sovreignty of the United States Government in 1825. In this peace treaty, both parties obliged themselves to keep the peace.

A new treaty in 1851 defined the following limits of the Teton Sioux territory: the Missouri River on the east, the Big Horn Mountains on the west, the Platte River to the south and the Heart River to the north. This region was 400 miles east and west and 500 miles north and south, and contained 72,000,000 acres with a population of about 35,000 Sioux.

The Teton Sioux lived a nomadic life as hunters and they needed this much land to support themselves. Prior to the advent of the white man, there roamed over their land some fifteen to twenty million buffalo, a seemingly inexhaustible source of commodities to meet the needs of the Indians. The meat was his food; the hides his clothing, bedding and tents; the bones utilized for utensils, glue and sizing. The buffalo kept the Indian strong, alert and healthy.

It was soon evident that a clash had to come between the white man and the Indian, as the whites were looking for more land and wanted the minerals buried in the soil. Roads had to be laid out and railroads built through the heart of the Sioux hunting grounds, so the white man could reach the gold fields of Montana and California.

It is little matter for surprise that in consequence of the many broken treaties, the invasion of the Indian lands and destruction of Indian property and buffalo, many white men lost their lives. The wonder is, why did the Indian use constraint instead of proceeding to extreme measures in the annihilation of the unjust transgressors who were allowed to over-run their homeland in violation of the treaties.

Unfortunately, the treaties were violated by not only single advenurers but by big groups. Even the Senate of the United States was unconcerned about treaty rights as were the many subordinate bodies. Other treaty violations resulted from the outrageous conduct of several generals of the United States Army. The South Dakota Historical Collecions, an authoritative source of accurate information, gives one example in Volume II, page 225.

"In 1855, General Harney invaded Indian lands and met the Indian Chief Little Thunder. The general kept the chief in conversation until the Federal Cavalrymen were in position to strike. Chief Little Thunder gathered from the conversation that everything was settled peacefully. Ready to leave, he wanted to shake hands with the general, but Harney refused, and told him, 'Go and fight', and Harney forthwith gave the signal to his soldiers to attack. One hundred and thirty-six Indians were killed and the entire Sioux camp was destroyed."

This incident is called the Battle of Ash Hollow. The account in the South Dakota Historical Collections continues: "Though hailed as a great victory and as additional plume in Harney's crest of fame, the

Battle of Ash Hollow was a shameful affair unworthy of American arms, and a disgrace to the officer who planned and executed it."

This same General Harney appears on the stage once more in company with four other generals. This is an act, which in its final development, brought about the tragic death of Colonel Custer's command. And with it, in revenge, was wrought the final and ruthless subjugation of a not unfriendly tribe, the whole of the Teton Sioux.

In 1868, Generals Sherman, Sanborn, Harney, Terry and Augur, with two civilians named Taylor and Tappan, met with the Sioux on the banks of the North Platte. On April 29th, they concluded and signed a treaty according to which the Indians should live on a permanent reservation. However, the Indians were granted the right to hunt on their old hunting grounds, "so long as game remains to justify the chase".

This stipulation of the treaty is contained in Article II, and the subsequent events make it noteworthy. On October 7th of that year, the commissioners met in Chicago, and despite the vigorous objections of the two civilians, Taylor and Tappan, the five generals voted unanimously to abolish the clause granting the Sioux the right to hunt outside of the reservation. Indian Commissioner Mannypenny wrote in his book, "Our Indian Wards", that this act was done without the consent or the knowledge of the Sioux.

Although the United States Senate did not endorse this treaty violation, neither the Senate nor the War Department challenged the legality of the vote. In fact, the order was issued by the War Department to the Army in the field, that any Sioux Indian found hunting on the hunting grounds recognized by the treaty, should be treated as a hostile.

As if purposely trying to provoke the Sioux into action, the Army sent Colonel Custer on a surveying expedition into the sacred Black Hills in 1874. This act was a direct violation of the treaty which excluded soldiers from entering this territory.

There were more provocations in 1875. That summer had been especially hot and dry, and the Sioux who lived in the northern part of the reservation had but one choice; go on a hunting expedition west of the Black Hills or starve. They notified the Government Agent of their desire to hunt. He could not oppose their wish, as he knew it was their right. In Washington however, the War Department prevailed upon the Commissioner of Indian Affairs to recall the hunters. The Commissioner issued an order that the hunters had to be back on the reservation by January 31st, 1876.

The letter containing the order, reached the Indian Agent on December 22nd, 1875. The runner forwarded the message to the Indian hunting party and was unable to get back to the agency until February 11, 1876, because of the snow and bitter cold weather.

General Sheridan reported that the army had to suspend all operations, but the Indians were supposed to take the same hardships meekly. Of course it was impossible for the hunting party to return on time, so on February 1st, the Secretary of Interior turned the handling of these Indians over to the War Department.

Immediately, General Sheridan gave the orders to reduce the Indians to complete subjection. The Indians who were still on the hunting grounds now knew that the die was cast, and that they would have to fight for their very existence. Chief Red Cloud, however could not be induced to join the declaration of war.

His words were, "I have signed the treaty of 1868, and I intend to keep it". In point of honor, he towered far above the five generals who signed the treaty with him.

CHAPTER ONE

Marriage and Capture

"Wake up, wake up!" echoed the voice of the camp crier. His loud intonations broke the stillness of the early morning. "Don your best garments, for this is the day of jubilance! To-day will bring the birth of a new family." A shrill ceremonial cry followed this information. As he slowly made his way around the Sioux camp, he repeated his declaration which was always followed by the ceremonial cry.

In anticipation of the big event, sleepy eyes soon cleared, and everyone prepared to spend the day with much merriment. Food for the feast which accompanied the forthcoming marriage had to start cooking early.

Young dogs were tied to stakes and clubbed to death, so their tender bodies could be put with the cooking food for an added zest and spicy aroma. After being thrown on the bonfire to singe off the hair, the young dogs were scraped, cleaned and dismembered. When chopped into small pieces and cooked with wild turnips, dog meat was considered a delicacy to be served only on very special occasions. Choice, dried venison and buffalo jerky were cooked with dried corn for another savory dish. Beverages were made by boiling herbaceous plants: Crushed corn was mixed with the tallow of the buffalo and the honey appropriated from the bees, to make wasna. Many varieties of sauces and deserts were made of wild berries to complete the menu for such a banquet.

Even with all of the various activities, the day was long, and toward evening the restless people tiring of games, cooking, and joking, were looking forward to the hour of feasting.

It was at this time that Chiefeagle, the old and respected leader of the camp, called all of his band together.

"My relations", he began strongly, "this day my heart is very happy, even though I am a little sad; sad because my lodge will lose a strong youth who has become very dear to me. This young brave has learned many things in the few short years of his life, things which most people of this land will never know."

His voice now becoming choked with emotion, the old man cleared his throat before continuing. "With wisdom and a noble purpose, he has taken a great road with a vow to follow it to the end. He has captured to his heart a fragile flower from the great white way; a beautiful flower who will bring him much comfort and enchantment."

The pause was long, the people were quiet while waiting for the next word. "My voice can say no more, but my heart wishes them well. In the name of my people, I ask the Holy Mystery to give them the fortunes of happiness."

Slowly Chiefeagle turned and looking at the ground he walked to his lodge amid the thundering approval of the people.

Regaining his composure, the old chief returned to announce that the feast was ready. The whole community then proceeded to devour great quantities of food, until they could hold no more. But still they summoned the servers and refilled their bowls and containers. This had been a generous feast, and what they could no longer consume they saved for later. The Sioux had known too many famines to think of wasting one morsel of food. It was no accident that not a scrap of food was left in the cooking pots.

All through the supper the people were solicitous in their attention to the bride and groom. Turtleheart was greatly admired for his bravery and generosity and he was liked for his shy and sincere demeanor. All hearts were happy that this grandson of their respected leader, Chiefeagle, should take for his wife the fair, blue-eyed one who had become one of them.

During the feast the bride and groom remained standing as decreed by custom. Evensigh's light skin stood out in deep contrast with her blue-black hair. Unbraided, it plunged down around her oval face in a cascade of natural waves which seemed to flow with the gentle breeze. Her blue eyes were large and expressive, and the lips of her full and sensitive mouth were the color of the wild cherry blossoms.

Evensigh's vibrant natural beauty was accentuated by her clothing. Clad from shoulder to feet in white doeskin, replete with porcupine quillwork of the best Sioux workmanship on the moccasins, leggins and dress. Her proud and straight form was indeed a striking sight, with the waist as lean and slender as that of an active youth and her hips narrowed with the grace of many years of horsemanship.

By now, the hollow tones of a drum could be heard. The young at heart are impatient, and even before the elders had finished their meal, several of the young impetuous braves took a large, decorated ceremonial drum to the center of the camp circle and started to beat out the slow rhythm of the round dance. As the drum beat gathered strength, singers chimed in with a love song dedicated to the bride and groom.

At the end of the chorus, all of the noise and singing abruptly stopped, except for a lone drummer who softly thumped the half beat of the first dance. Turtleheart arose with his bride, and with shy movements, put his left arm around Evensigh's waist. Side by side, their entrance into the dance area was slow and stately. Right hands clasped together, and with hardly a glance at the surrounding, they danced in a two-step fashion. Once around the circle of spectators, the remaining drummers took up the beat with much enthusiasm.

This was the awaited-for signal for the women to rise and ask the men of their choice to dance. Couple after couple fell into place behind the bride and groom, taking up the steps of the rabbit dance.

With light steps, Turtleheart moved his body gracefully in time with the beat. His shiny black hair was cut even with his shoulders, its tips brushing lightly on the muscles of his neck column. He wore a single spotted eagle feather on his head, its tip resting between the strands of hair. His medium height frame moved with the nimbleness of a deer, an indication of the athletic activities of his life. His copper red face was endowed with a masculine beauty and his eyes shone with proud dignity.

As the dance ended, shouts and all manners of war whoops filled the air. Above them all, the camp crier's voice intoned, "Take one last look at the lovers before they blend forever."

With the well wishers' cries still ringing in their ears, Turtleheart and Evensigh melted into the darkness which was now enveloping the plains. The dance would continue till sunup, but the newly-married couple had a journey to make.

Leaving the sounds of revelry behind them, they traveled into the night, and not until the stars started to lose their identity in the light of dawn did they stop. They chose to begin their nuptials in the privacy of a narrow canyon which was strewn with tall pines and luxuriant grass. Here they laid down their blankets near a bubbling spring and stretched out to rest. Because of the inherent shyness of Indian youth, they would not look at each other, even though the desire to do so was strong. At long last, when what seemed to be the longest silence of their lives had elapsed, Turtleheart found the courage to speak.

"Evensigh," he murmured, "the strangest type of shyness is now strangling the outward expression of my heart. Soon may its wild beating stop."

"Oh Turtleheart, my loved one, my heart is also acting wildly. It is only for you that it beats this way."

Any further words by Evensigh were smothered by Turtleheart's embrace. The silence had been broken and the shy fears of the man and wife had been conquered. The ensuing period of blissful seclusion was shared by the newlyweds until a new crescent moon appeared in the western sky. According to legend, this was a favorable time for important undertakings, and the wedding had been carefully timed to coincide with the new moon. To disturb the bride and groom at this time meant banishment from the tribe, the ultimate penalty for any serious violation of tribal rules.

The day waxed and waned over the earth, and there was a faint breeze coming up the canyon when Evensigh stirred. Waking, she opened her eyes to one of nature's phenomena, a wondrous sunset which colored the earth with its red glow. For a time she lay half asleep, but still cognizant of the changing colors. Reality seemed so far away; far, far away. It was only with some effort that she brought herself to the realization that she must gather firewood before darkness enveloped the canyon. Her mind was reluctant to accept this fact, because to awaken fully would be to break the spell of enchantment.

The days passed quickly, and it was time to start the journey back to their new lodge. Filling the water pouches at the spring, they were filled with remorse at having to leave this place of beauty.

"Ne ye!" Sioux! Do as I say! I have others with me, so do not try anything you will regret." The tranquility of the past few days was suddenly shattered, and the harsh realization of trouble entered Turtleheart's mind. "Back away from that woman. Lie down over by that dead tree." Turtleheart had now recognized the dialect of a Santee Sioux, and his brain was whirling with the knowledge that the voice was not friendly.

Dropping to one knee, Turtleheart glanced over his shoulder and realized the voice was speaking straight. Three white men emerged from the thicket of bushes on the edge of camp. He looked at Evensigh with eyes which seemed to say it would be useless to resist the command. To do so, would surely result in his death, and injury or worse to her.

Evensigh was unable to take her eyes from the face of her husband. Although she remained outwardly calm, her heart was racing wildly. Stories of these people who had white skin like hers raced through her mind and she was frightened. Her forearms and wrists dampened with fine perspiration. She could not understand the mutterings of the three white men as she watched them remove Turtleheart's weapons. The Santee was standing to one side, watching her with hawk eyes that did not miss the beauty of the girl and the fineness of her clothing.

Walking slowly toward her, he inquired, "Do you speak Sioux?"

She nodded, unable to speak, while watching Turtleheart's face for any possible instruction.

The Santee warrior turned his attention to Turtleheart. "My name is Thin Bird, and by what are you known?"

"I am known as Turtleheart," the young Sioux replied in an even tone. "What is it you want?"

"We wanted your ponies. We need them to continue our journey. We do not wish to harm you or your woman, but now, because of her, we must keep you with us until we cross the Paha Sapa. If you made your way back to camp, you would bring others to pursue us. We are on our way to the place of the yellow metal beyond the Black Hills, as the white man calls them."

"That is the sacred ground of my people, the Tetonwan. Why do you take these men to this sacred area? What kind of man are you, to be a traitor to your relatives?"

Turtleheart spat upon the ground. "Think of yourself! You are the same color as we are, and you belong with us, not on the side of the white people whose hearts and tongues are against our people."

"Your tongue should not ask these questions, Turtleheart." Thin Bird turned on his heel and motioned to the beardless white youth to accompany him to the horses.

After this bitter exchange of words, none other passed the lips of either Turtleheart or Thin Bird. Instead, silent preparations were made for travel.

For many days the small group moved, ever wary of detection. Thin Bird very skillfully avoided the Indian camps which lay along the way. Always traveling in single file, Thin Bird was the leader, followed by Evensigh. The three white men came next and last was Turtleheart. This order of travel was the idea of Jim, the beardless one, since he realized that Turtleheart would not try to escape without Evensigh. He also knew the Indian would be the best man to prevent attack from the rear.

Thin Bird informed Turtleheart that if they were attacked from the rear, the white men would take Evensigh's life. With this in mind, Turtleheart took every precaution against any possible attack. Sometimes he rode into the occasional forests of trees to the side of their route, and sometimes he back-tracked to conceal signs of their trail. He was always hopeful of being able to communicate with his people before they could attack, so he could formulate a plan of rescue.

After bedding down each night, the beardless one would set up a schedule of watches. Turtleheart knew he was the real leader of the group, despite his youth, and that Thin Bird was merely a scout for the party.

Evensigh was always kept separated from Turtleheart, and her movements were always kept under close scrutiny. She was the insurance for safe passage through the Teton Sioux Country, and they all knew it. Not one spoken word was allowed between the young couple, and their only means of communication was with their eyes and an occasional silent hand signal.

One night, after a hard day of travel through rough terrain, Turtleheart was looking at the stars through unseeing eyes. He was wondering how Evensigh could keep going at the cruel pace set by Thin Bird. Unaware of Thin Bird's approach, he was startled by the sound of the Santee's voice.

"Turtleheart, it is hard on your woman to be traveling as we have. It will soon be over. We have been pushing fast since crossing the Missouri River and we should reach the Yellowstone in about three days." Pausing, he sat down wearily. Thin Bird appeared nervous, a sharp departure from the cool assured manner of his past behavior.

Continuing in a low voice, he said, "Jim says that he will release you and your woman. He also said that he will let you take the two lame horses. We will soon be out of your domain and you will no longer be of value to us."

"That is good," replied Turtleheart. "I do not believe that she will be able to go much farther. But why are you with these pale ones? You and I are both Sioux and we must speak with a straight tongue as one brother to another."

"Well spoken, Turtleheart, but you do not know what I know." The Santee stopped in search for the right words. "In thinking of all the people I know, I can see a long procession, both Indian and white. In these past winters, mostly white."

A hard bitterness crept into the voice of Thin Bird. "In the land of my childhood, we lived as free people until a few winters ago. Now the old life is gone; the pale ones are highest in authority. With their many blue coats and weapons, they have taken all of what was ours. We are no more than driftwood left after a flood. White men own most of our land, not with his brothers, but by himself. They strive to own more than the next, and in seeking these possessions, they fight between themselves. Right and wrong seems the same to them."

Thin Bird fought to control the emotion on his face. "On my people's side we have no goals, no aims. For many, the only purpose in life is to get drunk; not to retain that which they and their brothers have had for hundreds of moons. Also, many refuse to change their habits of living, because freedom is to them the right to hunt, to feast."

"Thin Bird," interrupted Turtleheart, "to do what you are doing compares with the courage of a mouse. We are a proud people, and what we do now will determine our destiny in the sacred Paha Sapa. If we fail to act, we are cowards. Only fools would lay down their weapons and surrender. We must make the white people understand this. We must fight them and show we are not children. Ho, it is better to die in battle."

Thin Bird laughed bitterly before replying. "I'll tell you. Understand my words and you will not be so shocked at my story."

"Some time ago, I became a scout for the blue coats, the horse soldiers of the government. I will not attempt to tell all the reasons why I did so, but I was one of the remnants of a band of Santees who were crushed by overwhelming forces of white soldiers. All of my relatives were killed, and so was my spirit. I had nothing but my body, and in order to feed it, I joined the soldiers. They provided me with food and clothing. In return I was to help them by being a scout."

"I soon became the leader of the scouts, and of course, this enlarged the opportunity to help my people. I also came in closer contact with the blue coats and developed a sort of friendship with them, and a close friendship with the beardless one, Jim. He taught me English and the ways of the white man. He upheld my talking thoughts and my actions. He was my only true friend among the whites."

As if talking to himself, Thin Bird kept talking in a low monotone, "One day, he got into trouble, which was of great concern to the other blue coats. When he asked me to scout for him, I said yes. He told me his officers would not like him leaving the army post, so we must leave while the others slept. That night we sneaked away from the fort with two others and started for the gold fields."

"Since I was the chief scout, it was easy for me to get horses and provisions for our long journey. The pace was hard on the horses and they were very tired, when we happened on your camp. We intended to steal your horses, but you stayed so close, we could not. Jim and the others wanted to kill both of you, but I convinced them this would be bad."

Tapping Turtleheart on the knee to emphasize his words, Thin Bird went on. "When your relatives discovered the wrong, they would track us down like wolves to avenge your deaths. It was best to take you as hostages, so your people would do nothing to bring you harm. And now we are here where you will be released to go home."

"My heart lies on the ground for you, Thin Bird. I do not agree with you on many things, but I must thank you for sparing our lives. When we are free, you will never need to fear our telling on you. Evensigh will understand this. But she cannot understand the white men, because she has lived as a Sioux since a tiny baby, and has grown up under our culture. Tell me, Thin Bird, what do the white men say of her?"

"Since the first day, I made them understand that the first man to lay a hand on your pale face woman would die like a dog, with a knife at his throat."

"I do not trust the one called Jim, the beardless one." Turtleheart warned. "I do not like the growing desire in his eyes as he watches Evensigh. Her safety is my concern. He may be your true friend, but the passion for a woman can do strange things to a man."

Instead of answering this question, Thin Bird rose and walked away. It was only after he arranged his bed on the far side of the fire that he looked at Turtleheart. With gestures of his hand in sign language, he said he would watch the actions of Jim.

Knowing that Thin Bird spoke with a straight tongue, Turtleheart lay down on the ground which pressed comfortably against his aching body. But tired as he was, to sleep was impossible. Too many things were in his mind. And he must make plans on how to get back to camp after release.

CHAPTER TWO

The Lashing

Like an animal, Turtleheart sensed it before he saw it. The eye of the warrior was trained to detect imminent danger, and the slight movement near Evensigh was enough to cause his body to become tense. Someone was in the act of molesting his bride and had to be stopped. With a sudden and powerful spring, Turtleheart was upon the form of the intruder. With his legs he scissored the man's waist. With powerful fingers around the neck, he gave one quick jerk and his opponent went limp. The spinal cord had been broken so quickly there was no chance of an outcry.

Lifting Evensigh, Turtleheart's mind was searching for a plan of escape. There was no alternative now, so he must act quickly and quietly. Two white men lay, still sleeping, but there was no sign of Thin Bird, so the one he had killed must have been a white man.

"Quiet," whispered Turtleheart. Gently lowering her so she could walk, he whispered, "Because of Thin Bird we can't risk getting our ponies, so follow me."

Taking Evensigh's hand, he quietly led the way north through the cover of the woods. Dawn was awakening in the east, but it was not light enough to distinguish the many branches and brambles of the underbrush. Evensigh made every effort to adapt her pace to the long steps of her husband. To keep from moaning as they tore through the tangled underbrush, she clenched her jaws.

Reaching an especially dense thicket of brush, Turtleheart bade her lie down in the darkest spot and to keep quiet. "I will be back soon," he whispered. "I must get the horses or turn them loose. We have no chance to escape if they have the horses."

The crack of a gunshot in the distance caused Turtleheart to scramble back into the thicket beside Evensigh. The twisted and grotesque limbs of the wild plum trees were a perfect screen for their hiding place.

There would be little difficulty in avoiding an encounter with the white men in these jungles, but Thin Bird was a different kind of foe. Would he join in the search? And how good was he at tracking? Having made his decision, the couple pushed forward to lengthen the distance from those who were by now pursuing them.

Collapsing beneath the hanging limbs of a large pine tree, Evensigh suddenly felt violently ill. Rolling over onto her side, she vomited convulsively until nothing more remained in her stomach. Still the retching continued, the uncontrollable heaving sapping her little remaining strength. Turtleheart appeared, carrying some water in his breachclout. The pure, sweet water made her feel much better, and now she was aware of the numbness in her legs. They felt paralyzed.

"We shall rest here until sundown, then we must move on to a sheltered spot. That is where I got the water," Turtleheart was trying to soothe her.

However, nothing seemed to matter to Evensigh by now; she did not even feel worried about capture. The only thing that mattered was rest for her tortured body, even if it meant death.

Hours later, Turtleheart returned and gently picked the exhausted girl up in his arms. Instinctively she put her arms around his neck, and muzzled her face against his chest. A sharp flash of pain skipped down her legs and she became angry at having been awakened. Her angry response shocked Turtleheart into exclaiming defensively, "I am sorry, but we must go. We must go to a safer place where there is some water. It will be worse if we do not reach safer ground."

Evensigh was acutely aware of Turtleheart's movements as he carried her, and it seemed an eternity until she heard the comforting sound of water as it murmured down a little valley. Gently depositing her on the grassy bank of the stream, Turtleheart made sure her aching legs were immersed in the cooling waters of the stream. Evensigh could feel her tired muscles relax, and she started to feel as though life was again worth the struggle.

Turtleheart warned her not to move and that he was going to find some food. He would be right back, he assured her, and he strode up the little knoll and disappeared from sight.

She lay staring out over the hillsides, her hands clenching the long grass which brushed against her thighs. Her mind ran in circles, but when she thought of their escape from the white men her spine stiffened. A surge of pride and defiance rose within her bosom, as she knew that she had earned that right. Hadn't she proven to her husband and to others that she was strong and could withstand the trials of hardship? Feeling better, she soon fell into a sleep of exhaustion.

Dusk was beginning to enshroud the countryside as Turtleheart was cleaning a cottontail rabbit. A twig snapped and as he whirled to face the sound; he saw a shadow coming down on him fast. A sharp thud and he fell prone, the earth pressing against his nostrils until he could hardly breathe. His sudden whirling movement saved him a full blow, and he lay on the ground only half stunned. In the fog of semi-consciousness he could hear the voice of Evensigh pleading, and the familiar voices of two white men as they cursed. Try as he might, he could not move, and the fogginess of the unconscious world closed in on him until he could no longer hear.

Regaining consciousness, Turtleheart painfully became aware that he was laying over a partly buried log, and that he was stripped naked. Trying to move his arms and legs he discovered that they were tightly bound with rawhide to stakes driven into the ground.

"He tries to move," a guttural voice exclaimed. It was impossible for Turtleheart to see the man, but as he felt the lash across his bare back and hip, he knew who it was. The splitting noise of the whip caused Turtleheart to flinch as much as the searing pain. He did not utter a sound, and his hard breathing gave the only clue to the punishment he endured. Time after time he felt the lash. At each stroke, he clenched his teeth until the jaw and neck muscles stood out in cords. His back arched before each blow and flattened after each stroke.

Turtleheart was conscious of Evensigh's voice, her cries sounding far away, her sobs like those of a deer. They gave him super-human strength, a grim determination to endure the lashing and to kill the men responsible. Feeling his blood running down his torso from the diagonal gutters cut by the whip, he made a silent vow of vengeance.

His executioner tired, and gave the whip to the other man who proceeded to follow his companion's example by making a bloody pattern across Turtleheart's back from the other side. By now the merciless lashing had ceased to move the tortured body. Unconsciousness had eased the pain, but the man continued until the pattern on the back was made up of bloody squares that stood above the skinless channels of bloody flesh.

Convinced that the Indian was dead, the whipper at last lay down the lash, expressing satisfaction with the deed.

During the entire exhibition of brutality, Evensigh had been held helplessly in the strong grip of the white men. Each stroke cut deeply into her mind and spurred her spirit, giving her strength to struggle against the whites. As the whipping continued however, the anguish in her vitals took its toll, and her only reaction was to give the pitiful wails of Indian women at the time of death.

When the lashing ceased, the only sounds to be heard were the wails of Evensigh and the heavy breathing of the two men. She knew that no human could endure the excruciating pain Turtleheart had suffered, and live. Yet hope, which is common among womanhood, forced her to whisper over and over, "Please . . . Please . . . let him live . . . he can live . . . please . . ."

Impressed with the pleading of her voice, the man holding

her relaxed his grip and she ran to the prostrate form. Dropping to her knees she caressed Turtleheart's head. The white men stood transfixed and uncomfortable as they watched her gently brush her lips over the pale face, the shoulders, the bloody back. The blood on her face added to the expression of shocked horror on her features. Unable to watch any further, the men turned away without a word.

Evensigh now lay alongside the prone figure and rubbed the tips of her fingers through the black hair. She told herself it was all over, and that if Turtleheart died, she also wanted to die.

Rising to her feet, she ran to where the white men were kneeling and grabbed at the knife one of them wore. He struck her arm, deflecting it, so did not see her foot as she kicked him in the groin. He writhed on the ground as she faced the other man.

This was no longer a hysterical girl, but a woman who was ready to kill as the puma would kill. Flinging herself upon the astonished white, she sank her teeth into the flesh of his face and tore out a piece of his cheek. One man was down on the ground moaning and the other was holding his face in his hands when she spied the knife.

With an oath of hate, she picked up the knife and was about to plunge it into the red beard's bowels, when a firm hand grabbed her wrist and wrenched the knife away. Throwing the knife across the clearing was Thin Bird.

"No! No, Evensigh, the knife is too quick and much too merciful. They must die by the whip, as they did unto your man."

Turning on his heel, Thin Bird gave the full force of his hand to the one with the torn cheek, knocking him sprawling. A shot rang out and Thin Bird clutched his chest as he fell back with the mark of death already on his features.

CHAPTER THREE

A STRANGE ENVIRONMENT

Evensigh was only a physical being, without mental comprehension as to what went on around her. The crunching sound of the horses hooves and occasional words of her two companions were unreal. The only thing of which she was aware, was the rope around her neck with one end tied to the saddle of one of the riders. The night was dark, but not nearly so dark as the deep despair within her soul.

The cool air of the night eventually revived Evensigh, causing her brain to clear so she could understand her plight. With a strange resignation, she decided it was a relief to face the truth ... the loss of courage to fight back against the inevitable. Without courage, the feeling of desolation was rampant and she hated the earth with its cruel beauty; the white men she had been warned about by her instructors; the whole world. She longed to be free from all of its evil.

So oblivious of her surroundings was she, that she had not seen the flashing of lightning in the night sky. The spatter of rain on her face startled her, and taking notice of the sky, she saw that dawn was already spreading across the eastern horizon. The men appeared to be neither conscious of her nor of the approaching daylight. Slouched in their saddles, they showed the fatigue of long travel without sleep.

As the overcast sky lightened, Evensigh could see that they were now crossing rolling plains, the outline of the dark mountains at her back. Her perspective was beginning to clear now that light had returned to the earth. From somewhere within her being came a scolding murmur — she had completely forgotten her Indian mother's advice. Now her words returned — 'Do not let your faith in survival grope about as blind men do, have faith. There will always be a stronger hand than a human hand to guide you.'

Evensigh's present circumstances seemed to belie her mother's words, but those words were now of great comfort. She must have faith, even if she was forced to walk, led like an animal. With the revival of spirit, Evensigh knew that the Great Holy would make her life bearable, but it was up to her to make it possible.

The renewed hope within her breast however, was not a measure of her present appearance. Her moccasins were mud-stained and soggy, her once beautiful dress scarred from neck to hemline, grim evidence of her ordeal. The long hair which was always a source of pride was now a tangle of snarls with strands of damp locks hanging down in her face. At camp she had been told she was mocking a wild woman by not binding her hair, but such statements were made in good-natured, admiring jests by her friends. If they saw her hair now, all matted with leaves and blood, they would surely . . .

But, to get back to the present, she knew that she must cut her hair short like the older women do when they are in mourning for a cherished one who will never return to the life on earth. She must also cut gashes in the flesh of her arms and legs in remembrance of Turtleheart.

She was so lost in her thoughts, she did not realize that the horses ahead of her had stopped. As she raised her head she noticed that the men were looking at her in a strange fashion. She returned the gaze and steadfastly refused to lower her eyes. They could not endure her contemptuous eyes and averted theirs.

Without looking at Evensigh, they fixed a meal and gave her a portion, without saying a word. She did not think that she would be able to eat the food, but she knew she had to, to keep up her strength. The men made no effort to move on, and her woman's intuition told her they could not and would not make any move to molest her, so she lay down to sleep.

The uncomfortable sensation of being too warm awakened Evensigh, and her movements attracted the attention of her unwanted companions. Motioning to her, they conveyed the idea they were to move on, even though the sun was at its highest in the sky.

There was some satisfaction in noting that the rope had more slack, and that the horses were moving at a slower pace. The knowledge that the men were treating her more gently did not quench her desire to see them punished.

The sun was only a hand's width above the horizon when the party neared a settlement. From the type of strange lodges, Evensigh knew that this was a white community, and once again misgivings entered her mind. These were not her people, and considering her experiences with them, there would be little to expect.

Some distance from the settlement a small group of men on horses met them. They talked in their strange language for some time and occasionally became boisterous. From the many glances passed her way, Evensigh knew the men were discussing her.

To show her disdain, she shook her head defiantly while trying to brush away the flies which were buzzing around the group.

Evensigh concluded that these men were giving her a visual appraisal so as to put a price on her head, much like the braves do when a horse was placed in the village trading circle.

As the conversation progressed, there was evidence of some disagreement and an occasional word of anger. To her surprise, the two men who were captors shrugged their shoulders and allowed the strangers to disarm them. One of the strange men then removed the rope from around her neck, and he was so gentle, it surprised her.

The young woman who was taken into the cluster of strange homes was a very bewildered creature, but this soon turned into resentment as men, women and children of all sizes came out to watch. To be displayed like a prize pony was annoying.

A squatty, but pleasant looking woman took charge of Evensigh, and led her into a small log lodge. This woman fascinated Evensigh, and all the things she did were a source of wonderment. The woman was preparing food in a ridiculous manner, using odd cookware. The smell of the cooking food was very tempting though, after the type of fare served to her the past few days.

To sit in chairs at the white man's table was another new experience for Evensigh, but the strangeness of it all did not prevent Evensigh from consuming all of the food in sight. She was ravenously hungry because of the short rations of the past meals.

The white woman looked at her in amazement as Evensigh shoveled the food from her plate into her mouth with a piece of bread. Grateful for the food, she abided by the Indian rule of etiquette, which dictated that the host must not be insulted by leaving food on the plate.

Doubts about the stories told by her elders, skirted the edge of Evensigh's mind. This was the first person to show any friendliness or warmth toward her, and she was white. It was possible not all whites were evil.

With a sigh of resignation, the woman dipped her ladle into the pot for another helping, only to be stopped by Evensigh tugging at her sleeve. The girl put her hand to her face and the woman smiled at her and motioned to the top bed which was in the room.

So physically tired was Evensigh that she did not take off any of her clothing except for kicking off her moccasins, and immediately climbed the ladder to stretch out on the high bed. Even though sleep should have come soon, she did not go to sleep at once. The room was too hot and stifling for one who was used to the openness of the Indian lodge.

Lying on the pallet, she studied the room carefully and with awe. She had never seen a lodge like this, where the bed was off the floor and there were things to sit on and eat from.

The bedding seemed strange too, no skins or robes, just white, thin coverings. And the bed was much too soft. How could anyone sleep on something which gave with every movement and squeaked every time she turned on it?

She pondered for a long time about the strange appearance and behavior of the woman who was so kind. The kindness was just as unbelieveable as the cruelty of the two men who had lashed Turtleheart.

At the thought of Turtleheart, tears welled in her eyes. He was so warm, so tender and thoughtful of her. So friendly to everyone else. He was such a good person that he never said so much as a bad word with any of his people. They were all very proud of him, but not nearly so proud as Evensigh.

In her mind she thought that perhaps she did wrong in claiming Turtleheart as her very own. Maybe it was not meant for her to capture his heart. If he was destined not to become her mate, maybe the spider creature had put a curse on the marriage and doomed them to a tragic end. These thoughts pained Evensigh and left her heartsick.

As she felt the drowsiness surrounding her as the fog, she experienced a queer sensation of growing wings which would enable her to soar above the earth away from this place and to the land of her many friends in an Indian village among the rolling hills. There would be a valley and it would have cool, clear water; many trees; long grass and . . . the picture faded as the sleep of exhaustion overtook her.

The following morning there was a knock at the door. A middle aged white man dressed in buckskins stepped into the room after the light knock was answered. After speaking briefly with the woman he turned toward Evensigh and spoke in the language of the Sioux.

"My name is Reynolds and I work for the army as a Sioux interpreter." Upon hearing the man speak, Evensigh's eyes opened wide with interest. "The two men who brought you in, told of finding you with an Indian, and the commander of the post here has arranged to have you returned to your own relatives . . . do you know where they are?"

"Oh yes," she fairly shouted, "I am from Chiefeagle's band of the Teton Sioux."

"Not back to the Indians, girl." Reynolds summarily dismissed her statement with a casual wave of his hand. "You are a white girl. They want to send you back to your own family."

"Chiefeagle's family is my family," she insisted.

The interpreter shrugged his shoulders and left the cabin.

He returned by late afternoon. The pioneer woman gave him a cup of coffee and the two talked while glancing toward Evensigh who stood by the window. At last, Mr. Reynolds spoke to her in Sioux. "Do you speak English? No? Well the post commander says it is out of the question for you to rejoin the band of Chiefeagle. He has arranged for you to be taken to St. Louis by a couple who are going there on a business trip. Mr. Callahan owns a big store in St. Louis, and you could do a lot worse, girl. They have offered to bring you up like a proper young white lady."

"I do not want to go. Why do they want me?"

"Well girl, the way I understand it, both of their boys have grown up and left home. Their daughter died a couple of years ago and I guess they plan on making you a part of the family. You sure do not look nor smell like a Callahan, but you sure are pretty." Reynolds voice droned on, telling Evensigh of the plans waiting for her in St. Louis.

Her mind moved quickly. If she was to be held among the whites, she would be better off with someone who asked for her. "I will go," she answered hesitantly.

CHAPTER FOUR

The Vow

The sound of a hundred bird voices echoed in Turtleheart's ears as he regained his senses. How long had he been lying there? A cold wind sent shivers up and down his spine, the ripples sending arrows of pain across his raw and bloody back. A prism of sunlight filtered through the trees, striking him in the eyes. The eastern sun. He had been there all night — or had it been two? His body felt as though a herd of wild horses had trampled him, and to raise his hand took all of his strength and courage.

Hazily looking at his outstretched arms, he could see they were still bound. The rawhide cords were wet because of an extremely heavy dew, and hung with much slack. The Holy Mystery was surely on his side to permit this. And his medicine must be strong as he still lived.

With his right hand, Turtleheart clawed at the damp earth around the stake. The exertion brought beads of nervous perspiration out over his body, despite the coolness of the early morning. With desperation his fingers gnawed steadily at the ground until the stake loosened. With the last of his strength he pulled the stake from the earth as the grey fog of unconsciousness crept over him.

Turtleheart fought this momentary lapse with all of his being, as he knew he did not have much time. The sun would soon be high enought to shine on the strips of rawhide and they would tighten to cut off the blood supply to his hands and feet. He worked furiously to loosen his other hand, and when successful, tried to raise himself with his arms. The effort sent currents of scorching pain across his back. It was unbearable and he fell back on his chest, his body quivering. With eyes closed, he made a supreme effort to gain a position from which he could free his feet.

Now he thanked the Holiest One for helping him, and vowed to take the Sun Dance for his deliverance if he could make his way back to his village. Turtleheart was thankful, too, that he had taken heed of his grandfather's wisdom, and had strengthened his body to the highest peak of condition.

With every joint and muscle aching from the long period of forced inactivity, he struggled to his feet. His knees were weak and Turtleheart stumbled backwards to fall over the body of Thin Bird. Landing on his back, he, like a snapping bow, flipped over to his front side and lay waiting for the sharp edges of pain to recede.

Looking into Thin Bird's sightless eyes, he could do no more than stare at the inert form. When his reeling brain steadied, the young brave put together the story of all that which must have happened.

"Evensigh!" The thought of his bride caused the youth to stand. She was nowhere to be seen. The full story of the scuffle and killing of Thin Bird was plainly told by the signs he read on the ground. He also saw where two men and a woman had mounted horses and left. Evensigh was still captive.

Turtleheart staggered to the stream and lowered his aching body into the cold waters. They cleansed the wounds in his back and soothed the burning fires in his body. When he was able, he smeared wet earth across the lash marks, and took Thin Bird's clothing for his own. The garments would shield his back from the sun and would give him the identity of an Indian, in case his people should find him.

With an aching heart, Turtleheart knew that he could not follow Evensigh. First he must recover from his wounds. Not to do so would be foolhardy since he would surely die, a fact he could not accept. Next, he must see a Yuwipi man, his own grandfather. His advice would be most welcome.

The trail he left on his way to help was a weaving one because of his weak condition and blurred eyes. But Turtleheart tenaciously made his way in the direction of where he knew his grandfather waited. As he walked, he thought of the eventual destruction of the hated gray ones. He would carry the lance until Evensigh had been avenged.

To Turtleheart, as he looked in all directions, the countryside seemed to be so lifeless. For the first time in his young life, the things of nature did not appeal to him. His mind refused to accept nature's magnificence; he was no longer interested in the things which surrounded him. Conscience and mind were both tethered to Evensigh and to her safety and rescue.

Obligation arises from relationship, and theirs had been so intimate and mutual, that the difficulties they had shared since meeting Thin Bird had to be avenged. Right or wrong, no matter what methods he might use, he must follow the dictates which lay before him.

If he performed them well, he would stand high in the esteem of his people as would be expected of him, the grandson of Chiefeagle. Not only his family, but the wider sphere of those composing the seven council fires, would demand that he take such action.

The stumbling gait of Turtleheart became even slower as he tried to ponder the words of his grandfather. Without realizing it, he stopped, and the words became more coherent. He could hear those words of wisdom by Chiefeagle as if they were just being spoken. "My son, the duty of doing is in the doing for each and all; both the strong and the weak, and to the best of your ability and strength. To give up when all is against you, is a sign of being weak and cowardly. If you are confused and cannot think the straight way, take the vow to dance the Sun Dance. The Holy Mystery who watches over us will grant you the strength to attain your answer . . . !"

As the words faded away in Turtleheart's mind, he could see his grandfather s form in a hazy mist. Raising his arms, and with great emotion, Turtleheart began a prayer which came from the depths of his soul. There were no audible sounds, but only the movements of the lips as they formed the words.

"Oh, Holy Mystery, my guiding power and Master, look at me and take me by the hand. I am a poor and groping youth who is lost in the vastness of the unknown. I need strength, the strength only You can give, to face the tomorrows. Today the sun does not shine for me, but is hidden behind the dark clouds of despair. My heart is laden with sorrow, and I know that the most precious things of life are obtained through sorrow, but my spirit is burdened with more than I alone can carry. I invoke You to comfort me as I carry this great pain. Oh Great Spirit, I need the power of will, so that I may find my beloved Evensigh."

"To thank You for permitting me to live and to gain the vital strength of mind and body to do what I must, I now take a vow to dance to Your most powerful symbol, the sun."

His silent prayer ended, Turtleheart remained with outstretched arms until waves of color swirled around and engulfed him. The sound of Thunder was roaring in his ears, he had his answer from the Almighty above. Slowly his knees gave way and Turtleheart dropped to kneel on the ground for one moment before crumpling to a prone position.

Lying on his side, his hands grasping at his folded knees, he was acutely aware of being more tired than he could ever remember. Stiffening legs tastified to the great strain he had endured. His hands felt numb from being tied to the stakes. His back felt as if there were a hundred fires burning into his flesh. Pangs of hunger gnawed at his vitals. Hated but uncontrollable tears were coursing in dirty furrows across his cheeks. Even the strongest of men sometimes weep in self pity.

Recovering his composure after a few moments, he knew he must go on. There could be not rest, no peace, no comfort until he heard Evensigh's voice, her thrilling laughter; and could touch her and hold her in his arms.

There was no shame within Turtleheart concerning his tears. They were the life blood of man's emotions, but they should never be shed in the presence of others. This type of behavior was frowned upon by his people; the proud would look down with disdain, the merciless would reproach him, as tears were thought to be an indication of a man's crumbling courage.

Turtleheart was alone in the embrave of the bosom of Mother Earth, so he could shed some of his sorrow in unabated tears, proud tears which the Holy Mystery would understand and approve of. The lonely warrior cried himself to sleep as the sun silently sank below the horizon.

The warm glow of the rising sun was making itself felt when Turtleheart became aware of the daylight. The warm rays were soothing to his body and seemed to break the sense of fatigue which had held him in its grip. With the instinct of the wild animal, the Sioux youth knew that the early sun was of great benefit.

Turtleheart lay there rubbing the dried matter from his eyes and reflecting on the evening before. The pangs of the hunger in his stomach became too much to bear. He craved meat; fresh meat with the blood draining from it. To one weaned on this diet, meat hunger can grow into madness. He must have meat!

Rising gingerly to his feet so at to not start his back to bleeding again, Turtleheart made his way down to the banks of a small river which was only a few yards away. With his clothing off, and the cold water caressing his naked body, he could feel the fatigue leaving his aching muscles.

Leaving the cold water, he allowed the warm sun to dry his skin before dressing. Wishing he had some oil or fat to rub on his wounds, the youth looked around for signs of game. With luck, he would soon have meat to appease his hunger and fat to soften the skin of his lacerated back.

Knowing the skill of the hunt, the brave knew he must find a place to wait for the game to come to him. He decided to remain where he was, as his condition would not permit him to travel very far. After many hours of patience, the sun had crossed the top of the sky before he noticed a slight movement in the brush. The eye of the hunter is trained to see that which is not a normal part of the terrain. Survival depends upon being alert to any foreign movement.

Thanking the Holy Mystery, Turtleheart picked up the bow and quiver which had belonged to Thin Bird and waited behind the low sage brush he was using for cover. The deer, unaware of the hidden human, trotted into the opening adjoining the river. Its nostrils were quivering in an attempt to smell an enemy, when the arrow sped to its mark. Sore limbs and aching back were momentarily forgotten as the Sioux skillfully loosed two more arrows in rapid succession. The young buck reared up and fell over, struggled to his feet, ran a few steps and fell again near the edge of the stream.

Turtleheart had a segment of a shattered piece of flint which he used as a knife to disembowel the deer and cut out the liver. With the hot blood running down his chin and ribs, the Sioux ate part of the liver before turning his attention to the building of a fire.

To start a fire with dried moss and a piece of flint struck on a stone was easy, and a sage wood fire was soon blazing furiously. While he waited for the fire to die down into a bed of coals for roasting, Turtleheart sliced a thick slab from the rump of the deer. As the low flames cooked the venison, the savory smell was almost more than he could endure.

The hurried consumption of the large piece of meat, washed down with water, would have made a civilized white man deathly ill. But not so for Turtleheart. Only too often the Indian had to starve until there was a successful hunt, then gorge himself as if there would never be another meal. This was the normal way of life for the true nomad.

The rich food and another night of rest revived the body and spirit of Turtleheart and enabled him to travel for the next several days toward his home. While walking along, the figure of an Indian on a horse topped a rise in the near distance and stood there silhouetted against the sky. This was a beautiful sight for one who was lonely, and the impulse to give the howl of the wolf took hold of him. The echo of this cry of friendship was good to hear. It had been many days since he had heard the sound of his own voice.

The lone sentry who had been watching Turtleheart thread his way through the brush and trees, waved his acknowledgement and rode slowly down to meet the wanderer on foot.

"Hunka! Hunka! My son, my son." was the incredulous cry of the rider. Jumping from his horse and running to Turtleheart, he embraced him. "What has happened to you? Where is Evensigh?"

"Hunka Ate, I carry bad news. Some renegade white men, deserters from the blue coats, set upon us without warning. They lashed me until I could no longer feel the whip. They stole her from me. They stole her and I could do nothing."

The feelings of the Hunka and the Hunka Ate toward each other run very deep, and Turtleheart was very thankful that this should be the very first person he should see. The relationship of the Hunka is difficult to define, for it is neither brotherhood nor of blood kinship. It binds the two individuals in a pact much stronger than friendship and sometimes stronger than when they have the same parents. The Hunka Ate is the older of the two and is almost the same as a father. This has been true among the Sioux since the very beginning.

"Come. A temporary shelter, which I have set up, is just over the hill. We will go there and I will make up some medicine for your wounds. You sleep and then we will talk."

Gall, a war chief of the Hunkpapa Sioux, asked his Hunka to lie on his bed of skins. Carefully stripping the clothing from the boy's body, his hands trembled. Gall then gently rubbed warm bear oil on the tortured back.

A sense of guilt lay on Gall's conscience, as he felt he was to blame for the whipping and Evensigh's abduction. As Hunka Ate, he should have kept a close watch of his Hunka to protect him and his Evensigh from possible danger. He,

Gall, should never have consented to being Hunka Ate if he could not protect his ward. It was only natural that Turtleheart was too enraptured with love to be alert against danger.

"My heart lays on the ground, my son. My grief is a burden I must bear for you. I will carry the lance for you. Now sleep, my boy, and you will feel better."

Knowing he was safe with a trusted friend, Turtleheart was soon in a world of dreams. In this dream he re-lived the current of events which led up to his adoption by Gall.

There was the day when a band of Hunkapapas came to his village to seek help in fighting the whites. The leader of this band was called Yellow Forehead by his followers, but he was called Gall by Chiefeagle and his village. A strong friendship between the famous Gall and himself developed, and Gall was his idol. The deep understanding between man and boy impressed Chiefeagle, so his Grandfather contrived to have a Hunka ceremony set up so Gall could adopt the boy.

With vivid memory, he was seeing again the parts of the Hunka Ceremony; the buffalo skull with horns attached, the two rattles, the sweet grass and sage, the ear of corn, the fire carrier, the special drum, the scaffold. Especially vivid now were the two Hunka wands, two of them of the same size. They were four spans long and the small ends were as big around as a man's small finger. About a third of the way from the big end were attached six quills from the golden eagle. When the rod was held parallel with the ground, these feathers radiated in a glorious circle. A third of the way from the small end, a bunch of hair from the tail of the horse was fastened in the form of a tassel. A similar tassel of buffalo hair was on the small end. The wands and the scaffold were both painted red.

Some of the details were hard to remember, as he was not very old at the time. His grandfather had often mentioned them since, such as the informal uses of the wands and rattles. The smoking of the pipe, though, was very clear. This had been the most important part of the day, as the pipe was the greatest symbol of prayer to Wakan Tanka, the Holy Mystery.

He recalled the great pride he had felt at being bound to Gall with thongs; arm to arm, side to side, leg to leg. A red stripe was painted across their faces from cheek to cheek and forehead to chin across the nose.

The conductor waved the horse tail over them and intoned, "You are bound to your Hunka, and he is as of yourself. When you put the stripe on your face, you must remember that what you have, is his also. And what he has, he will give to you if you desire it. You must help him in his time of need. If someone harms him, you must carry the lance to avenge him, for it is as if you were harmed. Your horses, your robes are his and his are yours. His children are as if they were yours. If he is killed in battle, you shall not be satisfied until you have provided a companion for his spirit. If he is sick, you should take presents to the man with medicine to make him well. That is all. You are now Hunka."

The feast and the dance that night, given in honor of the new Hunka Ate and Hunka, was something he would never forget. The give-away dances, the round dances, the honor dances and the enthusiasm lasted until dawn. He was dreaming of a great event.

CHAPTER FIVE

Gall Speaks

Turtleheart's dreams were so profound that Gall had to shake him repeatedly. "Hunka, your thoughts are far away. You were talking in your sleep. Come back to this place. I have warmed you some herb soup, and it will be good for you. Drink all of it, it will be of comfort to your stomach."

Gall set the steaming bowl beside Turtleheart and sat facing his Hunka. "While you are drinking your soup," said Gall, "I will tell you why I am in this country, so far from my village." A few moments passed while he wondered how far back to go in time. Perhaps it would be best to start with the time of the Hunka Ceremony which was now twelve winters past.

Turtleheart sipped at the hot soup and waited. He knew that Gall was thinking of what to say. Breaking the silence, Gall continued. "I did not get any volunteers from your village the first time I knew you, possibly because Chiefeagle picked the most remote part of the land to set up his lodges. Your people do not come in much contact with the whites and they are not familiar with the trickery of the white man in his conquest of our land. They do not know that all around them the pale ones are turning the ground upside down, killing the buffalo, and putting the Indian on small areas of ground. They do not know that the people on these reservations are forced to live on small amounts of food, hardly enough to keep them from sickness."

Gall's voice had begun in a dull monotone, but as it continued, it grew more and more angry. To ease his fury, he rose from his place and walked about. To Turtleheart, there was something curiously magnetic about this brave man. He had the tongue of an orator, and his gestures were almost a second language of accompaniment to the spoken word. These gifts compelled all to listen and admire what he had to say.

Gall was calmer now, and sat down again. "The days of families visiting one another; the fun and relaxation of the old men in the shade; the women laughing and gossiping and playing the hand game; the children without worry, play-acting like elders; they will soon be over. The mighty Sioux will lose those days, just like their cousins to the east, unless they forget their differences and join all of their might against the whites."

Gall paused to clear his throat, then went on. "I was warned by Little Crow, a chief among the Santees, not to smoke the white man's smoke, or drink the white man's fire water, or eat of his food. He warned too, that to live like the white man would destroy our heritage. The white would not help the Indian. Instead, he would take away from the Indian and never give him rest. He spoke with a straight tongue, as the men of the traps agree." Bitterly now, Gall's voice kept on. "The chattering white savages have broken many treaties. They talk with a crooked tongue." He acted as to shake out the unpleasantness in his mind.

To Gall there were but two things a man could do to others; love or hate. Gall chose to hate all white people, not because of their pale skins, but because most of those he knew or had known, did not show honor. It was much better to be defeated in battle by an enemy Indian, than to suffer defeat at the hands of those who broke promises.

The man actually shivered at the mere thought of being conquered by the heartless whites. To his people, war was not a business of extermination, but a test of courage. The hunt of buffalo on enemy land, the stealing of horses and the combat between enemies was done by small war parties, and was worthy of high honors.

"We have tried to avoid battle with the invaders," Gall stated, "until a thief's road was built through our land to the yellow iron found beyond the Powder River. Forts were built to protect this trail. We retaliated by attacking and killing a band of blue coats near Fort Kearney."

"It was two winters before that, when we were surprised by those blue coats who killed many of our families . . . even babies. Since that black day, I have been on the path of war. I have helped at the battles of Fort Kearney, Wagon Box, Horseshoe Station and others."

His face now livid with rage, Gall was now walking like a caged bear. He continued his exhortation while pointing one hand toward the Black Hills. "The Paha Sapa is the last remaining symbol of our people's great might. We must not permit the whites to violate this sacred ground by digging for the yellow iron. These hills are sacred because of their symbolic nature, the expression of the Great Spirit."

Silently, Turtleheart reflected on the truth of what Gall had said. His thoughts were interrupted by Gall's finishing statement. "Hunka, I am sorry for permitting my innermost thoughts to stand out like war paint. But I must speak like this when I know our way of life is on the brink of a chasm that yawns wide to swallow us. Please forgive me for forgetting that you are suffering a great hurt, and not letting you tell your story."

With a great deal of hesitation, because of the emotion in his voice, Turtleheart started at the beginning of his marriage when he and Evensigh left for the wedding journey. He told all of the details and was very particular in the description of the white tormentors. As he brought his narration up to the point where he had first seen Gall, Gall spoke for the first time since the start.

"You have endured tortures men many times your age have never had to suffer, Turtleheart. It is because of these things that your heart is old. Your heart is strong and your honor is of the highest degree, so you will allow nothing to block your path in doing what you must do. You will keep your vow of the Sun Dance to the Great Holy."

"I have paid the closest attention to that which you have told, and I find that I do not know the condition of their heads, not even Thin Bird. My stomach turns over at the thought of a Santee betraying his own. Perhaps his actions were the result of the white man being his associate. The greed rubbed off the white skin to his own and he could not see the straight way. This thing I do know."

In a thoughtful mood, Gall picked up the empty soup bowl, idly turning it over in his hands. In a meditative tone he seemed to talk to himself. "It is in my mind they laid the lash to your back to send your spirit to the place of the dead. Your body was left for the wild animals to feed upon. You had good medicine and your body was strong, so you did not die."

There was a short silence while Gall searched for appropriate words. Turtleheart was dismayed at what he heard. "It is probable that Evensigh is alive, but she may be sold for a slave, as they did in the east. We must keep our ears open for news of her. For you to be patient will be hard, but if you keep your head, you will surely find her."

For many minutes no word passed between the two men as each was lost in his own thoughts. Gall broke the silence by saying, "Two days ago, I arrived at your village with a message for Chiefeagle. I volunteered to bring this message for two reasons. First, I wanted the opportunity to see you in your new manhood, to see the quality of man you ripened into. To deliver the message was second in my thoughts. Upon delivering the message from Red Cloud, Chiefeagle called a council of all the clans at his camp. Red Cloud had appealed to all the Sioux to talk of leasing the so-called mineral rights in the Black Hills to the white man. The elders decided that the whole village should go, since it was so small. You and Evensigh were the only absent ones. They did not waste time in moving and I stayed behind to await your return."

Considering these words carefully, Turtleheart finally questioned, "Why are these strangers trying to impose themselves on us? There is not much game left, as they have killed most of the buffalo. It must be this yellow iron you speak of that is so important. Red Cloud told us a few moons ago, that there were so many of these pale ones across the Father of Waters that they are living on top of each other. Maybe that is why."

Turtleheart had touched upon a subject about which Gall could speak with much oratory, so Gall began to speak with all of the dignity of a wise council chief. "A man is made to pace out his life in accordance with his own people; he must be able to walk into their arms. To refuse to do so shows a wall of ill-will through his mind. I have grown up with a proud heart among proud people, and when I walk through the Paha Sapa and let my mind rest on its meaning to us, my pride turns to a spirit of humility. The beauty surrounding me is more than my words can describe. No language can tell of its Holy Glory."

With a wry smile, Gall now looked at his companion. "You must forgive me, my Hunka. I have been getting away from your thoughts, and have not answered your question. I do not know why the white man feels as he does. I have seen that color only on the belly of the snake creatures who crawl in the grass, but I do not believe that the color of the skin matters."

"It is what is in a man's mind that matters. They look much like us and they pay homage to the Great Mystery as we do, but unlike us, they worship Him in lodges they call churches and use images of people. I do not understand these things."

"The Great One who watches over us, made the earth, so why use things He did not create. We pay homage to Him through His own creations, the sun, the earth, the winds, the thunder, the lightning." Gall was warming to his oratory and he was now on his feet to conclude his speech with a thundering voice. "The Paha Sapa is His sacred ground, and it must not be spoiled by men who worship in mere lodges."

Turtleheart's eyes were wide with awe as he watched Gall. In Gall's presence he felt like a small boy, so it was in the questioning tone of a child that he asked, "Have you ever lived among the white people?"

"No!" was the retort. "Never by all that is Holy!" The sharp reply was accompanied by a clenched fist swinging through the air. "Many times before the treaty was signed at Laramie, I came to know fur traders and trappers. They lived among us from time to time, but they were men of honor, like us. They were good men, respected by all. Hidetrader was one of them. Have you heard of the man called Hidetrader?"

"Yes, I have even seen him when he came to our village. He is as remarkable as the many stories they tell of him. It is hard to think of a white man to be as one of us."

"He is a very remarkable man," emphasized Gall. "He is as one of us. Did you know he fell in love with a Sioux girl and married her, according to our custom? He and his woman are now living where the Rapid Creek is swallowed by the Cheyenne River. It was he, Hightrader, who taught me much of how the white man lives. Sitting Bull also told me about the white man's culture."

Now sitting on his knees and gently rocking back and forth, Gall peered at the younger man's face with a blank expression. Turtleheart waited for Gall to reach for the words to describe something which was beyond him. Finally Gall spoke in quiet tones.

"Hidetrader always spoke with a straight tongue. You can believe the words he speaks. He has never told a false word to any of our people in all the years he has been with us. He has always been fair and has always been on our level. Once he told me that the Indians would never have to worry about losing their land to the whites because the Great White Father had passed a bill four winters ago. This bill he called the National Indian Policy Action, or something like that."

"When I asked Hightrader about the broken treaties, he did not answer. He believes as I do, that white men's scratches on paper say we have rights, but they can be burned and so mean nothing. I told him he was good in trying to make me feel better inside, but that it was not easy to believe the White Father when he acted in bad faith."

"When men come to us in solemn treaty, knowing that it will be broken, that is evil. Honor with prayer and mention of God while doing these things is mockery. So is it strange that we should look upon these treaties as nothing?"

Turtleheart started to speak and then checked his words. Gall was talking to himself as much as to Turtleheart, so words of answer were not needed.

"Red Cloud and the others may as well sign away the Black Hills. They will take it anyway. There are too many of them. For me to go to council with Red Cloud would remind me of the many broken promises and my heart would weep. I know what is to happen, peacefully or not, and in this knowledge, I am bitter."

"I, for one, am ready to die in battle. It is better to die for what you believe than to crawl on the belly."

CHAPTER SIX

Unheeded Advice

The flap to Chiefeagle's lodge was closed and fastened so the people would know that they were not to disturb the Patriarch and his grandson within. An important conference was being held inside, as Turtleheart sought the advice of one with more years of wisdom than he.

"Your arrival here has brought pleasure to my heart, my son, but knowing of Evensigh, a siezure strikes my heart. I have seen to it that all of the different bands know of her disappearance. She will be found. Do not give up hope. We must be patient and strong while waiting for word of her." It was Chiefeagle who spoke with the manner of one who tries to comfort a child.

"You have come to me to seek advice, and this I will try to give to you." Chiefeagle took his pipe out of its richly beaded pouch and proceeded to fill it with native tobacco. His hand trembled as he reached for a dry twig and struck its small end into the hot, low burning fire. He waited a moment and lit the contents of the pipe. Drawing and blowing out a great puff of smoke, he seemed to Turtleheart, an old, tired man.

"This is good. It is your privilege, and it shows that your mind is big enough to swallow what I have to say to you. Always remember that your mind must be like a tipi. Leave the entrance flap open so that the fresh air can enter and clear out the smoke of confusion."

Leaning forward to peer intently into Turtleheart's eyes, he took another draw on the pipe before continuing. "My grandson, you are of my life, and I must share the load which is on your shoulders. You must be willing to share your deep sorrow with me, and that is why you are here."

This time, the old man took several puffs on the pipe and watched the smoke as it swirled up toward the peak of the tipi. Wisdom does not speak with haste, so he was taking time to consider his next words. "You, my boy, are now learning that anything of worth does not come the easy way, and that the pain of mind and heart must be carried through all life."

Another puff on the pipe to make sure it was still lit. "Turtleheart, the Chiefest of them all, The Great Mystery silently made nature for us to use and preserve. But nature also imposes its obligations on us. This thing is meant to be. That is why we are Tetons, the camp makers."

"In this, our life, we could say we are men on the move, and when you bring all of our lives to a pointed thought, you will know that we are only passing through life on the way to the Happy Hunting Grounds of our ancestors." Chiefeagle's words were slow and measured.

To Turtleheart, the next words he was to hear seemed to be more of a command than advice. "Stay here, my grandson, and wait for Evensigh. You must wait for her return. That is the way it is meant."

"Wait! Stay here and wait?" Turtleheart's words were fairly shouted. "To stay here is to die of doing nothing. It is better that I die while doing."

Chiefeagle raised his hand in the signal of silence. "Yes, wait. You must wait. If she is alive, she will return. If not, remember, we are only passing through this life to a better one."

The tone was stern, the words clipped, as the old man's voice continued. "Go from this lodge and walk on the earth of this camp until you have thought over these things I have told you. When you have finished with the struggle of your thoughts, return. Whatever you have to say, I will listen. But now I must go meet with the others at the lodge of Red Cloud."

Chiefeagle's band was camped at the extreme northeast corner of the encampment. They lived the farthest away from the council fire, owing to the late summons they had received.

Representatives from the far flung reaches of the Teton Sioux were at this site, chosen for Red Cloud's council with the government men. Ogalalas, Hunkpapas, Minneconjous, Sans Arc, Brules, Blackfoot; they were all there. There were also a few Yanktons and Santees from the eastern branch of the Sioux Nation, plus a few Cheyennes and Arapahoes.

Each evening, Chiefeagle called the men of his band together, and gave them the details of the day's progress in the council. On the first day, every member of the band was near the lodge of Chiefeagle, to hear his words. As the days dragged on, they lost interest and relied upon the elders to keep them informed.

Late in the afternoon of the seventh day, Chiefeagle entered his lodge with bent shoulders. Worried and tired, he crossed to where Turtleheart waited. To Turtleheart, his grandfather had aged since he last talked to him. He stood to help the old man to sit down.

Grandfather Chiefeagle sighed and said, with a thick voice, "All of our talk came to an end today. We cannot sign their paper and they refuse to look at our side. They offered to lease our land for a great amount of what they call money. Money means nothing. The Paha Sapa is everything."

Leaning back onto his back rest, the old man angrily fussed with the buffalo robe he was sitting on. "Some of our Chiefs think the white man's offer good." †

"I cannot consign my people to a reservation, knowing they will starve in a few winters. Most of the other chiefs agree with me. The white men were angry. They feel we are being without thought and selfish."

† The offer made amounted to a total of $400,000 a year lease for the right to mine gold and to set up farms in the fertile valleys. A counter offer of $6,000,000 for the outright purchase of the Black Hills was also made. The Sioux had to agree to buy their supplies and to remain on a reservation.

"I see unhappy years ahead for the Sioux. The white men will show anger for years to come. We must pray to the Holy Mystery and ask that some day the white man will better understand us; that the seeds of their conscience will awake and grow. I must go and tell my people of what has been done."

Turtleheart helped his tired grandfather to his feet, putting his hands on the thin shoulders with pangs of regret. "I must leave you, grandfather. You can see that I wear my heart on my forehead for all to see. I feel well enough now to travel, and I have decided I must start my search."

"The only reason I remained this long was to give you support in your talks with Red Cloud and the others. I know that I should stand beside you, but I am anxious to go."

Chiefeagle stood with bowed head as Turtleheart lifted the skin flap and paused for another word. At this time of need, when all of the young warriors should rally to the defense of the Sioux, Chiefeagle could not approve of Turtleheart's rash action.

The wisdom of age could not stop the impatience of youth, and he made no move to stop his impulsive grandson. The stoic face showed no emotion, but as his grandfather looked at him for the last time, Turtleheart saw the look in his eyes which mirrored the sorrow within his heart.

CHAPTER SEVEN

MURDER

Driven by the hunger within his heart, Turtleheart searched the emptiness of the hills and prairies for his woman. Once, he was told of a fair-skinned woman who lived with a band of Indians. He followed their trail to the northern country, only to find she was a half-breed. Discouraged, but ever hopeful, he turned to another direction.

The longing desire for Evensigh would not let him sleep for any length of time. Rising before the first shafts of sunlight struck the earth, he made preparations for the day's travel. Once astride his pony, his spirits would rise and he would say, "Today is the day I find her."

Turtleheart was so intent upon his search that he did not heed the signs which foretold an early winter. His only thoughts were of Evensigh, thoughts which seemed to have a life of their own.

A solitary figure on horseback, he wandered from camp to camp, until he had covered all of the Teton Sioux territory west of the Missouri. At some camps he lingered a day or two while waiting for the return of a hunting party, but he never took part in any activity. Sympathetic women would manage to get him to consume a bowl of buffalo soup or rabbit stew; but when the warriors returned and Turtleheart questioned them, he would leap on his horse and ride off.

The women and old men, who were referring to him as the Lonely One, noticed the signs of the fever sickness in him, but Turtleheart heard only the words he wanted to hear. "If we see this Evensigh we shall send word to Chiefeagle. Do not fear, you will find her."

The air had now become bitterly cold, but the passion in Turtleheart's heart gave him the courage to challenge the snow and wind of the first blizzard that swept the high plains. It was the fatigue of travel and diet which finally felled him.

As the fever mounted, it replaced the tumult within his restless soul. Finding shelter, and with wood in abundance, Turtleheart decided he did not have the strength to go on. He laid prostrate in his robe for eight sleeps with little food or heat until the fever burned itself from his body.

He brushed the cobwebs from his brain, and thinking clearly again, he realized how foolish he had been to wander all over the country without a plan, without knowing where to search. During all of those long weeks of driving his body to the point of exhaustion, he had really been trying to drive the torment from himself.

Why hadn't he remained with his grandfather, who needed him? Any news of Evensigh would reach his grandfather just as fast as it could. Only by mere chance could he find her this way.

The decision was made, and Turtleheart made his way to the lodges of his grandfather. Welcomed with cries of joy, the young man was escorted to the lodge of the sister of his grandfather. "It is good to see you again. This time you must remain until the evils of sickness are driven away."

"I am thankful to be home," confessed the youth. "I am very sorry now that I was so selfish in my thoughts and in my actions. It is bad that I left my grandfather when he needed me at the council."

He watched the woman's face twist with grief, and he thought, with a frantic sinking sensation, that she had heard bad news of the girl she had raised as her own daughter. "You have heard news of Evensigh?"

"No, my son. No word of Evensigh has come. None of the bands have seen her, but we ask each to keep looking." It was not the habit of things close to the heart to be spoken of, but they both knew how deeply the loss was felt by the other.

With a mother's eye, she noted the gaunt frame and the sallow complexion of Turtleheart. "Somewhere, you have come down with the sickness of the white man. Again I say, you must remain here until the shaman can drive the sickness from your inside."

"It is not the white man's sickness. It was a sickness of my own making. In my search to the four winds, I drove myself until my body weakened to save me from my own mind."

"It was the will of the Holy Mystery, and He has shown me that I have been searching the earth with blind eyes." With a flash of the old smile, Turtleheart asked, "May I speak with my grandfather? He is far more wise than I and I need to seek his advice."

At the mention of Chiefeagle, the old woman's eyes filled with tears and she turned away with a stifled sob. "Two full moons have passed since your grandfather went to the land of our ancestors." Turtleheart looked at her with eyes that stared with disbelief.

"No! No! No!" Each no echoed with increasing volume as the full impact of her words sunk into his brain. Shaking his head, he fought to hold back the tears which were forbidden. Suddenly, he jumped to his feet and rushed from the lodge. He must go away to make amends with himself. What has he done to bring this misfortune to his grandfather? Thoughts of self-sacrifice were uppermost in his mind as he walked blindly from the village.

The cold air caused him to shiver and he went back to camp to enter the lodge of another relative. Entering, he demanded, "Tell me of my grandfather. I want to know all there is to know. Do not be afraid to tell me."

The woman of the lodge was upset at this sudden intrusion of her privacy, but soon recovered. "I will tell you. But why weren't you here when it happened?" Reproach was in the voice. "You could have done much, but you were gone."

Seeing the misery on Turtleheart's face, she softened her voice and spoke to him with moderation. "Some of the young men were given spirit-water by a passing band, and they became crazy in the head. They continued into the night and became very coarse. Some of the family men went to Chiefeagle and complained about the actions of the young ones. The camp was in an uproar. Chiefeagle was very angry and spoke harsh words to the crazy ones." In telling her story, the woman had difficulty in controlling the sobs which choked her throat.

"The next morning Chiefeagle did not appear, and we all thought he was not feeling well. His sister went into his lodge to see if he was still sleeping. She said he was covered with more than the usual number of robes and thought him ill. Later she went in to waken him and when she threw back the robes, she found your grandfather's throat had been cut from one jawbone to the other, and his tongue had been torn out."

"She screamed, and we went to her side, Whirl Woman and I. Red Feather found out what happened and called a council meeting immediately. All men had to go, and when Two Lance and Iron Feet did not appear, we knew they did this in anger for Chiefeagle's scolding of them. Their horses were also gone, so the elders of the council pointed the finger of guilt at them and ordered the Akicita to hunt them down."

Turtleheart was still trying to convince himself that his grandfather would never speak to him again. Thinking of the lance, he brusquely asked, "They were found and punished?"

"No, the dog soldiers hunted them for many weeks with the best trackers, but the rain helped them get away." Now she assured him, "They will be caught some day and made to pay for their deed."

"I must carry the lance for my Grandfather. It is a bad curse to have our honored and respected leader killed by his own people. Those responsible must die like a dog!" He was now able to understand his grandfather's prophecy when the old man said, "I see many unhappy years ahead for the Sioux."

CHAPTER EIGHT

Strong Echo

This mid-summer was far different than the others Turtleheart had known. The bad signs were many, and the weather extremely hot and dry. The sage grass was not even a finger span long. The choke cherries were few and not yet fully formed. The few buffalo cows in the area were thin, not fat as they should be at this time of year.

Everything was bad, and out of cycle for this season. The bad sign was even on the old men of the council. They often cast wisdom aside and entered into loud arguments. The dissension over even the smallest detail was a thing Turtleheart could not understand, and he grew to detest the wrangling of the elders.

No longer able to stomach this way of doing things, Turtleheart fled the encampment. As he walked with long strides toward the last place of his beloved grandfather, his thoughts became more and more troubled. These were bewildering days. Fearful times, with foreboding clouds, lay ahead. There was a time of life, he remembered, when the day was simple and uncluttered with the thoughts of white men. Now this life was becoming increasingly difficult, and the old ways seemed long distant.

"What was it Chiefeagle used to say? 'Strangers bring fear.' " The strangers were now getting to be many, as the leaves on a cottonwood. How does one stand up against those who are alien to our thoughts and actions? How can you fight people whose ways are so strange?

Turtleheart did not attempt to answer his own questions, but he knew he could not stop in any struggle against these forced oppositions of the Sioux way of living. One does not give up in an easy manner when the land that abides with old memories is threatened. The beliefs he was born with and lived with he must defend with honor. In his heart he knew the way of the future would be long and bitter. He knew he must accustom himself to the life of discord and tension.

Only after looking at the burial rack of the old Sioux leader did he find a balance of mind and spirit. In the mute silence of the prairie he felt nearer to his grandfather and to the Great Mystery, the Father of all.

Turtleheart slowly turned away and started back to camp. Standing in the path was the form of a broad, powerful man. He stood quietly, waiting for Turtleheart to complete his meditation before Chiefeagle's burial rack.

With the sign of friendship, the man stepped forward, his arrow case flapping against his thigh. As he stepped forward, Turtleheart noticed the black stripes across the bowed nose and broad cheeks.

The stranger spoke after the clasp of hands, his voice deep and resonant. "After leaving the council fire of your elders, I went to your lodge, but you were gone. An old woman told me you had walked in this direction. You walk a fast pace."

With noble gestures the man signed respect for the dead, then continued, "Here lies a great man, one who was of wisdom and vision. His ability to heal the wounds of our people will be sorely missed. I do not speak of Chiefeagle with hollow words, but with the deepest feelings of my heart." He placed his hand over his heart then signed the words for Wakan Tanka.

"Since my return to the land of my forefathers, I have heard many voices speak of him, and all are good. Many words have been spoken in your favor, Turtleheart. You must carry on for your grandfather instructor."

"From one of your rank, your words are good to the ears,

but I do not remember you," answered Turtleheart. "I cannot place you among any of my relatives or friends."

"Accept my straightforwardness with an apology," answered the warrior. A smile relaxed the stern features. "I am known as Strong Echo of the Good Voice band. For the past twelve winters I have been east of the great river. I have been to the white man's school. I returned only four moons ago."

"When I first went to live the way of the white man, I believed I could raise myself to a higher plane of life. But when I tried their ways in their world, my life was empty. I also was not accepted. I was an Indian and not to be trusted." Pausing, he rubbed his chin thoughtfully.

"I do not blame them entirely, as my greatest obstacle was myself. The internal life of my being rebelled and would not change. My emotions were too deeply imbedded with my heritage, and because of this, I could not work for the white man. They called me an educated savage only because I would not accept their worship of money." These words were slow in forming, as if he were trying to find justification for being born a Sioux.

"Perhaps, Strong Echo, the one thing which brought you back was that which is called bitterness. Perhaps you failed the white man's society because you failed to keep up with them?" Turtleheart's direct observation was tempered with a smile.

"Yes, you are right. There is no doubt. But I returned for two personal reasons. I had lost the means of living close to Maka Ina, our mother earth. My spirit as I had known it was dead."

"Also I came back because of my mounting concern for my people. The public back to the east worry about the Indian wars. Their talking paper always spoke of these wars, and my hardship kept mounting because I was an Indian. My color and my heritage were my enemies."

"In search of more understanding, I joined the religion and went to their house of worship. But even here, the hunger of my inner self could find no refreshment. Perhaps that was because their beliefs were based on their way of life, I do not know. I felt that the only thing which had been left for me was the will of my inner self."

"This second reason I returned for, the concern for my own people, gives me a heavy heart. As you know, there has risen to the great detriment of our way of life, a different way of living. Like a dense cloud, it is spreading across our land, and already it is breathing on you. I know that most of you have not had as much as a light contact with the contour of this mighty way of life. I also know that I do not want my people to suffer the tragedies of the red man to the east. I do not want them oppressed. I do not want them forcibly marched to what they call the Oklahoma Territory on legs that are bending with the weight of too many tragedies."

"Turtleheart, you and I and the others must think about the possibility of being conquered. To submit is to change. We will have to find a way to adjust."

"I am glad to learn these things, Strong Echo. Perhaps our minds should dwell more on the possibilities of defeat, and how much our people would have to change. It is good that you have returned to help us. If we are to survive we must rely on each other and stop the quarrelling which has come over the elders."

In the long, slow walk back to the village, Turtleheart used the silence to think. This man who walked with him had a strong and honorable inner self. He was a good friend.

Turtleheart stopped suddenly and with impulse asked, "Have you ever done the Sun Dance?"

Taken by surprise, Strong Echo looked at the younger man quizzically. "No, I have not. Why do you ask?"

"It would please me greatly if you would consent to be my sponsor and associate in the Sun Dance. I have not fulfilled my vow to do this dance and it has been almost a year since I made my promise."

"The time of the year when the clans gather together is now past, Turtleheart. The Sun Dance is always held at that time. How can you talk of the Sun Dance now, when all of camps of the different bands have returned to their own areas? Do you expect to send runners to the other bands and recall them for your Sun Dance?"

"I know that, Strong Echo. My grandfather told me the vow of the Sun Dance was sacred, and it should be held when the bands gathered in the early summer. But I was ill and unable to do it. It does not violate the sacred spirit of the dance if held later, and the rest of the Sioux bands need not be present. The important thing is that I have taken the vow to perform the Sun Dance within the summer following."

"Let us speak to Higheagle. If he approves we shall make haste to notify the chiefs to make preparations," assented Strong Echo.

CHAPTER NINE

PREPARING FOR THE SUN DANCE

The time for the Sun Dance was drawing near, and everyone in the village was preparing for the event. The inhabitants are always a part of the dance ceremony. Among the items needed were the presents for the poor; a dried, untanned buffalo hide; a dried buffalo part; a supply of red, green, blue and yellow paint; a red banner; drums and sticks for the drummers; the head of a newly killed buffalo; and a covering for the dance lodge. All members of the camp were deployed to obtain these items.

The site for this event had been previously selected on a level place near the banks of the White River, about four hundred yards from the camp.

Turtleheart and Strong Echo, under instructions from Higheagle, the Yuwipi, were gathering the necessary trappings needed to complete their part of the dance. Each brought a deer skin, a red painted apron, a cape from the skin of the coot with the feathers attached, rabbit skin anklets, buffalo hair arm bands, a decorated eagle bone whistle and a willow hoop painted with the colors of the rainbow.

When all of the articles had been procured, they were purified by Higheagle, who held them one by one over the fire of wild sage and sweet grass.

While the people were carrying out the details of preparing for the dance, a council of chiefs and advisors was assembled. It was this council which selected the dance officials, the intercessors who would be in charge of the dance itself, and the Dog Soldiers, who would see that all of the rules were obeyed.

The council was quite discriminating in appointing a man to the role of intercessor, since he represented the people in his prayers. If he is not a man of unquestioned integrity, the Great Holy might not answer his petitions. Even worse, there could be the possibility of a disaster befalling the people.

The drummers, rattlers and singers were selected according to their skills, along with the diggers, whose job is to dig the hole for the pole used in the Sun Dance. The greatest caution is used in choosing the marshall and police, since they were to maintain discipline.

The bands of Sioux who had been invited to the dance were now arriving, and were busy setting up their camps. Small groups of young braves wandered noisily from tipi to tipi while looking for old acquaintances, exchanging bits of news, telling humorous stories, and boasting of their accomplishments.

Turtleheart thought he recognized a familiar voice now and then, but the voice always moved on so quickly that he was never sure. His sense of curiosity made him long to go out into the camp, but custom required that dance candidates remain apart from camp activities. Higheagle could go out, but never did, and Turtleheart wondered why he did not. It could have been that Higheagle considered his withdrawal an expression of religious ethics.

Turtleheart's thoughts were interrupted by the appearance of a stranger in the doorway of the lodge. Of medium height and wide frame, he was conspicuous because of the deep and numerous wrinkles which covered his entire face and neck. His expression was one of triumph as he detected an air of non-recognition among those present.

"Higheagle, can it be that your mind is getting too old to function?" With this question, the stranger's face broke into a wide grin.

The yuwipi's face wore a look of perplexity. "Highlance?" His face relaxed. "Biglance. Yes. It has been many winters, many, many winters, since we last talked." The stoic calm of both men was lost as they embraced each other laughingly.

"Bring some hides for this poor old man, so he can set his carcass down in comfort," ordered Higheagle. As this was being done, Higheagle pulled his pipe out of its beaded bag, filled it with tobacco, and lit it. Giving it to Biglance, the guest took it and drew a few casual puffs.

"I must not tarry here much longer. I do not want them to interrupt you, Higheagle, and I do not want to be blamed for causing your mind to be confused. I would rather talk to you when we can laugh and joke. Yes, after the Sun Dance."

When Biglance reached the lodge entrance, he turned and apologetically announced, "This will cause you much sadness, but I have been chosen as intercessor for this dance."

"No, they must be crazy in the head." Higheagle could not control his laughter. "Why didn't you say so when you came in?"

"To be thrown out?" Chuckling to himself, Biglance disappeared.

Higheagle adjusted the tipi flap after Biglance left, to seal out the beam of light, then turned to face the candidates. "Biglance is a very courageous man who has won many war honors, and he is highly respected by all of the elders. You are fortunate to have him as an intercessor."

"Knowing Biglance, he has already sent a scout to locate a live cottonwood tree. It will have to be straight and four times as long as a man's outstretched arms. When he locates this tree, the scout will paint four red circles on the trunk to make it sacred."

"He will then report to Biglance and say that he found the enemy. And then, as you know, there will be a big search for this painted tree and when found, the finders will rope it and declare it captured."

The candidates had heard of this before, but they listened as if this was a new story. Higheagle was telling it with a great amount of vigor and action. "Four of the bravest Warriors will step up to the tree and strike it with ceremonial war clubs while telling of their bravest deeds. This will subdue the tree spirit."

The voice softened. "A young maiden, whose purity is above reproach, will come forward to fell the tree. As it falls, there will be much shouting and singing; the warriors seeking the right to wear the black face paint, will sing songs to petition success in battle."

"Now all the limbs will be removed and red paint rubbed on the trunk. Expectant mothers will gather the twigs as a charm against the bad spirits."

The animation stopped and Higheagle changed the tone of his voice. We have our own things to do, so we must think of these. We must turn our minds to the purification of those who are to do the Sun Dance. The sweat lodge is being prepared now and tomorrow is the day for the sweat lodge ritual where you will cleanse your bodies."

Higheagle was still giving instructions when a voice came from outside the lodge. "Higheagle, please forgive the interruption but Biglance requests your presence at the dance area. The tree is being brought in."

"I will be on my way." In a soft tone, Higheagle turned his comments back to the dance pole. "It has been lifted on sticks and is being brought in by the chosen ones. Enroute to the dance area, they will make three stops and a medicine man will howl like a wolf each time. You will soon be able to hear the procession sing as they follow the pole. And you will also hear the medicine man as he drives the evil spirits from the camp." With an air of expectancy, he turned and left.

The night was warm and Turtleheart's thoughts would not let him sleep. His reflections caused him to smile as he thought of his first experience with the sweat lodge, one which he was allowed to help build.

The lodge was about as high as the average warrior, its hive-shaped frame made by sticking the large ends of willows into the ground and tying them at the tops. The first willows were always placed to the east and formed the entrance. The next two were to the west, then two were placed on the north and last on the south. The green sticks were bent to be tied over the center of the lodge. He had been so excited at being allowed to help, that he was careless in tying them together.

The hoots of derisive laughter rang again in his ears as he remembered how the willow sticks pulled loose and suddenly snapped upright, just when the old men were trying to throw the buffalo skins over them.

As sleep gradually overtook Turtleheart, the thoughts grew dimmer and dimmer, but the smile still lingered on his face.

The morning gave promise of a hot day, so the sweat lodge was sure to be a test of human endurance. "This thing is good," quipped Turtleheart. "The sweat will roll on this day." They all laughed at his remark, happy to see Turtleheart smile as he used to do.

Turtleheart was still smiling as they approached the sweat lodge. Each candidate removed his breechclout, entered, and turned to his left to go around the lodge, the first one in stopping just before reaching the entrance again.

In the center was the familiar square hole, about the length of a man's arm across and deep. A bucket-shaped hide filled with water was near the hole. A buffalo tail brush and sweet grass was handed into the holy Yuwipi man and the entrance was closed to seal out the light.

The outside noises were muffled and the inside was dark. Turtleheart could just make out the naked forms of the others. As he turned his thoughts to the ceremony, a medicine drum echoed with the drummers thudding beat. The voice of the drummer rose in a sacred song. When the voice and drum stopped abruptly, it was deathly quiet.

The voice of the Yuwipi man startled Turtleheart as he began his chant. The sacred words of the chant were sung four times before he stopped to light the pipe. Taking four draws, the holy number, he handed the pipe to his left. Strong Echo carefully accepted it and took four puffs before handing it to the left.

The pipe was sent around the circle, each drawing the required number of four puffs until it reached the last man. He handed it back to the one on his right, who passed it on without smoking it. Reaching the Yuwipi, Higheagle repeated what he had done before, he took four puffs before handing the pipe to the one on his left. After this procedure was repeated four times, the pipe was laid on the altar.

"The hot rocks," Turtleheart said to himself. "It is time to call for them." And that is just what Higheagle did. Rolled in under the skin covering the entrance, Higheagle placed them into the pit.

The Yuwipi chanted a prayer as he took the tail of the buffalo and sprinkled the first rock with water. As the steam rose from the pit, each one silently assessed his ability to stand what he knew was coming. This taste of heat was only the beginning. This first rock was for Wakan Tanka. The next two would be for Father Sun and Mother Earth. They would be followed by seven more rocks for the seven council fires, plus more, until the pit was filled.

The sinister sound of rattles sent shivers running up the backs of the participants, even though they knew it was next to come. With this sound of the rattles, the priest of the purification rite began another chant. Interposed in the chant were melodic phrases extolling secret symbols; words that had been handed down from generation to generation.

Each time Higheagle dipped the buffalo tail into the water and sprinkled the hot stones, the heat became more intense. Now the pungent smell of the sage brush which had been fastened to the willows grew overpowering. The air was so thick it was getting harder and harder to breathe.

The chanting prayers were interrupted so Higheagle could ask his relatives in the spirit world to pray for the cleansing of mind and body so they would be pure for the Sun Dance.

All of the men took turns to present their prayers, and it was now Turtleheart's turn. He closed his eyes and began to chant to the Great Holy. He hoped to avoid being overcome by the heat and aroma by concentrating on his prayers. He must forget himself and think only of what was to be done. He was so engrossed he no longer tried to wipe his body with the sweet grass.

After the last rock had been placed and water sprinkled over it, the heat became unbearable. Turtleheart felt of his slick, wet hair; he placed his hands flat on his chest and pressed downward. The perspiration ran in rivulets from his skin, to disappear in the grass covering the floor of the lodge.

The chanting stopped. The rattles ended their nervous and monotonous rhythm. The silence was overpowering. Higheagle arose, threw aside the flap and stepped outside. The other participants rose one by one to go to the right so as to keep from crossing the entrance. It was a bad sign if anyone should cross it from the left.

With Higheagle leading them, the occupants of the lodge quickly ran down to the river and plunged into its icy waters. The naked bodies glinted in the sun as they ran.

Turtleheart was surprised that he did not feel cramped after the long hours of sitting. His muscles felt relaxed and his bones felt like green sticks that bent with every step. The sudden immersion in water strangely caused no shock and he felt completely at rest.

Walking up the slope of the bank of the river, Turtleheart turned to stand and look into the water. He saw the wavering reflection of a tall, lithe and well-built figure looking back at him. Jumping like a young colt horse, he went to pick up his belongings. Light of limb and free of the sweaty, rancid smell taken by the spirit of the waters, he must remain in a spiritual cleanliness until the dance.

The building of the Sun Dance lodge was completed during the sweat lodge ritual, and Biglance was scattering incensed sweet grass around the center. It was now a sacred place.

At the outer edge of the dance area, shade was provided by stretching evergreen branches and robes over forked sticks. The entrance was to the south, and was partially blocked by a new tipi where the candidates would make their last minute preparations for the dance.

In the center of the area was the hole dug to receive the "enemy" pole. Behind it was the altar prepared by cutting out a large square of grass down to the virgin soil. While this was being done, Biglance sang a chant four times. "Four times I pray to the earth; a place I will prepare, oh tribe, behold."

Almost immediately after the chant, there was a piercing cry of a warrior's whoop, followed by the ear splitting responses given by the others. The drummers bent to their drumming with enthusiasm. The flutes with plaintive notes and eagle bone whistles combined in a shrill, tumultous noise designed to run away the bad spirits.

Higheagle had already escorted the two candidates to the preparation lodge, where they would remain until they started the ordeal which was fast approaching.

The sun was getting low in the sky when the silent signal was given. Biglance and the other officials led the people in a circle around the camp area four times, the chants echoing down the river bottom. Another signal for silence and the feast was announced ready.

The old, the orphans and the poor were fed first. The others had to wait until this was done. During the festivities which followed, the poor received gifts. The rest of those present would receive gifts during the giveaway dances.

At sundown, Biglance and Higheagle left the noise of the camp behind to go to the top of a nearby hill where they held the pipe to Wakan Tanka. They offered it to the sun, because he provided the light and warmth for the things on earth. They offered it to the earth because that is where the food and clothing come from. They offered the pipe to the east, the west, the north and the south, because they were the homes of the four winds. The whole ceremony was a prayer for the people.

Throughout the night the old men would shake their rattles and chant. The old women gathered up the wood and twigs for the fires. The sub-ordinate medicine men wound their way all through the camp to keep the evil spirits at bay.

CHAPTER TEN

Fulfillment of the Vow

As the first rays of sunshine tinged the early morning sky, Biglance led his assistants to the dance lodge to make the final preparations for the three days of the Sun Dance.

First he began preparing the place of the Sun Dance pole, by placing sage grass and sweet grass on the bottom of the hole. These objects symbolized the offering of mind and spirit to the Author of Supernatural Powers. Next, some dried buffalo meat was placed in the hole as a token of the good things of life.

As intercessor he made ready the Sun Dance fetish. Four wands of choke cherry wood, a wisp of sage grass, a bunch of sweet grass, a bit of buffalo hair. Rising to one knee, he imparted to the fetish the potency of the Buffalo Spirit with a whispered prayer. This fetish was tied to one of the two branches left at the top of the pole.

Silently, Biglance extended his hand and one of his assistants produced another bundle of charms tied with a thin strip of buffalo hide. Another gave him a small figure of a man and one of a buffalo. Both were of buffalo hide and painted black.

The intercessor imparted to these figures the potency of Iya and power of Gnaski. These were all tied to the top of the pole.

On the second branch of the pole he tied a red colored skin made from the hide of a deer. Four strong ropes woven from the tail hair of the horse, were securely fastened a little more than halfway to the top. Four men grasped these ropes and the pole was lifted into position, the earth carefully tramped into place at the base.

Biglance stepped up to the pole and speaking for it, he sang, "Sacred I stand; behold me. It is said for me that I stand watchful at the center of the earth; stand watchful, while praying for the people."

The Akicita was waiting outside of the arena, and they were ordered to drive the obscenity from the camp. They did this by riding around the pole and shooting down the figures. The onlookers were now many and they trampled the fallen figures into the ground.

Raising his arms in prayer, the confusion of the moment ceased, and Biglance chanted a prayer to the Great Holy, as he placed a dried buffalo part and a pipe at the base of the pole. The pipe was to maintain decency among the people and the buffalo part symbolized the perpetuation of the Tetonwan.

As Biglance completed the last of the rites, Strong Echo and Turtleheart were having their hands and feet painted red by Higheagle. A blue stripe was painted across the shoulders of each. Higheagle asked for the totems of the two and receiving no answer, rapidly drew a cloud on Strong Echo's chest and a turtle on Turtleheart.

Throughout this procedure, not a word was spoken. Now Higheagle held up a bowl of mud and looked questioningly at the two. They remained silent, so he discarded it. Had one of them decided to be released from the vow of the Sun Dance, he would have smeared mud on his hair, arms and legs.

Chanting softly, Higheagle hung the red colored breech-clouts on each man. He attached the wrist bands and the anklets, fastened sage and sticks into their hair. Handing them each a staff, he stepped back for an appraisal.

"Ho, you look fit enough to fulfill your vows, but this performance is going to take more than just good looks. Finish and you will know great satisfaction. Fail and you will be given to the women."

Higheagle lowered his voice. "My relatives, everything is in readiness. There are four other dancers waiting outside right now. You will follow me and they will follow you. I have spoken."

Higheagle stooped to pick up a buffalo skull from near the entrance, threw the flap open and stepped out. With a motion for the others to follow, he took long, slow, deliberate steps to lead the dancers into the bowery.

In the language of signs, the dancers were told to sit on the beds of sage grass. Continuing to the altar, Higheagle approached it four times before placing the skull of the buffalo upon it.

The drummers and singers slowly entered the arena, the spectators following at a distance. By the time everybody had taken his place a fire of sage was burning on the altar, and Higheagle was purifying articles in its smoke.

Tension was beginning to mount as the spectators were straining to observe all of the things which were going on. The pipe was lit by Biglance, four puffs and he passed it to the dancer sitting on his left. Thus signalled the end of Higheagle's duties. Biglance, the Intercessor, was in charge.

A murmur was heard from the watchers as the drumming roll of the great ceremonial drum began. All six dancers, eager to begin, jumped to their feet to fall in line. Side by side they faced the sun, their arms raised in its direction. The drum became silent, the dancers lowered their arms, hands along the thighs. Biglance walked with ceremony down the line of dancers and thrust eagle bone whistles into their mouths.

Stopping at the last dancer, Biglance clenched his fist, and with a sudden movement, brought his fist across his chest in an arc. The drummers took the cue and to the accompaniment of many rattles, the dance started.

Turtleheart's heart raced as he kept time to the drum beat, raising himself onto the balls of his feet and dropping to the heels. The up and down action of the dancers was in perfect time to the rhythm of the drum, and the shrill whistle of the eagle bones was piercing to the ears. The monotony of the movement, plus the sounds of the dance, cast an eerie spell.

No word was spoken by the dancers as they kept up without break all morning, their eyes mere slits as they looked at the sun. Biglance kept pacing in front of them, offering words of encouragement.

As the sun reached its zenith, the spectators who kept drifting back and forth from the dance, all came back to see the dancers rest and to yell their words of approval.

Commanded to lie down by Biglance, the dancers were only too willing to comply. A short rest was welcome. As they lay on the couches, Biglance spewed water from his mouth upon them and an attendant gave them small bowls of dog broth.

The rest interval was short and the dancers were soon back to their bobbing step to keep on until the setting of the sun. After a full day of the dance, the men were unsteady in their walk and their eyes were red and swollen when they were released from the dance by the intercessor. Although very tired from their exertion, they could not lay their tired bodies down until given permission by Biglance. To stumble and fall would bring cries of derision and they would be taunted as women.

At the end of the second day there was no pretense of toughness of body. The candidates simply dropped in their tracks from exhaustion. At the end of this day the women relatives were allowed to help them to their couches.

As the sun approached its high point on the third day, the excitement of the people was rampant. After the short rest, the dancers were going to give of the body. They had already given of the spirit and the long awaited command by Biglance for the "tying up" was greeted with absolute silence.

The warriors of the Buffalo Society had been performing the buffalo dance a short distance away, and now they came running into the dance area. In simulated battle charge, their weapons were brandished with vigorous enthusiasm.

The prey of the warriors were the sun dancers. One was stalked by a hideously painted character with a war lance. Another was attacked with the tomahawk. A third wards off the flashing blade of a knife. The howls, the cries, the savage gestures were impressive and the watchers gave forth with loud whoops of pleasure at the show.

Turtleheart and the others were soon captured and thrown to the ground with no evidence of gentleness, to await the torture. After a short dance of victory, the Buffalo Warriors consulted among themselves about the manner of torture selected by the individual dancers.

The upper left arm of the first dancer was gashed fifty times with a sharp knife. The second dancer had pledged thirty gashes; the third, forty gashes. The fourth dancer had pledged one hundred and twenty cuts. Fifty on each arm was his share, the remaining cuts to be accepted by the women of his family.

The scarring ceremony was anti-climaxed by the smoking of the medicine pipe. Each of the four dancers took four puffs as the pipe was passed to the left. After the smoking of the pipe they were dismissed. With their arms over the shoulders of their relatives, they walked half supported, with stumbling steps. Collapsing to the ground out of the area, their wounds were treated by the medicine man. The cost of treatment depended upon the wealth of the family.

The ends of the horse hair ropes hanging from the pole were being split by the Buffalo Warriors. The split strands had to be long enough to reach the ends of the wooden skewers which would be inserted through the flesh of Turtleheart and Strong Echo.

The pointed sticks made from the wood of the wild cherry were in place on special pads to keep them holy. The hushed quiet was disturbed by the rolling beat on the drum. The sounds of the turtleshell rattles seemed vague. The time for the supreme torture of the Sun Dance was at hand.

The air of the hot day seemed charged with the arrows of lightning and as the tormentors dropped to their knees, one expected to hear the roll of thunder come from the clear sky.

The medicine man of the Buffalo Society drew his awl, and with much ceremony presented it to the four winds. He bent over the prostrate Turtleheart and grasped the flesh of the chest just above the nipple with his teeth. When he felt that the flesh was numb, he deftly forced the bone awl through the muscle to form two punctures. The blood was running freely when the skewer was inserted into the wound. Involuntarily, Turtleheart closed his eyes. He again closed his eyes when the same procedure followed on the other side.

The medicine man went to Strong Echo and Turtleheart felt the blood going down his abdomen. After the skewers had been inserted through the flesh of Strong Echo, the candidates were motioned to rise by Biglance. Led to the pole, the skewers were attached to the rope. Biglance gave each of them a few elm leaves for sustenance and a lance.

As Biglance raised the pipe to the Great Holy, the drumming ceased. After the invocation the pipe was offered to Turtleheart, who really did not care to accept it. A small fog of smoke appeared four times and the pipe was given back to Biglance, who now offered it to Strong Echo.

From the lips of the singers came the words of a sacred chant. The bodies of the watchers began to sway in cadence and from the throng could be heard the sounds of dull bells as many feet kept time with the rhythm of the drumming.

Securely fastened, Turtleheart began to pull steadily backward. The flesh of his breasts resembled two bloody horns. Strong Echo was jumping wildly about with the motions of a wounded animal.

By mid-afternoon, the singers had completed all of the twenty-four sacred songs of the Sun Dance and were starting on the second round.

Sharp, searing pains stabbed through Turtleheart's chest. The weight of a buffalo robe was upon the ropes holding him to the pole. He fell to one knee in agonizing anguish, his thoughts whirled as he barely heard a woman's voice. "In my small way, my son, I have tried to help you."

Staggering to his feet, Turtleheart began to jerk spasmodically against the restraining rope. Blood streamed into his breechclout and perspiration poured from every pore of his body. He jerked and felt one of the skewers tear loose. An awed silence fell upon the crowd as he fell to both knees, unable to rise.

He must tear loose from the other skewer. Knowing that the longer he stayed on his knees, the harder it would be to get up, he forced himself upright while feeling great pride that no outcry had passed his lips.

In one instant his body stiffened, his arms jerked and he was free. His mind was strangely clear, but his body crumpled to the earth, completely sapped of strength. He was free, free! He had preserved his honor.

The thunderous roar of approval increased in volume. Biglance announced that the last skewer had been broken. Both men were free! This was a good omen. It was the fulfillment of the vow!

CHAPTER ELEVEN

Dawn Country

Arriving in St. Louis with the Callahans, Evensigh was astounded at the size of their home. In her shy way, she made no effort to conceal her surprise at the beautiful carpets, the ornamental chandeliers, the pillars, and her fright at the first ascension up the wide stairway.

Shown to her room, she explored it like a delighted child. Smelling the draperies, laying on the canopied bed and fondling its covers, she was in a dream world. The many bars of soap fascinated her with their fragrance and she bit into one. Making a wry, funny face, she quickly spat it out.

As Evensigh became familiar with her new way of life, she soon realized that the life of a white woman such as this did not require the physical strength of a Sioux woman. There were other differences too; the customs, the attitudes, the patterns of habit. Her first impulse was to reject this life.

However, Evensigh earnestly tried to learn and understand what was going on. The differences were great and she spent many months adjusting. Mrs. Callahan was very understanding and patient, and taught her to read and write; to dress properly; to set the table and cook; how to dance and curtsy, and the many other things important to the people of St. Louis.

At the end of her first year, she spoke English well enough to be included at the dinner parties the Callahans had. She was a naturally sensitive girl and at these functions she could feel rather than see that there were many who were jealous of the Callahan family.

Really, she told herself, the people here were no different than those at home. If they were lazy and worthless, they had little. If they were brave and had honor they were highly respected.

Evensigh and Mrs. Callahan spent many hours together when Mr. Callahan was away on his many business trips, and the two women grew very fond of each other in the way of women who can understand another's feelings.

"You are very much like my mother at home," Evensigh said one evening. "You are very kind and thoughtful of others, as she is. You can understand how I feel."

Mrs. Callahan rose from her chair and gave the girl a warm hug. "You could not have pleased me more if you were my own daughter, Julie, who died so long ago. You are just as I always hoped she would be." Her eyes were misty, and the two women embraced each other as mother and daughter.

Evensigh had come to think of herself as the Callahan's daughter. It startled her to realize she had become a white person. She kept reminding herself that she must not forget her past life. Nothing could change what had happened, and it was important to her. She must keep her Indian thoughts in a closed part of her mind, and make a determined effort to face the reality of the present. At night her dreams gave her away. She thought Sioux and cried out Sioux words.

In the spring following her arrival, Mr. Callahan brought a young man, Michael Peterson, home to dinner. He worked for Mr. Callahan's firm and was very good looking and pleasant.

By choice, he was Evensigh's escort to the concert after dinner, and the two of them spent a most enjoyable evening. Seeing that Evensigh was attracted to the young man, Mrs. Callahan managed to invite him to their home many times.

"My, Michael is squiring you everywhere these days, isn't he?" Mrs. Callahan asked.

"Yes, he does. He is very considerate and understanding, and he knows that I like him very much."

"You still think of Turtleheart," the frankness in her voice was not unkind, but sincere.

While she had kept the memory of Turtleheart locked in her mind, Evensigh never thought of replacing him with another. The idea drained her cheeks of color.

"Please. Please excuse me," she said hurriedly. In her room she felt disloyal to the memory of her loved one. Mrs. Callahan did know her secret and in a way she was glad.

It takes courage to salvage a dream. She realized the memories of Turtleheart must not become entangled with her present life. The memory was sweet, but it was just a memory, no more or no less.

Michael Peterson was a constant caller at the Callahan home. He brought flowers; or a book; occasionally a box of candy. He did not question Evensigh about her former life, but respected her inner thoughts and steered the conversation of the others away from it.

As they strolled through the Callahan garden one hot summer night, Evensigh asked him to sit down so she could talk. She told him about Turtleheart and his tragic death, and about her love for him. It was hard to tell Michael, but she felt it was his right to know her true feelings, even at the risk of a beautiful friendship.

There was a short, awkward silence as Michael was trying to grasp at ideas to ease the situation. Not meaning to say what he did, he asked, "Were you married against your will?"

"Of course not, why do you say that?"

"Well, uh, gosh, I do not know. It's just . . . Well, I guess I have heard stories about Indian girls and all of that."

"Oh Michael," she fussed. "That is not true. You must not believe all of the stories you hear." Seeing the consternation on his face, she had to laugh.

"To marry an Indian girl, a man has to have the consent of her parents. If they accept his present of a robe or something, he is acceptable if she desires him. If she rejects the robe, he gets it back." She shrugged her shoulders as if to say that was all there was to it.

"The groom has to prove himself to the family then?"

"Yes, if he has honor, is generous, is brave and comes from a good family, then he will provide a good home for his wife and will be a good father for his children." She paused then added, "His family should be able to give many gifts to her family, which shows they have good thoughts of the forthcoming marriage."

She rose and held onto Michael's hand as they walked to a little pond.

"Michael, my grandmother has often told me that if you stand very still before sunrise, before the morning star has stolen away, that you can hear nature. Do you believe that? I do. You can feel it in your whole body."

"Your thoughts are most beautiful and I must say, you are right. That is the quietest part of the day." Taking a deep breath, he asked, "Were you happy in the Indian world?"

"Yes. I have to say yes. Our way was different. As a girl, the Sioux is trained to be the mother of the band. She can cook, dry foods, tan hides, make clothing, do beadwork, make a fine home for her children. A good woman is very valuable and the man depends upon her. To marry a girl, persuasion may be used, but never force."

"You are a very remarkable and sweet girl, Evensigh. If only the others had the honest and sincere personality that you possess."

The next day, a parcel from the most expensive shop in St. Louis arrived for Evensigh. Inside was a beautifully designed friendship ring and with it, a card with the penciled words, "To my Indian Princess, with love, Mike.

CHAPTER TWELVE

The Council

The summer of 1875 had been extremely hot and dry. Now, blizzards swept across the high plains, as the bitter cold of a very early winter enveloped the area. Rations were very scarce, even among the Indians camped near the agency.

Abiding by the insistent demands of the people, Higheagle called a council of the chiefs. Among those asked to attend were Turtleheart and Strong Echo. On the dark, wind swept night before the council was to be held, the hungry populace congregated around the lodge of Higheagle, in the hope that some action would soon be taken to alleviate the growing fear of famine.

At the first light of dawn, the council members began to arrive. They seated themselves around the center fire with their robes pulled around their shoulders. Their position depended upon the rank held, and as Turtleheart and Strong Echo were newcomers, they were given a place in back of the established leaders.

Higheagle arose to address them. "Without doubt, many serious problems have been abusing your mind. The biggest problem which is in our minds is the fact that we are without food. The children cry and the old ones weep. If something is not done soon, we shall starve." He spoke the last statement with extreme emphasis, then paused. "The land has become a barren place and the white men have done nothing. It would seem they mean to destroy us. They gave enough food to feed children and that did nothing but weaken our bodies and our spirits. We are only half alive. Even our ponies starve and cannot travel far, for they only have dry, weightless grass. We cannot survive the winter unless we kill and eat our horses."

Strong Echo rose from his position and asked permission to speak. "Men of the council, we cannot exist as men anytime, because we are only half free. This fact weighs on all of our minds, and I think every man should speak his thoughts. That way, we might find an answer."

Nods of approval and words of encouragement gave Strong Echo added strength, so he spoke in a bolder tone. "By treaty we are required to live on the reservation. But this treaty gives us the right to hunt elsewhere, even beyond the Paha Sapa, our sacred ground. All we need to do is notify the agent of our need to hunt there, and according to the treaty, he cannot oppose us. Our people are starving. Some of the old ones have already walked off into the prairie to die, so as to leave their share of food for the children. This is a bitter way for a proud people to die."

"The efforts of the blue coats are against us. I know that they do not all feel this way, but they must follow the orders of their leaders. Many of them are good people and try to help us, but those in charge know that what they do will weaken us. When we are broken like a stick, they will take what we have left, and move us to the Indian Territory down to the south."

The voice of the crier was heard, telling the people what was being said, as Strong Echo paused for a deep breath. "I have been waiting," he resumed, "to tell you of what I read in the white man's written language. This was written thirty-five winters ago by a man named Catlin. He said on this paper, that thirty million white men are fighting over the bones of twelve million red men, six million of whom have fallen victim of the smallpox, the dread disease of the white man."

"I was born an Indian and was raised an Indian, but I have lived the road of the white skin. I am telling you that the problems we have now will catch up the white man when he is unaware. I have spoken with my heart."

The silence following Strong Echo's words was broken by many comments of praise and assent.

The chieftains now looked in surprise at Turtleheart, as he had given the sign for recognition. His honor and bravery was well known, but for a youth who has had no real experience to want to speak? They were curious as to what this young man might have to say.

"For too long I have rubbed the oil on my impatience. Many are suffering because we have been surrounded as the buffalo by the white men. Nothing is left of our spirits to warm the darkness of our lives."

Turtleheart was nervous and his voice was strained, but with some effort, he tried to speak in a normal way. "Out of respect for you with greater wisdom than I, I have suppressed the idea of taking the band of Chiefeagle on a hunt beyond the Paha Sapa."

The earnestness of Turtleheart's thoughts gave him the courage to continue. "I, too, have suffered hunger, and that I can endure, but to hear the children cry for food, the old ask for meat, tears my heart in two pieces. Can we do nothing but sit on our haunches and warm the earth?"

"Have we forgotten that strength comes from use? We must be like the young eagle which was driven from its nest by the mother eagle. We too, must strengthen our wings by flying. We must go on the hunt."

Turtleheart's throat was dry from nervousness. "My relations with the white man assure me that he will not give us back our land. My words are harsh, but my heart tells me that the white leaders are speaking with a forked tongue in making promises to give us hope. If you believe this, I reject you. I will lead my band to the hunting grounds in spite of you."

With one fist hitting the other for emphasis, he concluded with, "What I have to say is strong, but if I am wrong you will have to prove what you say."

Crazy Horse was on his feet before any of the surprised elders could recover. Without the recognition of Higheagle, he burst out, "Your words are good words and spoken with the good spirit. I am with you. I cannot stay here and die. To die in war is honor, but to fade away with the sunset is to be a coward. That is all."

Higheagle gave the sign for silence as Iron Shield rose. "It is good to hear a man of your bravery, Crazy Horse, but this is a council of honor." The stern words of Higheagle were as a command. "Iron Shield, you may speak your mind."

"You have spoken the thoughts of a wise man, Turtleheart. I, Iron Shield, look around me, and from what I see on your faces, I would say we are in agreement. We can no longer be slaves of the white man's ways."

The remainder of the meeting was dedicated to the plans of carrying out the means of accomplishing that which had been agreed upon. When free to leave, Turtleheart hurried to the lodge of his grandmother.

"A messenger is being sent to the agency, Grandmother, to tell them of our intentions to go to the hunting grounds on the Powder River."

"That is good, my grandson. We have waited a long time for that news. How soon do we leave?"

"Early in the morning, grandmother."

"Bring two horses and I will start to pack."

Turtleheart smiled as he said, "Strong Echo is on his way with them."

"Did he speak at the council?"

"He gave a strong talk, one that opened many eyes. But his heart is sad."

"Ah?"

"Yes. He feels he has been abandoned. He has to stay with the old and the sick and the children. He is to move them to the agency after we have gone."

At the sound of Strong Echo's approach with the horses, Turtleheart stepped out into the cold night.

Strong Echo handed the ropes of the horses to Turtleheart and complained, "I was counting on hanging at your moccasins, my friend, but my pleading was ignored."

"Strong Echo, a strong man of your talents is needed. I am sure Higheagle selected you because of your great wisdom of the white man's ways and tongue. You will help dispel the fears of our people who are going to the agency. Your mission is more important than mine, old friend."

"Your words are of comfort, but it was my great desire to take part in the buffalo hunt."

"Higheagle is a man of great wisdom, and he knows that if the hunt fails and we are unable to come back, no one else could help our people better than you."

Eager to change the subject, Turtleheart asked, "Why was Red Cloud absent from the council? I understood he was to be present."

"On my last trip to the agency I had a long talk with him. He told me he would not come; his band was faring better at the agency. He said he was sending his spirit of support even though he had grown weary of letting the hatchet fall on his people. He said that the wars always ended in treaties, and that treaties are not understood by red men."

Strong Echo shook his head at Red Cloud's reasoning. "He is a good man, but torn between paths. He still believes in the language of the treaties and is sad when they are broken. I have deep sympathy for Red Cloud."

"He is truly a noble man, Strong Echo, but his memory is growing fogged with age. Like a child he is persuaded into thinking that freedom is to live like the white man. I prefer to be free to hunt for the food, for the clothing I wear, the vision which gives me strength of spirit. This is the freedom Red Cloud has forgotten."

"Freedom means many things to many people, Turtleheart. Our freedom is our way of life, but to others it could be a different thing."

"I must go." He grimaced to show that while he did not like Higheagle's orders, he would still obey. With no further word, he disappeared into the darkness.

"Grandson, step inside. I have something which you should have." The voice of his grandmother called from the tipi.

In a lighter mood, Turtleheart stuck his head inside of the flap and quipped, "You do? For me?"

"Do not stand there like a clown," she pretended annoyance. "You are letting in the cold and I am the one who hauls the wood."

"Here is the winter count which your grandfather started many years ago. It is yours now. He asked me to give it to you when he was no longer here to keep the record." Her voice now choked at recalling the details leading up to the death of her husband. "This is the proper time. You are now our leader."

The old woman slowly handed Turtleheart two rolls of tanned hide, as she explained further. "This smaller winter count is your own personal calendar which your grandfather kept for you since the time he found you."

"I had forgotten about it, until I unrolled the band winter count and found it inside."

Turtleheart's eyes were shining with pride as he unrolled the smaller tube of elk hide to study its symbols. Allowing his thoughts to go back over the years, he remembered many of the events the pictures portrayed.

"I shall take care of it grandmother, great care of it. He was a wise leader, and his winter count must be preserved."

"He told me it was to be very valuable to you, and that you must continue the story it tells."

"Yes grandmother, I will do as he wished. No one knows how much this means to me." He rolled the smaller of the two winter counts carefully inside of the other and left the lodge.

Outside were two boys helping pack his grandmother's belongings, and after giving them some instructions to follow, Turtleheart left them to make the final preparations for the hunting trip. Soon, scouts were sent ahead to break the trail for the long journey to the country of the Powder River.

CHAPTER THIRTEEN

THE BUFFALO HUNT AND A MESSAGE

Making rapid time in spite of the difficulties of bad weather, the caravan, under Turtleheart's leadership, was traveling through the area southeast of the Powder River in what is now Wyoming, within a moon's time. Devil's Tower was to the north and the Black Hills were to their backs in the east. The trip was uneventful except for the merciless weather. The vicious winter storms howled about their thin garments and turned the skin blue.

Two braves were with Turtleheart as the trail ahead was scouted. The enforced stay on the reservation had corraled their spirits, and now, in spite of the miserable weather, they were rejoicing to be able to roam unfettered.

The remarkable fragrance of the woods was in his nostrils, and the unfrozen spots of water in the streams seemed exceptionally clear. He wondered if this was the reason why the story tellers referred to these streams as 'Medicine Water'!

Everything seemed beautiful. Even the snow that looked so threatening a few days ago, charmed him now with its bluish hue. Thus was the mystery of Wakan Tanka, and these are the signs of His veiled presence.

What was it Higheagle had said? "You have to know just what you are, in order to feel Him through nature. It is only through nature that one can gain communion with the Holy Mystery."

"Look. The open spot ahead! And the one to the right; and close to the horizon. Look!" The excited shouts of the scout ahead broke the thoughts of Turtleheart.

"Straighten my arrows! That is a band of buffalo. They are in our path. This is a good day. Let us go and get fresh meat for our relatives."

"I will ride ahead to scout for a cliff to drive them over."

"No, no," answered Turtleheart. "Look closely, they are on the move. We must strike now."

"Hee-YAAAH!" was the yell on their lips as the three men descended on the herd with their horses at full gallop. The sudden noise confused two full grown cows into colliding with each other. Both were shot while still off balance, and they collapsed where they stood.

The remainder of the shaggy beasts were now alarmed, and with tremendous speed and power, they were on the move. The scouts were after them as the buffalo plunged wildly into the open, heads down and tails up.

Dashing madly ahead, Turtleheart glanced to his left to see a young amber colored bull. He aimed and fired and the animal, which showed four winters of life, veered unsteadily then plunged down, the momentum of his great bulk causing him to turn end for end in a cloud of dusty snow.

Quickly surveying the undulating sea of humps, Turtleheart selected the largest beast near him as his next victim. Dropping his single shot rifle, he snatched the lance hanging from the side of his pony. Pushing his horse to greater speed, it was now difficult to see clearly through the white fog of snow.

He guided his horse in between the shaggy animals until he raced neck and neck with his intended prey, terror in its eyes. Turtleheart could see the slithering tongue as it ran with a mighty will to live. With all the power in his arm and shoulder, he drove the lance deep into the brown body. Enraged, the animal did not give him time to withdraw his lance, and lunged at the horse with its huge head and horns.

The breath of the pony knocked out, the buffalo and the horse went down in a tangle of bodies and legs. Turtleheart leaped clear, with a desperate effort, and landed on his feet. As the pony lunged to its feet, Turtleheart was on his back, eager to get going before the rest of the herd ran them down.

Looking for the lanced buffalo, the hunter saw him nearby. He was moving, but with considerable unsteadiness, as the lance was pulled out and thrust home again. This stopped the wounded animal, and the rest of the herd thundered on by. As Turtleheart dismounted from his horse with a flying leap, the buffalo fell with a thud.

The other scouts raced up shouting, "This is like the old days, eh? We got three of them, and it is a good feeling. How many did you get?"

"Two."

"Five in all. We will feast for the next few days. A day of rest and a belly full of food will be good."

"Come, let us cut these buffalo." stated Turtleheart. "We have work to do before we eat."

With the satisfaction of a full stomach, Turtleheart pulled his buffalo robe close for warmth. It was late at night and he was taking his turn at watch in the crotch of a tree overlooking the camp.

The people were fast asleep and this made him feel good. They deserved the chance to rest without the gnawing pangs of hunger. A man's song of thanks drifted up softly from the camp, and Turtleheart knew this was the song of relief.

The good feeling was to be disturbed the next day. The scouts rode into camp reporting they had seen about thirty of the horse soldiers with some Indian scouts who were probably Crow. They were only a half day's travel from the camp and were coming closer.

With some haste, the camp leaders assembled for a council, and the leader of the scouts told of what he had seen. As Turtleheart listened thoughtfully, he was making plans. He rose to speak when the scout had finished his story.

"My relations, this has been a truly hard and trying journey. It was long, but successful. We thought it best to stay in the open so we could not be ambushed, but now, after we have camped, the scouts bring word of horse soldiers and our old enemy, the Crow."

"Before you clog your minds with what we must do," Higheagle interjected, "I wish to say that Turtleheart's leadership deserves our highest praise."

The answer to this was many "hous".

"Hear me, my relations," the slow and resonant voice of Crazy Horse silenced the men. "We have just emerged from a storm of suppression where we were supposed to be sustained by the agency. We were hungry there, but today we are not hungry. We can step outside and feel the many deep spirits of the past, return. Our heritage reminds us that the Sioux life came from the earth, and should be nourished by the earth. We now talk of preserving this heritage. The sensible step toward the preservation of our band is to move on into the valleys of the Tongue and Rosebud Rivers."

"There we and the horses can regain our strength until the warm weather returns. Then we can move into the valley of the Greasy Grass for our annual reunion of the members of the seven council fires."

"An excellent idea, Crazy Horse, and well spoken. Is there anyone here who is unwilling to put his faith in the suggestion of Crazy Horse?" There were no words of disagreement, so all went out to begin the task of breaking camp.

Along the river of the Rosebud, the band found life peaceful, and they gladly resumed the old way of life. In the many lodges there was always plenty of meat and warmth. At night the inhabitants of the lodges sat around the fires and spoke of the lore of their forefathers. They laughed and talked of the Red Cloud Agency as though it were a nightmare of long ago.

It was on one of these nights that Turtleheart escorted a runner from the Indian Agency into camp. They were astonished to see a frost-covered rider who appeared hardly strong enough to sit on a horse.

As the messenger was ushered into Higheagle's presence, he remarked, "Well, if it isn't one of the agency Indians, one of the Loafer band. You look ill. Sit down and have some hot broth to revive you."

"I am not ill, but I am very tired. The long journey to here has made me tired to the bones. I carry a message to you from the Commissioner of Indian Affairs. You are to move back to a place within the reservation. You must be there by the end of January on the white man's calendar. If you do not, you will be treated as an enemy."

"What day of the calendar is this?" Higheagle was greatly disturbed at hearing the words of this Loafer.

"Let me count the sticks I have in my pouch. Each one is for a different day of travel." With this, he emptied a small bag of its contents and he and Higheagle counted.

"There are twenty-six of them, Higheagle."

"And by what day of the calendar did you leave?"

"I left on the day of December twenty-second, the same day the message was received by the Indian Agent. The storms and bitter cold slowed my journey, and there were many times I thought I would not find you."

"Then, what day is this in the white man's count?"

The two bent their heads to figure this problem, and when it became apparent that this was already the seventeenth of January, Higheagle shook his head. "We cannot return by the fourteen days time."

"This is another deliberate attempt to declare war on us. This will give the agent a reason to turn us over to the horse soldiers." With these words of anger, Crazy Horse stalked out of the lodge.

"After you have rested, you can exchange your horse for another to go back and tell the long knives that we cannot do the impossible." A wave of the hand by Higheagle, and he excused the messenger.

Sitting Bull and his band of Hunkpapa arrived at the camp a few days later, to find the people in a mood of dejection. Being told about the message they were also much concerned, as they had received a similar message while camping on the west fork of Beaver Creek.

Turtleheart doubled his force of scouts and dispatched them as far as he dared. They were to keep a sharp lookout for the arrival of blue coats in the area. Days and weeks passed without event, and the weather was too bad to allow any movement of the camp.

Early one morning, during a break in the stormy sky, a group of mounted Indians were sighted by a scout who recognized them as Cheyennes. They informed the scout that there were only a few left of their band. They had been camping in the bottom of the Powder River.

They were extended the hand of friendship and invited to come into the camp to tell their story of woe. They had been attacked by soldiers while they were asleep in their lodges. They told of the terror of being awakened by gunshots, and the shreiking of women as they were shot down. All of the tipis were burned, destroying the meat and robes inside.

They had been taken completely by surprise, and those who did manage to escape did so by scurrying into the nearby hills. Being desperate men of courage they afterwards recaptured some of their horses.

"Where were your lookouts?" queried Turtleheart.

Two Moons, the heavy set leader of the Cheyenne, spoke up. "We have not had much use for lookouts since the treaty of 1868. For the last seven winters we have lived in peace with the soldiers. Our only enemies were the Crow."

"It was only a short time ago a handful of troopers came to our camp to move us to the Sioux Agency. When they found we were Cheyenne, they apologized and moved on."

When the Cheyenne leader had finished his report to the council, Crazy Horse rose with a furious anger.

"I cannot endure any more. Yesterday it was the Cheyenne. Tomorrow, it will be us. Think of our losses since the first treaty, Higheagle. Think deeply. I am sure the time of avoiding the war cries and paint is long past."

Crazy Horse was bristling with anger. "I am war chief in this camp, and I direct Turtleheart to send runners to those bands of Cheyenne and Arapahoe who have cause to unite with us. They must be told that the chieftains of the seven council fires demand their presence on the Greasy Grass for our annual camp."

"Also tell them that it is better to die with honor on the field of battle, than to die of dishonor in old age."

CHAPTER FOURTEEN

A Silent Burial

The weariness of many sleepless nights weighed upon Turtleheart as he dropped onto a couch of buffalo robes to sip the steaming broth his grandmother had given to him. He had spent many days at a time scouting the far flung areas of the Rosebud and Tongue River valleys. It was only when his supply of pemmican and jerky was exhausted that he returned to camp.

"You look so thin and tired, my son. You must stay here and rest until you put some flesh on your bones."

He did not reply. "You still think of Evensigh." His grandmother did not wish to mention this subject to her grandson, but she wanted him to know that she shared his thoughts.

"Yes grandmother, every day of my life I miss her."

The old woman's wrinkled face brightened as she asked, "Would you like to know who just came into camp with the Brules and the Santees?" When Turtleheart showed no sign of interest, she said, "He is a very good friend of yours, my son."

She waved her hand, and a head immediately poked into the entrance of the lodge. "So this is how the brave men loaf! On their haunches, warming the earth. Why, I should spit on your couch." The voice was laughing.

Recognition stirred Turtleheart to action, and he jumped to his feet. "Strong Echo! The two grasped each other and indulged in loud shoulder slapping and a few playful cuffs. "When did you get here?"

"Just a little while ago. I was told that the great and fearless warrior, Turtleheart, was somewhere on the purple horizon looking for the enemy. We came in from the south, and did not see anyone, so where were you, oh great and fearless one?" In spite of the lightness of talk, this was a serious question, and Turtleheart answered it with a sober face.

"I was up north toward the Crow territory. We were scouting the area where the Rosebud melts with the Yellowstone."

Strong Echo examined Turtleheart's tired face and gaunt frame while shaking his head, but said nothing. Turtleheart was aware of his friend's thoughts, and he, too, said nothing. He asked, instead, about the old people who had been left with Strong Echo when the band left for the hunt.

"They are well taken care of. It was Red Cloud himself who took on their responsibility by putting them in his own band. When he received your message, he spoke in despair. He told his own people that to challenge the word of the white government would bring disaster. There were many, however, who paid no heed to his words and left for Two Kettle's camp."

"It broke his heart when his own son went with them. I think they will be arriving at the Little Big Horn soon."

"We will be looking for them with joy, Strong Echo. What do you think of the situation?"

"I am not a part of it yet. You and I both know that the long knives have forgotten their promise to provide the people with food. They are starving us. But what you don't know is that they are breaking the solitude of the Black Hills with their shouts and echoes. They are killing the buffalo within our sacred land. They are laying their curse upon our Black Hills."

Strong Echo scratched his chin. "The more I think about it, the more I realize that we are the declared enemies of the white man."

"I am glad you have cast your lot with us." Turtleheart lost his serious look and grinned.

"Strong Echo thanks you, oh worthy scout." He made a playful pass at Turtleheart, who ducked away. "You always knew I could not go with those whose tongue is forked."

"Strong Echo, you are the best medicine a man like me could have around. You keep me on top of my feelings."

With this feeling of comradeship, the two men forgot the time of day and talked far into the night, long after all of the others had settled into sleep.

"The tribe's greatest hoop is broken. Our respected and beloved leader, the holy Yuwipi man, is dead. Higheagle died during the night."

The sad intoning of the words of the crier as he repeated his message of death, shocked Turtleheart out of his drowsy early morning behavior. Already the grievous wailings of the women were being heard from tipi to tipi.

Higheagle's passing was so quick that we were all numbed," Turtleheart remarked to Strong Echo as he sipped at his soup. "Some think this is an evil omen, because Higheagle never mentioned the possibility of his going to the land of our ancestors."

"I do not follow your words, Turtleheart."

"Did you notice the haste of the burial? It was one of the strangest ceremonies I have ever seen. And the mourning was only for one night. The burial procession began so early this morning that the sun was not yet in the sky. And there was no eulogy. Higheagle was buried without the usual formalities."

"You are a leader. Why didn't you say something?"

Turtleheart frowned in puzzlement. "I do not know. It is something hard to explain. When I went into his lodge to pay my last respects, there was an aura of nobility on Higheagle's face."

Pausing, Turtleheart looked at the sky. "Even in death, his face bore witness to the power he possessed. When I tried to think of something to say, I felt incapable of heaping worthy commendations on his spirit. All I could do was stand there in silence."

"You didn't take part in the burial rites?"

"No."

"You, for one, should have been there," his friend admonished Turtleheart.

"A strange fear had crept into my thoughts, Strong Echo. You know that his sacred powers went beyond our knowledge, that he had performed phenomenal feats. His physical body did not make me afraid, but I feared the mystery of his spirit."

"Turtleheart, your thoughts are deep indeed. You are not thinking clearly, my friend. You start this conversation with an air of curiosity, then, as you tell me of Higheagle's hasty burial, you sound so different."

Strong Echo shook Turtleheart's shoulder. "Do you think that others feel as you do?"

"Yes. Yes, I think that is possible." Turtleheart put his hand on that of Strong Echo. "Now I do know that you are good medicine for me. You straighten the crooked thoughts in my mind."

As the two walked toward their horses, Turtleheart said, "This is the day I am to lead our move to camp a little more to the north, up near where the creek widens. Will you be my assistant, Strong Echo?"

"As I once said, I will follow your moccasins. You lead my way."

The rest of the day was spent in moving the camp. The united bands of Ogalala, Brule, Minneconjou, Hunkpapa, Santee, Yankton and Blackfoot led the way. The Cheyenne, Sans Arc and Two Kettle followed as Turtleheart led them along the Rosebud River until they arrived at the pre-determined council site.

The women silently went about the setting up of lodges, gathering firewood, and the hundred other things necessary to settling in a new location. The leaders met in council.

Sitting Bull was chosen to serve as spokesman for the consolidated bands and correlator of their movements. Before the camp crier was dispatched to tell of the announcement, Turtleheart informed Strong Echo of what had transpired in the council meeting.

"I am not happy over the selection of Sitting Bull. I was hoping that Gall would be marked to fill Higheagle's place, but Sitting Bull was quite effective when he appealed to the minds of the council members. I had heard he was a fiery orator and a man of many moods."

"Yes, and quite surprisingly," answered Strong Echo. "My grandfather had told me that Sitting Bull's parents had given him up as a reckless fool when he was but a youth. They were content to put him under the care of Four Horns, his uncle. His companions were few, because he was always getting them into trouble, and he was finally barred from a lot of ceremonies because of his reckless nature."

"How did he take that? Was he bitter?" asked Turtleheart.

"He must have been hurt deeply. It was then that he began to work on the skill of influencing people with his words. As Four Horns was a medicine man with the talent for words, he contributed his knowledge to Sitting Bull's training. Also, because of Sitting Bull's heritage, it was not too hard for him to gain the power of performance."

Turtleheart was an interested listener, so Strong Echo continued with his story. "His own band considered him to be an agent of the Yuwipi, so he easily gained the status of a medicine man."

"His is an interesting story, but how is he trained in the making of war?" Turtleheart wanted to know.

"The story tellers speak of him as not having the courage to participate in battle, but they do tell of his power of vision. He has a remarkable ability to dream, that I do know. He is always the hero, as he has a very high opinion of himself."

"Yes," nodded Turtleheart. "It cannot be denied that he has a way with people. I am sure that on occasions in the past Sitting Bull took the laurels that rightly belonged to Gall. Instead of being angry, Gall talks of Sitting Bull as being a great person Sitting Bull must have strong medicine to be able to do the things he does."

"I should tell you, Strong Echo, that I sat next to Gall in council. When the results of the voting were made known, Gall conceded the better man had won."

"He said that if war was to come, Sitting Bull was best equipped with the knowledge to deal with the white soldiers. Gall hates them so intensely, he feels his hate will rule over his reason of mind. He said Sitting Bull was also better because he is keen at voicing what is warm to our ears."

"This may be true, Turtleheart, but in the times to come, Sitting Bull will have to rely on such men as Gall."

"Being the showman that he is, he will depend on Gall and other great warriors, then keep the glory to himself." Turtleheart's head was moving up and down with each word.

"Sitting Bull is already following the advice of Gall and Crazy Horse. He has sent out small raiding parties to gather all the guns, ammunition and horses they can find."

The spring day was warm as Turtleheart and Strong Echo reined up their horses on a high rise overlooking the camp. After several days of scouting, the view was welcome.

"It always makes my spirit rise and sing to see the magnificent view of the entire camp below. On a clear day you can just make out the path of the Tongue River. When the eye sees this, the mind dwells on my ancestors and the wisdom they had to come to this valley." Turtleheart took a deep breath and sighed in a moment of happiness.

"Look." Strong Echo pointed a finger a little to the north. "See, all of the people are returning to their lodges from the dance circle. Something must be going on. Let's hurry down and see."

With the dust raising at their horses' heels, they rode at a gallop down the hill, in a wide circle. Slowing their horses, they made their way from the outskirts of camp to the center area. Gall was waiting in front of Turtleheart's lodge.

Greeting them with a raised hand and a smile, Gall rose from his sitting position. "You two look happy." He turned to Strong Echo and commented, "You must be good medicine for Turtleheart. His grandmother was just telling me today that until you came along, he was not living in himself."

"Your words are good to hear," chuckled Strong Echo. "I always knew I had to be good for something other than giving birth to blisters on my hindparts." He patted himself on the part of the anatomy he spoke of.

"I have good news today," Gall remarked. "My warriors have brought reports that there are now many camps along the Little Big Horn. Already there are four times more lodges than we have here."

"The Little Big Horn? Why are they camped there? They are not coming here?" Strong Echo was quizzical.

"No, it was a year ago that we all agreed that the Greasy Grass was the best place for this year's annual council of the Sioux nation," Gall answered.

Gall switched his gaze from one to the other several times before continuing. "Three days ago, Sitting Bull informed us that he would give his body to Wakan Tanka through his performance of the Sun Dance, and would offer the penance of one hundred gashes on his arms. Today, Sitting Bull told us of the message he viewed in the clouds over the ceremonial circle."

"He said the Sioux nation must join forces. He said that the white soldiers' destiny is death in battle and that we would be the victor."

"You got here right after the council had met. They have decided it is time to move to the Greasy Grass to hold talk of war. The time has come to act like men of honor."

"How many warriors will we have in the camp on the Greasy Grass?" queried Strong Echo.

"I would guess about four thousand," answered Gall.

"Four thousand warriors? Wahhhhah!"

CHAPTER FIFTEEN

Rosebud Battle

It was two days after Sitting Bull's Sun Dance, and Turtleheart was watching a long train of soldiers and equipment come from the south. They appeared to be going toward Rosebud Creek. After motioning to Strong Echo to join him, they discussed the matter. Going down to the horses, hidden in a clump of bushes, Turtleheart mounted to ride straight toward camp, as Strong Echo remained behind to watch the formation of troops.

The camp was aroused with curiosity when Turtleheart rode in at a full gallop. Reaching camp, he started yelling at the top of his voice. "Blue coats! The soldiers of the enemy are coming this way!"

As his horse came to a sliding stop in front of Sitting Bull's lodge, Turtleheart was hitting the ground with his feet. Stepping into the lodge, he exclaimed, "Blue Coats!"

"I heard your cries," said Sitting Bull, as he continued to dab medicine on his scarred arms. As Sitting Bull turned, Turtleheart realized there was another person present.

It was Hump, the great warrior chief of the Minneconjou. "Hau," said Turtleheart, as Hump acknowledged the greeting with a silent hand signal.

After advising Hump to see to it that someone called all of the chiefs to council, Sitting Bull turned to Turtleheart. "How far away are they?"

"Because they are so many, their pace would enable them to arrive here after a full day of travel, sunup to sundown."

"You have seen the enemy, so I think you should stay for the meeting of the chiefs. They will have many things to ask." Sitting Bull said no more, and resumed the application of the medicine to his wounds.

The sounds of people making ready for a hasty move had replaced the original confusion. In cases of emergency, the people knew exactly what to do, and the chiefs lost no time in assembling for a council of war. Almost immediately they were on the way to Sitting Bull's lodge, which they entered silently, and took their places.

When all were assembled, Crazy Horse rose to ask, "How far away are they?"

"Near the upper end of Rosebud Creek."

"How many are mounted and how many on foot?"

"There must be a thousand to fifteen hundred of them, and most are on horses."

"What are your thoughts, Sitting Bull?" Crazy Horse was now facing the medicine man.

"A soldier for a warrior and a warrior for a soldier. We are equal in numbers, but nearly half of our warriors are without the guns they need to fight," replied Sitting Bull.

"May I offer a plan?" The voice of Gall was unmistakable. All eyes watched him as he continued slowly and with great thought. "Our first concern is our families, who are now preparing to break camp. My suggestion is for Sitting Bull, who is still unfit for battle because of his wounds, to lead the old, the women, the children to the big camp on the Little Big Horn. All the warriors will remain here to fight. For us to run now, with night coming, would be disastrous!"

"We all know that our families move much slower than we would, and if the soldiers knew of such a move, they would be sure to attack. Sitting Bull and the camp must move quietly, and we must remain here to protect them."

"The soldiers must know of our camp in this valley, or they would not be moving toward us. They must be planning to destroy our camps and supplies, thinking to destroy our will and ability to fight. They know that if they do that, we must bury the tomahawk and remain on the reservation like the dog."

Gall continued talking quietly and quickly. "Our camp is being prepared now and will be moving out this afternoon. We will then have time to take up our battle plans and could meet the soldiers in battle tomorrow."

"Your thoughts are excellent, Gall," Crazy Horse commended. "At a given signal we can pull out of the battle and lead them into the hills, then make a fast break to join the camp at the Little Big Horn."

"We must be cautious and see what the soldiers do before we attack them. If only a small force of them leaves to investigate our abandoned camp, let them through. They will be scouting and unable to do much, and it will be easier for us if their main force is weaker." Crazy Horse was a man of battle experience and his words were immediately endorsed.

The whole plan was created out of emergency, but the experience of past battles with the soldiers told them this was a good plan. It must be carried out with no loss of time, and the war council was over as abruptly as it began. The final plans would be made and carried out as the events of the next day unfolded.

Turtleheart and Strong Echo spent the long night taking turns to watch the camp of sleeping soldiers. With the coming of the eastern light, the darkness which enveloped the plains began to crawl away. It was at this time that Strong Echo became aware of the movements of warriors on the west side of the creek. An equal number of warriors were coming up the creek on the opposite side. Turtleheart told Strong Echo the latter group was led by Crazy Horse. The warriors on the far side were led by Gall. Hump would probably be with Gall.

Now was the time to be patient. Secrecy was the key to any success they hoped to achieve. Turtleheart prayed that the leaders could hold the young, impatient warriors in check. Any attempt at personal glory would result in disaster for all.

Strong Echo's low words brought Turtleheart's attention to the soldiers' camp. They were moving around, and preparing to mount. The absence of fires disturbed Turtleheart. Could the soldiers have any idea of impending trouble? If so, there would be no possible chance of splitting the command, and the odds would be in favor of the enemy.

The thoughts in the mind of Strong Echo were imperceptible to Turtleheart, as the older man's face was impassive. Turtleheart was sure his heart was going to jump out of his chest.

Finally the first contingent of soldiers mounted, and with a command, started to move down the valley. The others were still on the ground and it was a little later that they too moved out.

As the second contingent of soldiers reached this point however, war whoops echoed across the valley. The Sioux were on the attack. Gall led his warriors to hit the front of the column on one side and Crazy Horse and his warriors hit the rear of the column on the other side. This maneuver caused the column to turn on its axis, the soldiers completely at a disadvantage.

The two scouts welcomed the opportunity to rise from their cramped positions. Concealment was no longer necessary, so they stood in full view to watch the battle develop.

Charging time and again, the Indians kept the soldiers milling around. Only one time did the Sioux let up, and a swift moving formation of soldiers got through. With rifles firing and swords flashing in the sunlight, the soldiers made a run to a small hill. A few warriors pursued the group for a short distance, then returned to the action.

The main body of soldiers were able to mass together in a small area, and with their superior fire power, kept the Sioux warriors at a more discreet distance. Most of the activity now turned into harassment, with the soldiers pinned down. From every direction, the warriors moved in at top speed to shoot the arrows, wheel around and ride back to a safer distance.

"Turtleheart, look! Look down the valley, the first of the soldiers are coming back. They will be caught in a cross fire! I will warn them!" Strong Echo's words were almost lost in the distance, as he was on his way, riding recklessly straight down the hill. Turtleheart watched until he reached Crazy Horse. The great war chief could be seen gathering his warriors, and leading them in a sweeping curve toward Gall.

Gall had his warriors under command and his group fell in behind Crazy Horse and his men. The entire party made one sweeping circle around the soldiers before heading off to the east and disappearing over a hill.

The first contingent of soldiers was now on the scene, but they made no effort to follow the Indians. Perhaps they were fearful of an ambush, but it was certain they were glad to have the seige lifted. They had many casualties and were unwilling to make any further hostile moves.

Turtleheart smiled in satisfaction as he mounted his pony. The battle plan worked perfectly and there were but few Sioux who could be counted among the casualties. There were a few wounded, but they were all rescued.

One of the last men into the big camp on the Greasy Grass was Turtleheart. He rode into view of the camp and paused to take in the sounds of revelry. The hour was late, but many persons were gathered in the center of the camp, and the crier was still extolling the victory.

Spurring his horse, Turtleheart rode to camp with the victory song on his lips. Great pride filled his breast as he edged his horse through the people toward the center.

There was a tugging at his leg and he looked down to see his grandmother trying to speak with him. He bent low to catch her words. "They are reserving a place for you in the council lodge. Gall said to split the time and come."

"We had a safe journey and Sitting Bull has been in a council since we arrived," she patted him on the leg.

A familiar voice broke into their conversation, echoing the grandmother's words. It was Strong Echo who continued the line of talk. "Sitting Bull has been fanning the flames of animosity since his arrival. I have heard that his influence has been enormously increased since he exposed the sun dance scars on his arm. I have also heard you are to attend the council of chiefs. You had better go express your thoughts. Here, I will take your horse."

Approaching the council lodge, Turtleheart could hear the voice of Sitting Bull as he spoke in his most flowery language. Entering, he found that it was filled to capacity with council chiefs, war chiefs and ceremonial chiefs. No one paid any attention to him as they were too engrossed with what Sitting Bull was telling them.

"Today we have tasted victory, but you should not have to strain your memory to know that defeat passes by no age, no race. We must unite to survive, to defeat the white man who is our greatest enemy."

"Because I am a Sioux, one who is proud to be a Sioux, neither time nor the forcing of another way of life onto me will change the enduring emotions I have for our lands, for my people."

"Your wants are my wants. Your despairs and glooms are my agonies. My old body has almost reached the limit of what it can stand, and my mind is getting too tired to know what is best to do, so I am asking you to give my words your great consideration, so you may help make the decisions."

"If you choose to bear the lance with me, we shall taste victory, and we will again dwell as we did in the times that followed Red Cloud's victory. Today was the battle on the Rosebud, and we won. We must continue to win."

There was a momentary silence before whooping and howling filled the lodge. Turtleheart felt a warm glow over his body; his spirit was raised by the force of Sitting Bull's speech.

Crazy Horse rose to his feet with a sign for silence. He was of slight, medium build, but his bravery and cunning had made him a giant among a strong people. The red and black of his face paint, as always, concentrated on concealing the scars of his chin and jaw.

With rapid words and with little inflection of voice, he cooly related the day's events.

"I measured the actions of our hereditary enemies, the Crow and the Shoshone scouts, and I found them cunning as the coyote. As long as they continue to help the enemy we must remain alert to insure their defeat."

Dramatically, he produced a pipe. Striding forward to the fire, he selected a firebrand and majestically lit the tobacco. He drew long on the pipe and presented it to Wakan Tanka and to Maka Ina. "This is to seal our alliance." He handed the pipe to Turtleheart who sat on the left of the entrance. A puff of the pipe and he handed it to his left.

CHAPTER SIXTEEN

Soldiers and Decisions

For the next few days, Turtleheart and Strong Echo spent from sunup to sundown checking lookout posts of the scouts. They now stood on a high bluff of the Wolf Mountains, thinking of returning to the camps on the Greasy Grass. Almost simultaneously, both spotted small beads moving up the valley that Sitting Bull had used when fleeing from the Rosebud Creek a few days before. Horse soldiers! Their position was north and east across the mountain from the Sioux camp.

When dusk fell on this day of June 24, 1876, the two men mounted their horses and rode toward the long knives. They moved cautiously, and kept their ears tuned for the slightest sound. They did not want to blunder into the blue coats or their Indian scouts.

"Strong Echo, you stay here with the ponies. We must be near where they have stopped to camp and I want to see if I can sneak up on them."

"I can see nothing. It is now too dark to see much."

"They are camped almost directly north of us."

"How can you tell? Are you sure?"

"Yes. Turn your eyes to the east. Now move them very slowly across the slope below us. You will find the tail of your vision will catch a faint glow of light more to the north."

Turtleheart spoke very softly, since the wind was from the south and he did not want the sound of his voice to be heard by any of the Crow scouts he knew to be around.

"Ah yes. There is a faint glow of a fire. It is not much. They are keeping the fires small so they will be hard to see. It must be that they are planning something."

"You stay here and I will be back as soon as I can see how many horses they have. When I can study the size of their herd I will know how many of them there are." With these words, his form disappeared into the gloom of the early night.

Turtleheart was thankful for the darkness. It made his task much easier. To be able to thread his way through the night was a skill he had developed over a long period of time. It was but a short time that he could see a couple of small fires. "They are very cautious," he thought to himself.

There were no horses! Perhaps they had them hid some distance from camp. That did not make sense. He knew the army commanders were too smart to make that foolish a blunder.

Dropping onto his stomach, he started to edge closer. There was a definite cause for wonder. Could this be another group from the one they saw from the ridge?

His mind told him there had to be horses around. The army could not travel without horses. Just as he decided to circle the camp, the sound of muffled hoofbeats reached him. A group of Indians and soldiers were bringing the herd up from the other side. Possibly from watering.

Under the cover of the noise of the moving horses, he was able to creep closer. With all of his senses straining to their utmost, he was trying to identify the sounds of camp and the sights of the moving figures. He lay unmoving as an Indian came his way.

"It was an Arikara!" he thought. "They are not near so dangerous as the Crow." The Indian turned to walk in another direction, so Turtleheart breathed easier. When his curiosity had been satisfied, he circled slowly away from the enemy to avoid the sentries. He was very careful not to excite the many bushes as he moved.

Returning to Strong Echo, he told him of what he had seen. The two warriors led their horses over the divide before mounting, Turtleheart to ride to warn the camp and Strong Echo to tell the other scouts.

It was after midnight when Turtleheart returned to the sleeping villages of tipis. Going immediately to the large lodge of Sitting Bull, he gave the call of his society to waken the leader. Sitting Bull listened intently to Turtleheart before sending messengers to the chiefs in the different camps. Late as it was, he was calling a council meeting.

Dawn was just beginning to melt away the darkness as the council convened to discuss the presence of the soldiers and the obvious nature of their mission. There was a sudden and loud commotion outside. Strong Echo's voice was demanding admission to the council lodge.

"The troops must be commanded by Yellow Hair. After I left Turtleheart, I went to Loneman and another scout and we returned to watch the enemy. Loneman sneaked up to the horse herd and recognized some gray horses used by some of the men under Yellow Hair. Also, they are on a forced night march!"

"Are you sure?" questioned Gall. In his face was the reflection of the hate within him for the army leader.

"Loneman is outside. He will verify what I have to say. He is one of the most experienced scouts, and he claims to know all of the groups of soldiers in this territory. He is well acquainted with Yellow Hair's command."

"Sit down, Strong Echo."

"No. Not now. I am stiff from riding, and hungry. If you will excuse me, I will eat something and walk around before I go back up the ridge." Strong Echo disappeared quietly.

"If this leader is Yellow Hair, he is considering attack. I am sure he will not be so merciful toward us as General Crook, the Gray Fox." Sitting Bull was talking to himself as much as to anyone else. He spoke louder as he continued his thoughts.

"He must not come in contact with Crooked Three Stars. Crook was to the south and Custer, if this is the hated Yellow Hair, comes from the north. They must be planning to meet"

Looking at Turtleheart, he asked, "You guess his force to be half the size of Three Stars?"

"Yes."

"He could decide to attack. He might follow the foolish coaxings of his pride. But he must not know we are here." The words of Sitting Bull were hesitant, as if he were not sure of his plan of action.

"If Yellow Hair is the leader, he has come to do battle. We are well prepared to take him on, if that is what he wishes. Why, just today, I rode around the many villages of our gathering place and saw how many warriors we have." Crazy Horse was up, speaking with the air of a confident war lord.

"I saw many groups of warriors making as if in battle. One group, mounted on their best horses, engaged in mock attack. I went as far as the Cheyenne camp, the one farthest down the Greasy Grass, and there I heard the beating of the war drum. The sound of the drum made my heart sing. I am happy at the confidence of our combined forces. We have a mighty group of warriors at our command."

Gall asked the courier to go out and tell the many people who were now milling around, to wait for further instructions. All of the camps must know. All drums must remain silent.

"Yesterday, I felt tension all day. I could feel that something was about to happen." Sitting Bull's face was glowing with the satisfaction of having stirred up the Indians into an emotional state of mind which promised great trouble for the enemy.

"If the blue coats attack us, they will be at the mercy of our best warriors and will be defeated." Sitting Bull was now speaking with his best voice, and his words were noisily accepted by the council members.

"How many warriors do we have, Gall?"

"Including the youngest members of the lowest societies, we have more than three thousand. Some will have their first experience in battle."

Sitting Bull rose and commanded, "Strike down half of the tipis. Hide them in the brush alongside the river bluffs."

Turtleheart recognized this order as being part of the strategy planned by Sitting Bull to encourage the soldiers to attack.

"Hunka," Gall spoke to Turtleheart. "You are the chief of the scouts. Keep your best eyes watching the blue coats. Bring in the others to help us. Every warrior is needed."

"I will do anything you ask. If you will now excuse me, I will go and see that these things are done. I will put my best scouts to watching the blue coats of Yellow Hair and to keep alert to any sign of Three Stars."

"Good. Our success will depend upon your information."

It was the hour before sunrise, and a lone Sioux scout was hidden in the rocks overlooking where the soldiers had stopped. Even before the gray light smothered the stars faintest glimmer, he was straining his eyes to watch them.

From his vantage point he could view all that was happening; the preparations of the soldiers to move on, and the movements of the Indian scouts. "A south wind is blowing," he said to himself. "A south wind is a good omen. Ah, now they are beginning to move about more. There are no bugle calls and but small fires. They do know of our camp and they plan to attack."

A horse was moving fast into the camp. He was ridden by an Indian, probably a scout. "It must be important, he is riding so reckless." The Sioux was talking to himself. "I will wait to see what else they do before I move. Where is the chief of the scouts? He should be back soon."

The first heat of the sun was warming him, when he felt rather than saw, someone moving up the slope behind him. "Turtleheart must be coming."

It was Turtleheart, who was making his way up a small draw. Arriving at the hiding place of the scout, he asked, "What have you seen?"

"Nothing yet, except for the hurry of one of their scouts who rode into camp. Look, now it seems as they are going to do something. See, they have mounted their horses. Now it looks as if they are going to have an imaginary attack. Ah, now they have their horses at a fast gallop and are charging up the slope. Now they dismount and go through the motions of firing their thunder sticks."

The two scouts watched the troopers make one mock attack before Turtleheart spoke. "You know, Sitting Bull is not a fool. Yesterday, I was thinking that he was too anxious to do battle. I thought he was willing to gamble away the lives of our relatives and friends to build up his reputation. Now, after viewing the enemy, I have to admit he had sound thoughts behind his oratory."

"Yes," agreed the scout. "If Sitting Bull had not talked as he did, we would be unprepared for the attack."

"They must know where our encampment is. They must be planning an attack today, or else, why would they march all night? See how those murderous Crows are returning from their scouting missions?" Turtleheart spat upon the ground. "They are very skilled at spying. You cannot ever trust them."

Another hour had passed, during which time the soldiers had mounted and started to ride across the slope and up the divide. "You watch them, and when you see them going down the west slope of the mountain, you ride with the wind and tell Sitting Bull and the council."

"I will go to Strong Echo and tell him I must see Sitting Bull. He is waiting for me down below." Turtleheart was gone with the silence of a shadow.

"What do you make of the enemies' actions, Turtleheart?" Strong Echo greeted him.

"They must plan to attack our villages today. The sun will be in the afternoon sky before they can do that. We do not have much time. I will tell Sitting Bull that they are on their way and will attack from up the valley."

As Turtleheart approached the large encampment from the north, he realized it was mid-day. Time was of vital importance now. He welcomed, yet half dreaded, the knowledge that the time for battle was fast approaching.

He beat his lathering pony to a faster run. Would he ever reach the first group of lodges? After what seemed a lifetime of riding, he galloped his horse through the tipis at breakneck speed, scattering the dogs as he went. Slowing down, he noticed many warrior were stripped except for breechclout, and they were painting their faces with the designs of war.

As though by some secret signal, everyone knew the soldiers were on their way. Some of the warriors leaped to the backs of their painted horses and followed Turtleheart to the camp of the Hunkpapa. Reaching the council lodge, he flung himself to the ground in front of the large lodge. It had its sides rolled up enough to see inside.

"The south wind is good to us today. I found you all in one place." Turtleheart spoke excitedly and dropped to the ground on both knees. Pushing the floor of hides aside, he drew a map of the enemy movements in the dust of the earth.

"Now that we know the soldiers are getting into position to strike, we know what we must do. We should send all of the women and children and the infirm to the flats at the lower end of camp, even beyond the Cheyenne lodges. Gather them quickly, this is an emergency and we do not have much time." Sitting Bull spoke rather slowly, but the orders were put together in few words. Messengers were dispatched to all of the camps with these commands.

"Broken Bow," called Gall, "Come in here." When a huge, elderly man came to the entrance and blocked it with his massive frame, the Hunkpapa war chief declared, "I want you to ride to the Sans Arc and the Cheyenne villages, and do this quickly."

"Have them ready to move their warriors along the creek until they reach the fork of the little river. They are to follow this until they are opposite the Minneconjou lodges. Tell the Minneconjou, they are to prepare to join with the Sans Arc and meet the Cheyenne on the creek. Tell each leader he is to appear here at this lodge as soon as he can. It is time to make the final decisions."

"Gall," said Crazy Horse, "I will take my Ogalala and move them up the creek and below the bluffs. We will be concealed in the ravines and brush, and will be able to strike the ones who will come in from that side."

"Good words," commented Gall. "Our medicine is strong today. Victory is in our reach."

"That leaves the Brule to reinforce the Cheyenne." It was Crooked Nose who was speaking. "And that leaves Sitting Bull and the Hunkpapas and my village, the Blackfoot to lay in wait for the enemy coming in on this side of the Greasy Grass."

"Good." emphasized Gall.

"You are right, Crooked Nose," said Sitting Bull. "But I will not be with you."

"Look," spoke Crooked Nose in a heated tone, "I do not intend to be put in charge of the women and children again. I am one of the most experienced warriors and will lead my own braves."

"No, no, Crooked Nose. You will not be in charge of the women and children. We need every leader and warrior for the battle." Gall soothed the irate chief. "You will be in command of your warriors, but Sitting Bull will be in charge of the whole battle. From this point here." Gall quickly drew a map in the dust to indicate the positions of the Indian placements.

"Not under any circumstances must any of you go to the aid of another unit. Not until your own opposing force is defeated." The assembled leaders nodded in understanding.

"Again I warn you as I repeat my words. Do not go to assist any other group until you have claimed victory in your own battle," Gall concluded with great emphasis.

"May I remind you," spoke Crazy Horse, "that each of you use our age-old plan of sending warriors out as decoys to draw the enemy into a trap."

"Yes, we will do that. It always works against the white men. They are too stupid to learn."

"Turtleheart, I need a good man to assist Hump," said Gall. "He will be leading some Minneconjous, Sans Arcs and Cheyennes. You will lead your own warriors in support. Just see that they are well hidden. When the soldiers come down from the east to meet Hump and his warriors, you attack from the side in a surprise movement."

"Some of your warriors are inexperienced, so keep them under control. A foolish movement by any of your men could be a disaster."

"My thanks to you, Gall. For a time it seemed as though I would have to join the women."

"It was a thought, my boy. It was a thought." The eyes of Gall sparkled at his words.

"Send your scouts to the four winds to spot any soldier movement. The Gray Fox may be close."

"The leaders from the other villages are beginning to arrive. We must now make our final plans," exclaimed Sitting Bull.

CHAPTER SEVENTEEN

Blood On the Little Big Horn

When the sound of gun firing flailed the air like a thousand sticks breaking, Turtleheart's warriors were getting their horses ready to mount; desperation in their minds. They could not see the fighting as the first attack was from up the Greasy Grass, near the Hunkpapa village. The low hills obscured their vision.

Turtleheart sent three Cheyenne scouts toward the engagement to find out what was happening, but when they could catch no sight of the battle, they returned to crouch down behind a small bank within sight of Turtleheart.

Wild yells piercing the air announced the discovery of a second prong of the attack approaching the village of the Minneconjou. The waiting warriors could see their comrades ride to the battle with swinging tomahawks, clubs and lances. While they watched the Cheyenne braves cross the river to meet the soldiers, Turtleheart was watching Sitting Bull moving about in all directions on top of a small hill. Astride a gray horse, he carried a crooked lance decorated with long banners, which he used for his silent commands.

Sitting Bull made an imposing sight on top of the hill, and he was closely watched by the chosen leaders at the battle scene. Interpreting his signals, they then relayed the desired information to the men in the battles.

Turning his attention to the battle, Turtleheart compared the Indians' attack to the actions of a school of fish. They rode to the attack in a broad sweeping curve to meet the blue coats who were approaching at a fast gallop.

Two riders were streaking toward Turtleheart's position, the froth flying from their horses' mouths. He recognized the warriors as Gall and Strong Echo. As they came to a sliding halt, Gall shouted angrily, "I have made a fateful blunder. There are soldiers riding down the other side of the river toward the Cheyenne village and that is where all of the women and children are. And the Cheyenne are going across the river."

A Cheyenne youth volunteered to go to the Ogalala village where the warriors were getting ready. "I will tell them we must brave a move to intercept the enemy before they reach my village."

"Move fast, boy," Gall commanded. "There is not much time."

"He has a long way to go. I hope he can make it," Strong Echo put in. Turtleheart echoed his thoughts.

Gall's voice was flat as he said, "When Strong Echo brought word that the soldiers to the east were going down to the area where our families are hidden, we wasted no time getting here. I could see them riding in columns of two across the open on the other side of the river and I knew we must change our plans." He was visibly upset at this development.

"Look, across the river!" Turtleheart pointed toward Crazy Horse and his warriors riding fast across the slope.

"Hah, it is a move to cut off the enemy," Gall spoke in a tense manner as he slapped his horse into a full run.

Turtleheart motioned to four Minneconjous to follow him, and instructed them with a terse statement. "We are going to help our Cheyenne brothers draw the enemy."

He immediately set out with the four braves following. As they mounted the first hillock of ground, he and the four warriors gave loud war whoops and joined forces with four Cheyennes. There were now nine warriors on the way to attempt to decoy the soldiers from the lower end of the encampment. This was a very dangerous and desperate maneuver, one that could be fatal.

They were less than one hundred yards away when the soldiers caught sight of them. There was a noticeable slackening of pace as the troopers were undecided as to which group to follow. One of the Cheyenne warriors carefully aimed his gun and fired. The leader of the soldiers grabbed his shoulder and the soldiers were no longer undecided.

The Indians turned and fled as the troops wheeled about and started after them. This was a gallant effort to draw the enemy, but it would be foolish and ineffectual to tarry longer. They raced for their very lives. Two of the Cheyenne were shot from their mounts. From the corner of his eye, Turtleheart saw two Minneconjous spin from their horses as rifle bullets struck them. These were no ordinary Blue Coats; they had an extraordinary skill with the rifle. The Indians were now pushing their horses to the limit while riding low alongside the horses' backs. All thoughts of heroics were gone. They had to reach the rest of the Indian forces or die.

There was sudden pandemonium as the concealed warriors left their place of hiding and charged the troopers. The air was filled with blood curdling screams intended to terrify the horses of the enemy and make them unmanageable. Turtleheart and his remaining companions turned their ponies and joined the flooding, screaming mass of painted Indian warriors.

Quickly scanning the area, Turtleheart could see the elite warriors under Crazy Horse's command sweeping in from the other side. The waters of the Little Big Horn turned red with blood in just minutes as wounded and dead men and horses plunged into the river. The Blue Coats were utterly confused at the sudden turn of events and were looking for an avenue of escape.

At close quarters the long rifles were of no use, and the Indians were deadly with bows and arrows and lances. The horses reared frantically and threw many of the troopers. Horses which had been shot, bucked and screamed, and some dropped dead with riders still on their backs.

The battlefield was filled with dust and black smoke powder as the troops frantically made their way up the slope of a small hill. Soldiers and Indians were engaged in hand to hand combat. Horses were running back and forth in terror, adding to the confusion. Warriors in groups of two and three were rushing at the enemy to express their deeds of bravery by counting coup, only to be killed by the soldiers for their reckless behavior. Many of the young and reckless braves crossed the death flights of their own comrades' arrows.

As the troopers began to dismount, Turtleheart could hear someone repeatedly ordering the Indian warriors to concentrate their fire on the still mounted soldiers.

Turtleheart and his men swept close to the hill where the soldiers were now concentrating, and he searched for the leading officer. He could not be seen; perhaps he was using his fallen horse as a breastwork. Circling to a stop, Turtleheart started to reload his gun. Looking around he was surprised to see that no man of the enemy was moving. The battlefield was quiet, except for the loud yells of the Sioux and Cheyenne, and these sounds echoed in a strange way.

The full comprehension of what had happened turned the terrible war cries into resounding tones of victory and joy. Accompanying these sounds were those of sadness and despair as men and women searched and found fallen friends and relatives. The death wails of the women caused Turtleheart's flesh to crawl.

Rubbing his hand over his forehead, he jumped from his horse and stepped over the sprawling bodies of the soldiers as he ascended the hill. His body crouched over, he carefully and swiftly scrutinized the individual forms. Around him, the many saddles, blankets, white gloves, rifles, boots and other items of clothing were being plundered by the victorious Indians. All of them were methodically scalping the dead and dying, so as to have hair to decorate their war shirts.

"Has anyone found the leader of the Blue Coats?" Gall's loud voice was unmistakable.

"Here. Over here!" someone answered. "He has yellow hair, and it is cut short."

"Yellow Hair," Turtleheart's body stiffened at the news.

"Loneman was right when he said our enemy was commanded by the hated one!" Gall's voice commanded the attention of many of the nearby Indians and they all rushed over to see for themselves if this was indeed the hated Custer.

Turtleheart and Gall were both running now, and reached the spot where Broken Bow was excitedly gesturing. At his feet was the lifeless form of an officer with short yellow hair.

"Gall," said Turtleheart, "you are the rightful one to lay claim to this leader's weapons."

"No! No!" Broken Bow was emphatic in what he said. "I say this man shot himself. He destroyed his own life. To take anything of his is bad. It will bring bad things to you, your relatives; all of us. No, you cannot take anything."

"You saw him do this thing?" There was a puzzled expression on Gall's face as he questioned Broken Bow's statement.

Broken Bow let his eyes rest longingly on the pistols belonging to Yellow Hair before answering. "In the last of the battle, the white handles on his short guns drew my eyes. He was crouched behind his dead horse and I was over there." He pointed to a few yards behind the slope. "I was about out of ammunition, so I lay there waiting for a soldier to die. When Yellow Hair stopped to reload his guns, I took advantage of his distracted attention and crawled closer. When he looked up and saw his forces crumbling all around him, there was terror on his face. He put a gun to his head with both hands and fired. When he did this thing, I knew I did not want his guns. I swear this is true."

Turtleheart looked at Yellow Hair, and noticed that blood had run over his chin and mustache. He was lying on his back, eyes closed. His right hand, covered with blood, still clasped the left hand fingers which still held the gun.

Gall drove a war lance into the ground next to the body, then bent to strip the bloody coat from the leader. He hung the coat on the lance, saying, "It is evil medicine and a bad omen to take what belonged to one who takes his own life."

"As you say, Broken Bow," continued Gall, "this man has had his hair cut short. That is why we could not spot him in battle. We always knew him with long hair, like an Indian.

That is all he ever did in common with us." Gall spat on the ground.

A lone horseman loped up to the group, and as he stopped he said, "My relations, my victorious friends, press the eyelids of every soldier to make sure that none are among those who live." It was Sitting Bull who was issuing the orders.

"There is one over there who lives. If he is not seriously wounded, bring him here and tie him." Gall gave the commands.

The young soldier was dragged over and tied in spread-eagle fashion to await Sitting Bull's disposition. Although bleeding and in a somewhat dazed condition, the youth did not appear to be seriously wounded.

An elderly woman pushed her way through the gathering and before anyone could stop her she had mercilessly struck the soldier in the head with a tomahawk. He had been hit twice before she could be pulled away, but it was already too late, as the prisoner was dead.

"I had to avenge," she screamed. "I killed him to avenge my son who was just found dead." The words were hysterical, and as she was carried away by her relatives she started a loud wail.

Sitting Bull strode over to ask, "Is he dead?"

Nodding heads affirmed the question.

"I need a live soldier to carry a message to Three Stars, and now this one is no longer able to do this."

Near the body of Yellow Hair, Turtleheart saw a soldier move his head. Bending over the form, he turned the blue coat over and pressed his thumbs on the closed eyes. A strong moan escaped the lips.

"Come here, this one lives!" he shouted. "His head has been creased. Come help me get him to his feet."

"Make sure that nothing happens to this man," Sitting Bull roared. "I want him to carry a message. Protect him from the old women if you can." There was a note of derision in his voice.

Looking around, Sitting Bull seemed to be impatient. "I want Strong Echo. Find him. He can speak the enemy tongue."

Turtleheart was reviving the wounded soldier when Strong Echo came riding up on a cavalry horse. "You look for me?"

"Yes," said Sitting Bull. "You speak the tongue of the long knives, so tell this white warrior to ride to Three Stars with a message. He is to warn them that they are not to come into this area. If they do, they will meet the same fate as Yellow Hair and his men. Let him tell them that we will not meet with them until they have removed all of the white invaders from our hunting ground."

These words were greeted by loud cheers. Still shaky from his wound and surrounded by unfriendly painted faces, the young soldier was badly frightened. Deep down, Strong Echo felt sympathy for the man as he helped him mount a horse.

Struck on the rump by Strong Echo, the horse jumped and started running down the slope. The wild and loud jeers of the Indians echoed in the ears of both horse and rider and frightened them even more.

Strong Echo grunted and laughed, "The way he rides, I do not think I could catch him, even if I had to."

"Look, the horse has stumbled!" A cloud of dust marked the spot where the horse fell. The horse rose to his feet and galloped away, but the human form lay still.

Turtleheart raced his horse down the same path the soldier had taken, but warriors from the banks of the river were there first. "He is dead," they observed without emotion. "The fall broke his neck." They shrugged their shoulders and rode off.

Without dismounting, Turtleheart knew they were right, so he wheeled his pony around and rode back toward Sitting Bull.

On his way, he saw his grandmother standing by an arroyo, so he detoured in her direction. She was watching other women loot the bodies and mutilate the naked forms. Her face brightened at the sight of him and she came up to his horse. "I am so glad you are all right my son. I prayed with my whole self for your safety."

Turtleheart jumped from his horse and took his grandmother by the shoulders. "You must dry your tears," he said. "I am safe, and will be here to take care of you."

"I was standing here, afraid to go look for you. I feared I would find you among the dead. I am crying because I felt the joys of ancient times when I saw you."

"Come, grandmother, I will take you to the lodge and you can rest. You should not be here watching this . . ."

"That does not disturb me so much, Turtleheart, I know that many mothers and wives have lost their loved ones to the guns of the invaders, so they must be allowed to destroy the ghost-spirits of the enemy."

"Just the same, grandmother, I am glad you are not out there doing as they are doing. And you must not watch."

Turtleheart looked out over the trampled hills and slopes. His heart was sick as he saw the desecration which was everywhere. "Grandmother, this morning that low hill was covered with tall grass waving in the wind, as the Holy Mystery intended. Look at it now; trampled and with the dead lying upon it. Man has defiled the goodness of Maka Ina. Some of those dead out there were nothing but mere boys, and it is wrong for them to die. It does not matter whether they are friends and relatives or white, this is wrong, all wrong. They should not have to die because of someone else. Come, grandmother, I do not want you here."

A truant curiosity lingered within his mind. Do the white women cry for their men who will never, ever return to their arms? In his heart he knew the answer, and the answer made him very sad.

CHAPTER EIGHTEEN

After the War Cries

With the intense excitement of the battle now gone, the following day was a tiring one. With the news of more of the blue coats coming, tempers were short. The relatives and friends gathered their dead, and the wailing of the women could be heard the full length of the huge encampment. No band was spared its share of victims.

Turtleheart stayed near the lodge of Sitting Bull and waited for messages from his scouts. He knew this was a very crucial time, and felt it wise to stay in camp. In the early afternoon he watched many young warriors go into the lodge of Sitting Bull. They were trying to get the medicine man to lend his weight to the demands of some to attack the other soldiers. However, he knew they should thank the Holy Mystery for being alive and that they should let wiser heads rule.

There were many of these hot-blooded warriors who, having tasted victory, asserted that the battle had just begun at the Little Big Horn. Flushed with the charm of victory, they all said this was the summer of good omen; now was the time to drive the palefaces back to the dawnlight.

By subtle means and promises, the medicine man persuaded the belligerent young men to hobble their emotions and wait. Many times that afternoon Turtleheart heard Sitting Bull say, "Why endanger our families when it is much wiser to wait for the fruits of victory? The white soldiers know that we have taken many scalps, and soon they will call me to council for the terms of peace which we will dictate."

Late that afternoon, Gall and Crazy Horse entered the lodge with unsmiling faces. They sat in front of Sitting Bull, who waited for them to speak.

"I hope that I am not the only one that these hot-blooded young braves have been pestering for permission to rub out the invaders," Crazy Horse spoke slowly.

Sitting Bull's voice was stern, "I watched you pull out for the flats, but I could not stop you. What, may I ask, was your reason for not obeying our agreed plan of warfare?"

Crazy Horse gave his story with unbiased detail. "Everything was going to plan, and we had the soldiers pinned down. Just as we were going to circle them, word reached us that our families were being attacked. This word spread like fire, and I took some of my men to ride to save our families. I thought that was where the biggest battle was being fought, and if the women and children were being attacked, we were needed there."

"As we crossed the branch of the creek forking toward the flats we saw the soldiers were already on the hill. We were all of one mind, and wasted no time in racing to cut off the long knives. The rest you know, so I have no further words." Crazy Horse waited for a moment expectantly, but when Sitting Bull said nothing, he quietly made his exit.

The silence was finally broken by Gall who said, "We can not stay here much longer. The odor of death is already in the air and will be unbearable soon. I vote that we strike camp and move to the Twin Buttes on the Grand River."

"Yes, this is a bad place to stay. There are going to be more white soldiers here to see what happened, and we should be gone. We will not be able to leave signs to tell where we have gone, as the Crow and Shoshone scouts will be able to read them."

"Call Turtleheart in," said Gall. "We can have a few of our scouts stay here under Loneman after we leave."

"Your words are wise, Gall. We will move to the Grand River and camp below the twin buttes."

When informed of the decision to move, Turtleheart answered, "I will select the scouts immediately. They have rested and will be anxious to get away to higher ground."

Stepping out of the lodge, Turtleheart saw a group approaching. His grandmother was among them, and he stepped up to put his arm around her shoulders. The leader of the group spoke with a smile. "I have heard nothing but praise for you. You are an expert scout leader, Turtleheart."

"Iron Shield, you make my spirits rise. Praise coming from you makes my heart feel good. Did you lose any warriors?"

"No, we were very fortunate. We had a few wounded, but none were serious. The camp crier said this morning we lost sixty-three warriors."

"We did lose sixty-three. I am sorry so many fell, but if we had been on the other side, we would be more sorrowful."

Turning to his grandmother, Turtleheart changed the subject. "I hope you are well rested, because we are moving to the Grand River, near the twin buttes. Everybody must be ready to leave this afternoon."

"My son, some of us are going to go with Iron Shield and his band. They are going back to the reservation." She spoke slowly, her eyes looking at the ground.

"Back to the reservation?" Turtleheart's voice showed his disapproval. "Why?"

"Control yourself," Iron Shield stated defensively. "If you will hear us out, you will then understand why we have made this decision."

"Understand? Your tongue speaks words that I find hard to understand. A short time ago we all starved on the reservation, and now you want to go back to starve again?"

"Most of my warriors are staying with you. They will do as you command, but some of us are fearful. The elderly and the women with small children feel they would be more secure on the reservation. The battle was not good for the young, and we feel there is more to come. We feel that no matter what happens, we would rather die among our loved ones who are still around us."

"We are tired, Turtleheart," his grandmother said sadly. "After what happened yesterday, we feel we are doing what is best for all of us. We do not wish to be a broken travois hindering your movements." She sighed wearily. "Iron Shield has spoken our thoughts of death, and we must face this. I know I am going to die soon and I want to pass into the great beyond near my brother's resting place. You must take good care of yourself, son."

The old woman turned away, tears in her eyes. "Always keep the winter count with you. Remember," she added fondly, "as long as I live I shall have hot broth ready for your return."

"Grandmother." Turtleheart paused, unable to think of what to say, as he was stunned by the sudden turn of events. Finally, in a voice choking with many unspoken words of affection, he said very quietly, "Goodbye, my dear grandmother." Not daring to say any more, he embraced her for a moment before turning away. Without looking back, he disappeared among the lodges.

Two days later Turtleheart felt a terrible loneliness as he sat thinking of how he had watched his grandmother leave with Iron Shield's small band. His stomach felt weak as he remembered her saying one time that no man will ever be able to control his destiny. Even the twin buttes seemed lonely.

As he sat there lost in his thoughts, he was unmindful of the scouts as they came into camp. It was only when he noticed the stoic faces cast a spell of foreboding, that he came back to the realization of the moment.

Only Loneman entered the open flap of the lodge. His silence gave evidence of bad news to those present. "I carry bad words, my friends. With troubled heart I must tell you what we have seen."

He sat, Indian fashion, with crossed legs, to continue his story. "We have scouted many blue coats on the move. There are more soldiers than I have seen in all of my life. They count many times greater than the enemy forces we have battled in the past. There are more groups than I have fingers."

"How many have you seen?" queried Turtleheart.

"Two large groups and many small ones. Strong Echo says they are well armed and have what he calls the deadly Gatling guns that shoot without stopping."

"What is this gun you speak of?" Gall's voice quivered with anxiety.

"Strong Echo," Loneman called.

"Yes, my friend." Strong Echo came in and stood expectantly with his arms folded across his chest.

"Tell about the Gatling gun the blue coats have."

"Yes." He stepped across the lodge and sat next to Turtleheart. "It is a giant gun. It shoots shells that explode, and they weigh two pounds, like a rock this big." He formed his hands to show the size. "I have never seen this gun used, but I am told it shoots fast, as fast as you can count. It leaves nothing standing," he concluded.

The silence was oppressive, and Gall finally asked, "How far away are these blue coats? In what direction?"

"At the rate they travel, I should guess not more than two days time from here, and mostly to the east," Loneman answered, while pointing with his hand.

The message was directed to Sitting Bull as their acknowledged leader, but he sat perfectly still, his eyes veiled in thought.

When he sensed all attention was on him, he shook his head and uncrossing his legs, slowly arose. He started to speak, but the nervous twitching of the corners of his mouth spoke more than words. The hard glint in his eyes gave way to fear.

"I do not see how this thing could happen," he said finally. "The enemy should be asking for peace, not searching for war." His words were emphatic. Now his forehead was wrinkled with thought as he admitted, "Thinking about these things makes my head whirl." He bowed his head and looked at the tipi floor as if the proper words could be found there.

"No, I just do not understand. Even Red Cloud did not kill as many long knives as we did, and he was given peace." Looking up, Sitting Bull directed his words at Gall. "I do not intend to be pushed into the narrow boundaries of a reservation. I will not forget our sorrow. I cannot forget our people's burden."

"Sitting Bull," Gall said flatly, "we have a choice of two plans. We can go south to the land of the "Spiolas", or we can go north, into the land of the Redcoats. Which shall it be?"

Hump jumped to his feet and shouted, "North, I say north." Hump was surprised at his own actions and now moderated his tone. "We have friends in the north, and they are treated with respect by the Redcoats. The Redcoats speak with a straight tongue. They will treat us right, not like dogs."

"Your words are true, Hump," Crow Dog interjected. "The north is a friendly country, our type of country. I do not think we can live very long in the heat of the south. And our enemies, the blue coats, would always be there to harass us."

Sitting Bull very slowly moved his eyes to look at each individual to see what their sentiments were. All voted "Hou" by a simple nod of the head, with one exception.

Crazy Horse shook his head. "Moving to the land of the Redcoats is only a temporary solution. The white man is taking over that country too. What is happening to us here will also happen up there." His finger was shaking in the direction of the north, and he now brought it down to point at the others.

"Iron Shield has already decided and left. More are now thinking of running away. We must remember that the things we fear will always be creeping up on us until there is nowhere to turn." Crazy Horse was pleading.

"Knowing my own thoughts, I am afraid that my hopes will never be realized if that kind of frightened Indian is at my side. This is not the time to act like a weeping woman. Wipe the clouds of self pity from your minds and face reality. Think, and you will know that we can regain our land only by violent action. If we must die to keep what is ours, then we must die."

Crazy Horse paused to let the full impact of his impassioned words be assimilated by the others. Clearing his throat, he raised his eyes above his audience and continued, "I have pondered this truth too long. We must never forget that this is our land. We are not guilty of making these times dangerous. We are not responsible for the fears and frustrations which tear at our people. It is the white man who is tearing our hearts out. It is he who steals and lies and kills the innocents."

Crazy Horse was now on his feet, his eyes ablaze with scorn. "When you are pitifully driven back from the land of the Redcoats, you will then help me carry the lance." He looked at his hand which he was unconsciously flipping over.

Defiance was in his words. "If my people and I must die, then we will die like brave Sioux. I go now to get my people and head for the Big Horn Mountains." Looking neither right or left, Crazy Horse scooped up his rifle and brandishing it, stalked from the lodge.

"Crazy Horse speaks with a straight tongue," sadly admitted Sitting Bull. "If only the bigger part of the Sioux nation, who are under Red Cloud and Spotted Tail, had remained with us instead of going on the reservation, it would be the white invaders who would be meeting difficulties now. In spite of all my attempts, I cannot keep our people united, and divided we are weak."

"I do not know what your plans are Strong Echo," whispered Turtleheart, "but I cannot go north." Before his friend could reply, Turtleheart rose to address Sitting Bull.

"Because of reasons, it is necessary for me to remain in this land." He put earnestness in his words, in the hope that the others would not think he was being a traitor and turning into a white man's Indian, a reservation loafer.

Sitting Bull's silence indicated deep thoughts and his reply reflected those thoughts. "A strong man like you means safety for us. I am sorry to lose you, but I can understand why you must stay. I wish to commend you and your untiring scouts for keeping such a keen vigil on the enemy. It was the efforts of you and your warriors that saved our people from being annihilated. You spoiled the surprise attacks. It is with a good heart that I thank you." The great emotion in Sitting Bull prevented him from speaking in his normal manner.

"Sitting Bull, I also choose to remain." It was Strong Echo who spoke. "I will follow the moccasins of Turtleheart."

"If that is your wish. You will be good medicine for your friend. Before you leave," the medicine man was appealing to them, "I would like to ask you to do us a favor. Will you see our old friend Hidetrader? See what you can find out about the white man's plans. If they wish to meet in a council of peace, send us a message. Hidetrader is full of information. He will tell you what the white man plans to do next."

"We shall do as you wish," Strong Echo promised. "We shall make plans to go there from here."

"We can leave for Rapid Creek today," added Turtleheart.

Evening was approaching as Turtleheart and Strong Echo led their horses out of camp. The wind muffled the small noises they made, and when a few hundred yards from the camp they mounted and rode eastward, zigzagging through the pines. No word had passed between them since they started, the silence a true indication that two friends do not have to speak to know what is in each other's minds.

Dusk had darkened the stirring grass at their horses' feet as they reached the summit of a high plateau. They were taking great care to stay to the high ridges to avoid the many scattered mining camps in the area.

Turtleheart was in the lead, since he was familiar with the country. In the darkness they would occasionally come upon an obstruction and have to seek another way. Turtleheart enjoyed the thrill of this fast travel, but was perturbed that the darkness hid the familiar signs.

When dawn sent arrows of light into the sky, the two men hid in a ravine close to a stream. Strong Echo slept while Turtleheart kept the first watch. This was in enemy territory so neither spoke as they exchanged places. The language of the signs was their communication.

After Turtleheart had rested, the two mounted their horses and again turned toward the east. The area was teeming with white people, and daylight travel was hazardous. There was something revitalizing in the presence of danger however, so both enjoyed the challenge.

As Turtleheart's spirits picked up, he seemed to be more like his old self. Once more he acted with the speed of his thoughts and the boldness of his action set a fast pace. They always kept to the high plateaus, their ponies moving fast across the open areas, and resting under the cover of the trees in a canyon.

It was late in the afternoon of the second day when they stood still in the bottom of a draw, covering their horses muzzles with their hands. A small group of white men passed them so closely, the Indians could hear snatches of conversation in their strange language.

The danger of discovery over, Turtleheart and Strong Echo led the horses through the thick brush, coaxing their nervous animals to ignore the scratching branches. Finding water, they stopped to let the ponies drink and to rub the legs of the animals to ease the tired tendons. When the horses were taken care of, the two men ate of the jerky in the saddle bags.

It was Strong Echo's turn for a rest when Turtleheart went to check the ponies again. He suddenly decided it might be wise to set his lookout post a little ways down, where they had heard thc passing white men.

The chattering of the white men was apparent before he reached the post at the mouth of the ravine. He stopped to listen. He could not understand what they said, but one of the voices nudged his memory. His body stiffened with recognition.

It had been almost two years since he heard those voices. Hot memories crowded into his mind as he crawled forward until he was only a few feet away from their fire. Through an opening in the brush, he peered at the men. There was no doubt.

His spine crawled with the thought of delicious revenge for the abduction of Evensigh. This emotion was soon replaced by a shrewd, detached calm. If he had followed his first impulse to kill, who could tell him where Evensigh was? A plan formed as he watched the two brew their evening coffee.

Coldly and calculatingly, he lay down his rifle and drew the knife. In the dark he felt for a rock just the right size, large enough to create a noise and small enough to throw accurately. His hand closed over one, and he carefully threw it over their heads. As it thumped to the ground on the other side of the camp, Turtleheart lunged. He was upon the nearest man before the white men knew what had happened. The knife went into his back to the hilt.

With equal swiftness, he pounced on the other man, who was stunned with surprise. Fast as a thrust of fear, Turtleheart had wrenched the beardless one's arm behind his back until he heard the bones crack. A cry of agony escaped the man's lips and he sagged, moaning, to the ground.

A sharp crack of a breaking stick and Turtleheart turned, with the knife poised for use. Strong Echo suddenly emerged and stopped at the sight of the knife. "What are you doing?" Strong Echo looked at the two white men. "You nearly scared the leggins from me with all of this commotion."

Strong Echo wiped his brow and exclaimed, "Say, don't you know you have friends when there is chance for combat? You do not have to be selfish and kill them both? Save one for me."

"Well, mighty friend, when I recognized these two, there was little time to search for one who sleeps. These are the ones who stole Evensigh and left me to die."

Strong Echo turned the body of the dead man over. "Look!" he exclaimed. "This one has two scalps. Two fresh Indian scalps." His voice mirrored dismay when he realized they were from a woman and child.

Turtleheart poked at the other form with his toe. "This one is not dead. When he revives, ask him what they did with Evensigh. See, he is coming back to reality now."

Strong Echo asked many questions, and the frightened man told him all he knew. As he watched Turtleheart with the knife, he pleaded for mercy. "Mercy he wants?" asked Turtleheart. "I will give him mercy." With a swift motion, he plunged the knife into the man's chest. With a cold stare of contempt, Turtleheart watched the man sink to the ground and die.

CHAPTER NINETEEN

Visit with Hidetrader

Hidetrader stood in front of his cabin beside Rapid Creek. He watched the approach of the two riders with eyes narrowed to mere slits. When he recognized them as Sioux, he straightened from his casual slouch and waved a greeting. His face was wreathed in smiles as he cried out his surprise.

Hidetrader was an elderly white man of medium height and frame. His beaver cap and beard made his face appear round as the full moon. The face above the beard glistened with shiny sweat and he laughed heartily as he pulled off the cap.

Turtleheart slid off his mount and grabbed the trader's outstretched hand with his own. "How good it is to see you again, my friend. How are your wife and boy?"

The trader's smile vanished. Choosing to ignore the question, he motioned for them to go inside the log cabin. Inside, they reclined on couches of buffalo hides while their host prepared food for his guests.

Turtleheart and Strong Echo had not eaten all day, and they devoured the broth and fry bread like ravenous wolves. Hidetrader said nothing, but watched them in silence.

When they had finished, Hidetrader tossed them a wet cloth for the wiping of faces and hands, before asking, "Which direction did you come from?"

"From the southwest and across the Paha Sapa. We went on around the miners by staying in the high places."

"You are either as wary as the puma, or just plain darn lucky. Those men are all over this country. Just a few miles from here is a large camp, and it is bigger every time I go there. Gold seekers come in every day."

Hidetrader quizzically turned to Strong Echo. "What is your name? I have never seen you before, have I? If you are traveling with Turtleheart, you are a friend of mine. Shake?"

"Strong Echo," was the reply. "When I was a youth, I was taken to the east, and I returned only a year or so ago. So you can call me James."

"Hidetrader, where is your family? You did not answer my question before, so I ask again."

The white man was silent for a long time, and did not look at either of his companions. Finally he spoke. "All of my life I have made it a point to ignore the differences of our skins. You Indians are happy with your skins and I was contented with mine. We accepted each other with mind and heart, and I soon learned to respect my red brothers. I even fell in love with an Indian maid and married her. She bore me a son who was the spittin' image of you Sioux. A good lookin' lad, he is. The very thought of them warmed my heart."

"After Custer had met his reward, they put up a lot of posters in the settlement. What with knowing what you did to General Crook, those posters offered a fifty dollar reward for every Indian scalp brought in."

"Now, that sure put me to thinking, so I hurried back here. I was too late. My family was gone. All I saw was the sign of some scuffling in here and outside. It was dark by the time I got home, and too dark to track. I spent the rest of the night searching the hills anyway, but I found nothing. No sign of my wife or my son. I did some crying too."

Tears welled in Hidetrader's eyes as his words trailed off. "When it was daylight, I came back here and picked up the trail. It led along the creek for about eighty paces, then it went off southwest. By the time the sun was up halfway, I saw them. It was the torture of a lifetime, seeing them dead . . . both dead . . . scalped." His voice was sobbing now.

Turtleheart and Strong Echo exchanged glances that warned each other this was not the time to mention the white men they had encountered, nor of the scalps they carried.

Regaining his composure, Hidetrader studied his gnarled old hands. "My eyes are open now. I have learned what you Indians always considered evil. From now on I will never live among the whites. I am no longer one of them. I belong to no one."

"You are wrong, Hidetrader," Turtleheart interrupted. "You are welcome among the Sioux. They respect you. When they learn of your sorrow, they will want you to become one of them."

"Thank you, Turtleheart. I owe your people more than I can ever repay. Until I came here and lived among you, life was no account. It was she, she and her people, who rescued me from a life of loneliness and taught me how to live."

Now, Turtleheart spoke with deliberate care. "My heart lies on the ground for you, but this is of little comfort, I know. Your loss is more than a man should have to bear."

"Now don't you go a feeling sorry for me, Turtleheart. I told you of this because you and your people are in danger. As for me, I do not want anyone to share my trail of sorrow. You have had more than your share of sorrow too." Hidetrader wiped the back of his hand across his mouth.

"Turtleheart, the death of your grandfather has been avenged. Fate dealt with Two Lance and Iron Feet for their foul deed. The two of them were shot from their horses the day after the posters were put up. They were trying to sneak out of the settlement real quiet, when a scalp-hungry miner saw them. There was a big uproar over this, since some claimed those loafer Indians were sure not worth fifty dollars apiece."

At the mention of the two Indians who had murdered his grandfather, Turtleheart's spine stiffened. As Hidetrader kept talking, he felt a tight bowstring inside of him loosen, and his body relaxed. The murder could never be undone, but the killing of the two eased his sad memories. He no longer would carry the lance for his grandfather. It was an odd twist of fate that within two days time he was free of his two vows of vengeance.

Turtleheart already knew the answer when he glanced at Strong Echo and back to Hidetrader, but he asked anyway. "We were at the Rosebud and the Little Big Horn battles, and now Sitting Bull would like to know if the white government is ready to meet in council with him?"

"Sit in council? That does not enter into their plans. There is serious unrest among the whites, and they are crying for the Sioux to be crushed. Custer was a hero and you have destroyed him and his men, so now I fear there will be no talk at council. They mean to destroy the entire Sioux nation."

"What have we done that is not right? Three Stars attacked us. Yellow Hair attacked us. We did the only thing we could do. Is it so terrible to fight for your families, your land, your right to live?" Turtleheart's voice rose with each word.

"Whoa, son. You do not have to ask me these questions. I know you did right. The others? All they want is your punishment, and the way things are now, it will be very severe. I know that I am telling you in cruel words, but you wanted to know and I have to tell you. We do not like these facts, but they must be faced. There will be no council."

Strong Echo clenched his right fist and smote his open hand. "This is unjust! It is wrong to blame us. We are not guilty of any peace violations. The whites have committed all the violations, and we are to be punished for protecting our families?" Strong Echo was on his feet, pacing the floor.

"We are of the same thoughts, Strong Echo, but who are you?" Jabbing his thumb into his own chest, Hidetrader practically shouted. "Who am I? Well, I will tell you. We are nothing! That is right, nothing. Who will listen to us? We are just Indians, you and I. All we can do is hope for the best and expect the worst."

The old man slumped down onto a buffalo robe, his breath coming in gasps. "Tell me, where is old Sitting Bull now?"

"Probably on his way to the Redcoat country with his followers."

"Good. That is the best thing he could do right now. I know the government is more fair up there. He will be safe as long as he stays. Where are you going? Maybe follow Sitting Bull? You will be smart if you do."

"No, we are going back to Red Cloud, back to the reservation, and try to make the best of what is to come." Turtleheart turned to Strong Echo and said, "It grows dark now. It is time to leave so we can travel at night."

"What is your hurry. You just got here. Both of you are in need of rest, and I say you should stay here and leave tomorrow night. No one ever comes around and I will be here to keep watch while you sleep. I insist that you stay."

The two Indians looked at each other for a moment, then nodded their heads in the affirmative.

"Now you are getting smart. This calls for good friends to have a drink." Hidetrader now smiled as he poured whiskey into three tin cups.

As he raised one cup, Hidetrader spoke his thoughts. "If old Sitting Bull is in Canada, I will be seeing him soon. I need to get away from this place for a few seasons, and the north country is where I want to go."

Turtleheart raised his cup a little apprehensively, and made a sour face as he sniffed the contents. The smell was repulsive. So this was the firewater he had heard so much about. He remembered the words of the wise elders of the tribe as they expressed their dislike for whiskey and those who drank it.

Strong Echo and Hidetrader raised their cups to their lips and downed the whiskey in one quick swallow. Hidetrader now said, "You do not need to drink this."

Turtleheart stuttered in reply, "I, ah, I. Oh, I may as well sample this poison. I, uh, just want to know why this is a curse to my people." He put the cup to his mouth and emptied it with one gulp. The hot taste took his breath away and he stood there sputtering. As the whiskey reached his stomach, he suddenly belched.

They all laughed and Hidetrader winked at Strong Echo. He filled the cups again. "If Turtleheart is a stranger to the effects of whiskey, it is time he became acquainted. Yes, well acquainted."

Strong Echo licked his lips. "Me," he said. "I can drink this, but I do not do so because it is a curse to the Indian. Tonight I will drink with you Hidetrader, because I know you will not scalp me or Turtleheart."

After a couple of drinks, Turtleheart's eyes were shining brightly, and as he watched the flickering candle flames, he suddenly became aware of their foreign origin. "Get those white man lights away from me. Do you hear, take them away!"

"Turtleheart, you can hardly see in the light. How could you see in the dark?" Strong Echo was leaning toward him. Turtleheart gave a violent shove and both landed on the floor. Strong Echo got up immediately, but Turtleheart just turned over and started to snore softly. Hidetrader just smiled as he covered the sleeping form with a robe.

The following morning, Strong Echo was the first to wake. His movements woke Hidetrader and the two of them started to cook breakfast. It was not long before Strong Echo noticed the robe move.

"Ho, Turtleheart," he cried out. "How does the drunk feel this fine morning?" The two cooks roared with laughter. "You should have cheered us with wise advice instead of becoming so drunk. You kept us awake all night with your buffalo bull snores."

Turtleheart shook his head as he sat up. "I do not like the smell of whiskey. I do not like the taste. I do not like the effects. My head feels wide enough to put a tree between my ears, and you laugh."

"That is what happens to pure people. We are not pure, so we do not have that problem. Ho, Turtleheart, how about a good, stiff drink to wake you up?"

"NO! Give it to our enemies, the blue coats, so we can just push them over."

CHAPTER TWENTY

A Decaying Indian

In the sluggish moments of awakening, Turtleheart's mind was not yet answerable to his will, but he remembered that catastrophe had come. It would be upon him the instant he became fully awake. He wished he could fall back into the vacuum of sleep forever. The more he tried, the closer he came to a full wakefulness. He opened his eyes, saw the walls of the tent, and knew where he was.

He remembered fully the details of the day before, and in his stomach area was an odd feeling. Yesterday he and Strong Echo had ridden into the agency and handed over their guns. The government agent also demanded their horses, reminding them that only Indian police and Army scouts were permitted to carry guns, and one horse would be allowed per family.

Strong Echo applied for work at the agency and Turtleheart accepted the invitation to stay with the Blue Thunder family on Wounded Knee Creek.

All of his world had been swept away from him. He felt lost and lonely as he stared at the canvas overhead. At the agency he was instructed to start a new way of life with new lights and new ideals. What lights? What ideals? His mind was conscious of the fact that he was utterly broken. He had nothing, only the clothes on his back, the winter count, and the bag of dried food issued to him.

Turtleheart remembered the words of the interpreter, "Unknowingly, you have been a renegade; a person fighting against your own nation." He did not understand what the man said, but he was glad that he did not tell that he had participated in the Rosebud and Greasy Grass battles.

As he lay there in the tent he pondered on his past life and was thankful Evensigh was not around to see and to feel this new kind of sadness. He wondered where she was. The white man had said she went back east to live with the whites. The door flap was open, but he did not notice it, so engrossed in his own misery was he.

Then a voice penetrated the fog in which his mind moved. "Turtleheart." It was a man's voice. "Turtleheart, come out and receive the benediction of the sun on your head. You will feel better." The elder Blue Thunder stood before him, his face narrow with high, protruding cheek bones. His face and frame bore the marks of many winters.

Outside, the warm sun felt good on his body and seemed to drive away the chill in his bones. The bowl of Indian tea he drank made him relax. The elder Blue Thunder came over with a handful of government beans and announced with the air of the knowing, "See these round white man's rocks? They are supposed to be eaten. My daughter-in-law, Alice, will be cooking them soon. She will have to cook them almost all day before they are soft enough to eat."

"Father! Are you trying to get him to eat those stones?" A middle-aged woman had joined the conversation. "As soon as Jim and the kids return with more firewood, I'll show Turtleheart how to cook them. This noon we will eat the baby teeth." She smiled at Turtleheart's look of disbelief. "Do not worry. Baby teeth is what I call government rice."

"Here come your firewood pickers, Alice," said Blue Thunder, pointing to the curve of the creek. Three figures with bundles of sticks on their backs were making their way toward them. To Turtleheart this was astounding. Men getting firewood?

"Last winter, when he registered at Red Cloud's agency, they gave my boy a new name." The old man shifted his weight from one foot to the other. "It took a little time, but he got used to it; the name they gave him. Jim Blue Thunder. Mine is David. My grandson here is Douglas, and he is twelve. My granddaughter is Mercy and she is nine. It took us many moons to get used to having different front names and the same back name."

"They added to my name too," exclaimed Turtleheart. "I am supposed to be William Turtleheart." He wished he could say it with a proud boast, but the name was strange and given at random. It meant nothing to him.

"Blue Thunder, do you see that little hill over there? Across the creek? Look carefully, see that small pile of rocks? That is where my real parents are buried." After a moment he added, "My Evensigh's real parents are buried there too."

"I know that all too well, Turtleheart. It was many years ago when your grandfather told me the story."

"Do the others know?" Turtleheart asked in surprise.

"Of the few families who live along this creek, I am probably the only one who remembers the day Chiefeagle brought you and Evensigh back to camp. We were visiting his band that time."

Blue Thunder wrinkled his forehead in thought. "Yes, I do remember that it was a chilly early morning during the moon of when the buffalo calves are born. Your grandfather and Hidetrader stormed into camp with you two little ones. Evensigh must have been nearly one winter in age, and you we guessed to be in your third year."

"I did not know you knew Grandfather back that far."

"Turtleheart, my pride is wounded that no one told you. Chiefeagle's father and my grandfather were both members of the Leading Bear band when the Sioux first came to this territory. As a young man I chose Chiefeagle as my Hunka Ate."

"Your words astonish me, but I am hearing good words, Blue Thunder. Tell me, what did grandfather say when he brought us back into camp? How did the camp accept us?" Turtleheart was hoping to hear something new on the subject.

He had heard the story many times from his grandfather and each time the story brought out something new.

"Be patient and I will tell you. This has been long ago." Blue Thunder cautioned. "He and Hidetrader trotted their horses into camp with you two in their arms. Yes, Chiefeagle had you wrapped in a small robe. They appealed to the women for help, and you know women. They practically tore you from your grandfather's arms to make over you, especially when they found you were both orphans. Ah yes, there were many disappointed families when Chiefeagle finally decided to put Evensigh in his sister's lodge and kept you for his own."

"Later that season, your grandfather brought me down here to show me the burial mound and he told me the whole story. He said they were returning from the Good Voice band and the sun was already set when they smelled smoke. They left the trail to search and found the smoldering ruins of two wagons. A child's cries brought him down off his pony to find a weeping girl concealed beneath the skirt of a dead white woman. There were no marks of injury on her but there was a bullet hole in the head of the white man."

"While digging the burial hole, he noticed another dark object further down the slope. He ran to the spot and found you lying naked on your cold mother. She still clasped the hand of your dead father. He said you tried to smile, but it was your black eyes that conveyed a feeling of trust."

Blue Thunder had to pause for a moment after his long oration. While collecting his thoughts, he put some Indian medicine in his mouth. "They never found out who the killers were, but from what they found, they knew they were not Indian, to leave babies."

They sat silent for a couple of moments. "Your names, yes, your names," Blue Thunder was thinking back over the years. "Chiefeagle said that the little girl cried outwardly all the way back to camp, so he named her Evensigh. You, you never made a sound, so he said you had a strong heart and he named you Turtleheart."

"Chiefeagle sent runners to all of the bands to find out who your parents were." Blue Thunder stopped and looked straight at Turtleheart before adding, "Anyway, you are an Indian, you have our skin color. That is all I can tell you."

Alice brought in some firewood and they watched her as she arranged it on the ground.

"How do you feel, Turtleheart?" Jim asked.

"Like a, well a, oh . . . A decaying Indian!"

They all laughed at his wry answer and the boyish grimace on his face. "It is good to see you laugh, Turtleheart."

"Blue Thunder, where are the families who belonged to the Bushy Band?"

"The few that live on the Wounded Knee Creek are all that remain in our band. Many of the young warriors joined Crazy Horse, Iron Shield, Hump and Gall. They have never returned. Some of the families went out to the soldier settlements to loaf and to drink firewater."

"Brother has turned against brother to seek favor with the winning side. Everything changes too fast. Our band, at least what is left of it, is in a coma of hopelessness."

"By order of the Indian police, we are not permitted to bring our lodges together as we once did. Our small band is scattered along the Wounded Knee Creek for about three miles." Jim had added to his father's explanation.

"How many horses do you have?" Turtleheart asked.

"We have one. Each family can have one and that is all. If we need another, we borrow one from the other families. I think our band has a total of fourteen horses and three colts." Jim turned to his father for confirmation and Blue Thunder nodded in accord.

"Handing out food to us is not a good thing," Blue Thunder was speaking. "To some of the people it is an encouragement to seek more, even by unfair methods. To the rest of us, it is the same as taking the heart out of us. All of this is bad and leaves us in despair. It has drawn us closer in brotherhood as we along this creek have learned to share our sadness so it does not hurt so much any more."

"We have four wagons," said Jim. "They are owned by the families along the creek, and we all use them to haul water from the springs and to gather firewood."

"The wagons. I remember the good laughs we had when they gave them out." Blue Thunder was chuckling.

"Father, tell Turtleheart about them," Jim encouraged the old man. "That was a good joke on us."

"We were all told to go to the agency for government rations," Blue Thunder began. "Most of us walked the seventeen miles. When we got there, there were big piles of food to be given to all the people. I never in my whole life saw so much at one place."

"Along with our regular rations there were some round loaves of something the whites call bread. Ptew!" He made a grimace at the thought of the tasteless loaves. "Each one who received these tasteless things was also given a can of wagon grease. One soldier told us to put some on the bread to make it taste better. Well, I have not felt the same since." He was grinning broadly.

"That is not all of it." Jim interjected. "After the soldiers started to laugh, we knew the joke was on us, so we all laughed too. Then a soldier told us to spread the wagon grease on the wagons. Brave Elk received a wagon frame without the box. They did not tell us that the boxes were coming in later. Anyway, I helped Brave Elk spread the black grease all over his wagon; the frame, the tongue. We ran out of grease. We were standing there wondering how the ignorant pale faces could stand to ride those greasy frames, when some agency men came around and started to laugh. I thought it funny too, but you should have seen Brave Elk. He started to throw anything he could get his hands on. I have never seen anyone so angry."

As the laughter died down, Strong Echo rode up, reining an extra horse. He dropped to the ground and went directly to Turtleheart.

Bluntly, he uttered words which caused the smiles to leave. "Nearly all of Iron Shield's band have been killed. They were caught at the Slim Buttes by General Crook. A few escaped, but all the rest, all the women and children, even Iron Shield, are dead."

"My grandmother is . . .?" anxiously queried Turtleheart.

"My heart lies on the ground. The only ones who escaped were the young warriors who could outrun the soldiers."

Turtleheart rose and philosophically said, "In my heart, I knew I would never see my grandmother again. When she left the Greasy Grass with Iron Shield, my heart told me that was the last time I would hear her voice. No, I am not surprised, but I am deeply hurt to lose the last one of my family."

Reaching beneath his buckskin shirt, Turtleheart untied the winter count which was about his waist and pulled it out. "This is my personal winter count. She gave this to me to keep up on my years. My grandfather started it when he found me on that hill. After he was killed, grandmother passed it on to me."

"A personal winter count? This is most interesting," said Blue Thunder.

"Now I must record my grandmother's death." He unrolled it for all to see.

"What is so different about a personal winter count?" It was Strong Echo who asked the question.

"As you know, winter counts portray history," Blue Thunder explained. "All bands have to have some sort of calendar, a method of recalling events of the past. The winter counts are kept by the winters, not like the white man's calendar of the years, months and days."

Blue Thunder paused to breathe deeply. "In each band, the keeper of the calendar consulted with the elders to decide the most notable event for that year. When this was done, he drew a picture on the tanned hide. Each picture tells of a year."

"This winter count is different. It does not tell of the band, but of Turtleheart. It is his personal history."

"Hah. It is a crude way to keep a history, but I can see where it can be favored by an individual,"said Strong Echo.

"You have just come from the agency?" asked Jim. "Is there any other news from there?"

"I have not been there long enough to be trusted, so I do not have any particular duty. I do odd jobs such as filling in as interpreter, messenger. The government men are facing quite a task in running the reservation with more and more of our people returning. I hear that the white chiefs are hamstrung by differences of opinion in their own ranks."

"See if you can get them to increase our food rations," said Blue Thunder.

"Yours is not the only complaint. I have heard many others complain of the rations being smaller each time."

"What do you hear of the rumor that the government people are going to make farmers of us instead of hunters? Is this true? There is much talk about this, but no one will say where the talk comes from."

"Maybe the government men do talk of this, I do not know. Last night," Strong Echo confided, "I was at a meeting and the agency men told us to forget our old way of life. We stand between the old and the new way of living. If we wish to survive, we must break with the past and face the new. At least that is what he said. They must have a plan."

"I am afraid many of us cannot wipe from our minds the past, Strong Echo. I cannot forget the days when there were more of the buffalo than of the arrows owned by the entire Tetonwan." Blue Thunder spoke with quivering words.

"When I think of the old days and compare them with the new, I am ashamed. We used to hunt for food, now we have to beg for what little we get. We go in fear and frustration. Now they talk of making us farmers. We do not know how. It is against our will to disturb the bosom of Maka Ina."

"Do not worry. They will help us to be farmers," Strong Echo reassured the old man. Then to change the subject to one not so disturbing, he turned toward Turtleheart.

"I told them about you at the agency, and they would like to have you on the Indian police. If you agree, this horse is yours to use."

Turtleheart looked longingly at the animal before speaking. "I would rather be on foot than to be a white man's dog soldier. My wounds are too deep. I have not forgotten my pains and my sorrows. I cannot forget my distrust of the white man."

"Well, maybe later on." Strong Echo said sympathetically.

This was the first time that Turtleheart ever felt anger against Strong Echo rise in his mind. He rose and left the gathering without answering. Soon this feeling turned to an anger against himself, and he knew he must make a decision.

Early the next morning, he made his decision and caught Blue Thunder away from the others.

"Blue Thunder, like the wind, I know no direction. I must find myself. It is on my mind that I must go on a vision quest. I have decided I must seek a sign, some advice. Maybe a vision will come."

"Turtleheart," Blue Thunder began as he put is hands on the young man's shoulders. "I am glad to hear you say you wish to walk in our ancient moccasins. You are mixed up right now, and a vision quest will ease your mind and give you the direction. You will know what you must do. Yes, you will know."

CHAPTER TWENTY-ONE

Vision Quest

Early the next morning, Turtleheart went to see an ancient looking medicine man. He had to get the advice of the elder on what was expected of him and to get his blessing. This man of medical knowledge would also give him the interpretation of his vision.

Having been instructed, Turtleheart was clothed in breechclout and moccasins and carried a scraped buffalo hide. He was ready to set out for his lonely vigil with the unknown, his vision quest. In his hand he carried a pipe. Attached to the thong of his breechclout was a pouch containing tobacco and whole leaves of the elm tree.

Bear Mountain was his choice for the vision quest as it was the highest point in the whole territory. He set out at a strong pace in the early morning sunshine, and by the next day he had reached the old Sioux hunting grounds. From here he could see Bear Mountain looming in the distance. The ground was barren of wild game; there was no buffalo sign. This was already becoming a void passage land for the whites who wanted the land of the Paha Sapa.

By early afternoon of the second day, Turtleheart stood at the base of the mountain. As he looked at the sky, he noticed the clouds of an impending storm form over the peaks. He filled his lungs with the fresh air of the green valley. Rain had treated this area more kindly than the plains to the east, where his band lived.

Turtleheart searched the tall spruce of the forest and he listened to the noisy communication of the leaves of the bushes. This was an enchantment he had not experienced for a long time. How comforting the nature of the forest is. How smooth and how beautiful, with everything well balanced and in tune. How protective she is by leaning over him, providing him cool shade.

The last time he was with Evensigh, it was in a place much like this. The poignant memory of her fingers caressing his cheek made the old days seem like a dream, something which perhaps never happened at all.

Turtleheart renewed his trek up the slope, the wind now moist with the smell of rain. Let it rain. He would not seek shelter. This was the prime enjoyment of life, life in the clasp of mother earth.

It was nearly in the evening when he reached the top of Bear Mountain. The sun was just beginning to dip below the horizon in the west and its slanted rays struck the rock of the summit.

Below him, the forested slopes he had come through were already caught in the darkness of dusk. The animal dwellers of the forest were busy preparing for the night.

A wide valley stretched endlessly north and west, its lower reaches lost in the darkness. In the valley were low hills, humped against each other, their dark patches of pine indistinct with the approach of night. He marveled at the beauty of the tops of the hills as they tried to stay in the fading light, as if afraid to succumb to the dark.

Along the tops of the Paha Sapa Mountains, the sun's coloring of the clouds turned from blood red to purple to a blackish gray. Suddenly there was no color and the wind sighed at its passing. The warmth of day was fast disappearing, so Turtleheart wrapped himself in the buffalo robe, and with his back against the trunk of a great tree, he waited for the long shadows of night to swallow him.

He was now quite alone within himself, as he listened to the many voices of the wind as it swept through the tall pines.

As he lay there, the events of the past and the uncertainty of the future kept his mind in a turmoil. He lost all track of time and was not conscious of going to sleep.

The purple hues of dawn were just beginning when he roused from his cramped and uncomfortable position. Rising to stretch his full length, he stood erect with the pipe to the east, to wait for the sun.

When the sun showed its forehead, Turtleheart sang his prayer. "Wakan Tanka, the Giver of all that my eyes can see and that my mind can feel, I offer to You, through Your power the sun, my humble thoughts. I stand here in solitude and pray. I pray with all my inner strength, that You will take pity on me, that You will be good enough to smile at my mistakes. In my humble way, I live a life of faith which has been handed down to me through the religious rituals of our tribal priests. You are the only one who knows that this is the right way; so with a deep sense of humility, I seek Your way through my belief. I pray that it is Your will that You may give me strength to meet the tomorrows ..."

The chant which emanated from the lips of the earnest young warrior was low in tone and slow in delivery. As he stood there, his hands and arms became increasingly heavy. And although he allowed his head to drop forward until his chin was against his chest, he did not waver. His voice was now a mere whisper. His fingers were turning numb from grasping the pipe. At last, the pain in his arms became so great, it disturbed his sense of balance. Only then did he lower his pipe.

By this time the sun was streaming over the countryside. The slow, warm breeze drifted westward as though carrying the warm rays of the sun with it. Turtleheart inhaled the air deeply and eagerly, and seemed to gain strength from this exercise. An uncontrollable urge to shiver seized him, not because it was cold, but because of the thrill of the experience. He had the feeling of floating into eternity.

All morning he stood facing the sun and holding the pipe, while praying for enlightenment by invoking the powers of the Holy Mystery. While meditating on this quest he would touch neither food nor water for three days and three nights.

At mid-day, when the sun was about to slip over into the western sky, Turtleheart raised his pipe to the four cardinal points and again stood motionless while offering his pipe to the symbol of the Holy Power. He stood there until no longer had he strength to continue.

Late that afternoon, pangs of hunger gripped his vitals. His legs felt paralyzed from standing in one position, and his feet ached with pain. By shifting his weight from one foot to the other he could lessen some of the discomfort, but the hunger was nearly beyond bearing. Finally, he dipped his fingers into the tobacco pouch and extracted a few of the elm leaves. This he consumed to help quell the twinges of hunger. His people had always eaten these leaves to quiet the contractions of an empty stomach.

As the sun approached the western horizon, Turtleheart again raised his pipe to the sun and repeated his tiring ritual. He had been conscious of it before, but now he found that it was becoming very arduous and difficult to hold the pipe to the setting sun. After an interminable time, the glowing orb disappeared from sight and Turtleheart was no longer able to trace its path. It was pure torture to make his way to his robe. Dropping to the earth and hardly able to move, he was satisfied with his day's expression of penitence.

Turtleheart had been taught from childhood that the reasoning behind a vision quest is primarily for the purpose of having Wakan Tanka's reflections accepted by the candidate. This was accomplished through intercessors; through any living object of nature. The only way for a candidate to be successful in this meditation was to withdraw his physical being from all human activities. Any human intervention during the quest would doom it to failure. Consciousness of self and self alone must be attained. When this occurs, the light of the vision rises in the mind. The mind may then be said to have penetrated itself, permitting the vision.

The mystical men believed that a man must have knowledge of these sacred and deep feelings within the mind and body before the total self could be attained.

Only too soon there was the dawn of another day. Wearily Turtleheart rose to meet the day's ordeal. He put a leaf of the elm in his mouth, picked up the pipe, and moving away from the tall pine, faced the east to await the sun.

As it began to appear over the horizon, he raised the pipe and began to pray in a low chant. "Close my mind to cowardice. Let me do the right things for my people. Not for the sake of merit, but because of the sacrifice of my people in this land which belongs to them."

The rising sun, breaking away from the eastern prairies, poured a sudden radiance of gold upon the tops of the mountains. He wished then, that the meaning of his own heart could be put into words. Surely then, Wakan Tanka would know his real thoughts.

This day was a repetition of the previous day, but he was more weary in mind and body. It was little comfort to him that the afternoon became stifling hot, with no cooling breeze. As the day ended he felt a relief of mind and body. There was peace and indolence. As he fell asleep, the land itself seemed to sleep.

During the dark of the night, Turtleheart heard a beautiful melody. It seemed to originate a long way off, but it was coming closer and closer. The sweet melodious voice enchanted every fibre of his body, and it somehow seemed familiar. Evensigh! The thought of Evensigh caused him to raise up, his ears straining to hear.

The soothing melody continued. He raised himself to his feet, shook his head, and tried to find the direction from which the song came. Now he was sure he was awake, and he could still hear Evensigh's voice.

Thinking the voice came from the scrub oak, he ran to each clump expectantly. With soaring spirits, he was realizing her voice was coming from the sky. Scanning the sky, he could see nothing but darkness, and her voice was coming from the whole sky.

He could hear her very clearly now. His heart was thumping as he felt utter despair settle upon him. "She is in the land of our ancestors," he cried. In answer, her voice moved to the east and the haunting melody receded into the distance until there was no sound except the whispering of the wind through the tall pines.

Turtleheart could feel all of the strength in his body leaving him. He faced the east, feeling remorse and a complete loneliness. He could sense how inadequate human character is during times of extreme distress. His legs could no longer hold him, so he collapsed to the ground, the pipe still grasped in his hands. Sleeping fitfully, he awaited the coming of the third sunrise, when somehow, he found the strength to rise.

All morning of the third day, he stood facing the sun as before, and repeated the invocations of the two previous days. His eyes were almost swollen shut from staring at the sun. At noon his pipe offering was very short and his chant but a moving of the lips.

In the manner of a blind person he felt for the bag at his waist, looking for the elm leaves. His mouth was extremely dry and as he bit down on the leaf, there was no trickle of saliva to moisten it. Easing the particles past his swollen tongue, the ticklish bits of elm started a feeling of regurgitation. He felt he was trying to swallow handfuls of young eagle feathers. The thought was amusing and he felt much better.

During the afternoon he felt the sensation of little puffs of cool air touching at points all over his body. The heat of the afternoon was stifling, so he was afraid to open his eyes, as that might disturb the pure relief of the coolness. The puffs grew stronger until the strange sensation of flying birds was vivid in his mind. He could even hear the fluttering of wings as they breezed about his torso and the calves of his legs.

Again he heard the sweet melodious voice of Evensigh. The soothing caress of her low voice was pure enchantment. Quickly, he opened his eyes, fully expecting to see her. She was not there and the fluttering bird wings were gone. The sound of her voice still continued from above.

It was raining. The whole countryside was being rained upon, but none of it touched him. Where he stood there was no rain. Curiosity made him step forward and extend his hand out beyond the edge of his position. The drops of rain fell against his upturned palm, and he withdrew his hand to dab at his parched lips with the moistened fingers.

Turning, he went to the opposite side of his dry area and knelt to pull at the wet grass. The singing voice of Evensigh was wafted to him on the eastern breeze. Wonderment filled Turtleheart. He was having a vision.

When the rain stopped, Turtleheart knew that his vision quest was successful. Upon returning to the Wounded Knee area, the success of the quest was immediately noticeable to the people. On his way to the medicine man, his body exhibited more strength instead of weakness after the days of the fast. The people were glad for him and everyone shared his pride.

CHAPTER TWENTY-TWO

Dancing Fires

Every day of the passing season, Turtleheart hunted the creek beds, the prairie hills, the flats, for small game. Always on foot, he was sometimes gone for two or three days at a time, but he usually returned with the wild fowl or a rabbit. At first he roamed the countryside to assuage the pain and shame of being a reservation Indian.

With the passing of summer, he began to realize the true value of silence. Silence was his constant companion and he came to know it as a priceless commodity. Much wisdom could be attained within its domain. It uncovered truth, bliss and sorrow, but it made him forget the sorrow for himself. He now gave very little thought to the old days, even when he thought of Evensigh. Only occasionally did he brood about the past or the invaders or become rankled at the defeat of his people.

When the north winds came with their lingering alarms, moaning a dirge across the country, he watched them squeeze the color out of the evening sky and beat against the cottonwoods to capture the last leaf. He saw autumn laying upon the earth its own colors of red, orange, yellow and brown.

When the pattern was ready, the white mantle spread down from the hidden shake of the sky. The snow-on-snow robed the earth and drifted deep in the gulches, to bring a beautiful but desolate look to the land. The cold was so intense it hurt the lungs to breathe deeply. The hunger was felt by the people because of the lack of meat in their diet.

Late in the spring when the government food rations grew meager, the spotted disease of the white man fell upon the Indians in their weakened condition. It came unannounced and unwelcome to spread until Wounded Knee Valley was filled with it. Those who recovered were marked by the deep pits to remind them of its terrible toll.

There were many who did not recover. The old, the young, the weak. Nearly every family raised the death chant that miserable spring. The people felt that death lurked in the very air they breathed.

The wave of disease took the lives of Douglas, the mischievous one; and Mercy with her wide eyed smiles. Blue Thunder took the loss of his grandchildren very hard, and for weeks he was not himself. He did not act like the Yuwipi man of the Sioux band. His face became very old, his actions very slow and tired.

Several weeks after the deaths of the two children, Strong Echo came again to the valley, reining a spare horse. He rode to where Turtleheart and Blue Thunder were seated and tossed the younger man a pair of woolen trousers.

"Kola! I brought these for you. I thought you might have use for them," he said as he slid off the horse to squat on the ground.

Turtleheart smiled. "I suppose I could," he answered after giving the pants a quick appraisal. "My leggins are in need of patching, and hides are hard to come by." He rose and went in the tipi. In a matter of a few breaths he emerged, wearing the serge trousers.

"A perfect fit," Strong Echo commented.

"I feel foolish in them, but they are comfortable."

"We were discussing dreams when you rode up," said Blue Thunder. "Will you join us?"

Strong Echo enjoyed a good discussion as well as the next Indian, but courtesy demanded that he not seem too interested. "I did not mean to interrupt your talk," he ventured. A chance to hear the renowned Yuwipi man, Blue Thunder, talk about dreams was an opportunity he did not intend to let slip by.

When no one spoke, he cleared his throat slightly, and to encourage the discussion he said, "Dreams are of many kinds. How do you classify them, Blue Thunder?" Protocol be hanged, he thought, the stubborn old man just wanted to be coaxed.

Blue Thunder settled himself on the ground, for all the world like one of Alice's government hens ruffling herself into her nest. "I was telling Turtleheart, that most dreams have a natural explanation. They are caused by physical disturbance, or sometimes by fear or by activities such as smelling or feeling."

"You mean that if I was sleeping and the smell of roasting buffalo was in the air, I would probably dream something of the buffalo?" Strong Echo was now becoming interested in the words of Blue Thunder.

"Why yes. It would be something like that, yes," Blue Thunder agreed. "I must also mention that one perceives distant things in a dream that are attributable to the extraordinary power of one's inner spirit."

"Is that the kind of dream which is brought to you? Does a dream like that give you trouble in interpreting it?" Strong Echo was now trying to sound profound.

"No. Explaining a dream is not difficult. The problem lies in trying to find out if the dream is a prophecy or an ordinary dream. Many people bring me dreams that are caused by pain or desires, or even past thoughts which they do not know are hidden in their minds."

"Now if a dream sounds as though it does have a prophetic meaning, I will perform a Yuwipi ceremony. With the aid of my prayer chants and some of nature's plant roots, I am able to feel the prophecy of the dream." Blue Thunder's words were slow and solemn.

The afternoon sun warmed them, and they sat in silence for a short while. Strong Echo was obviously impressed with such powers, and strangely enough did not ask questions.

"Is there much difference between a prophetic dream and a vision quest?" Turtleheart finally asked.

"Well, they can both be classified as a form of communication. In a vision quest, the individual has a certain purpose he wishes to attain. He has the deep meditation of his mind to help him probe deeply into the communication. When a vision does come, he understands the general story, but he has to come to me or to a medicine man to have the details in the vision interpreted."

Blue Thunder paused for a moment to readjust his position. "Now in prophetic dreams," he continued in a level tone, "the individual needs the assistance of a Yuwipi man's sharpened senses to unravel and expose that which is not obvious to the dreamer."

"Many people go through life without ever experiencing an extraordinary dream. And there are those who have the dream but fail to sense the prophecy, or do not recognize the dream as a message until after the dream has actually come true."

He looked from one to the other of his listeners. "I am holding the Yuwipi ceremony four days from tomorrow to help drive out the spotted sickness. If you would like to attend, I will speak to the others. They must give their approval."

"What needs to be approved?" Strong Echo spoke bluntly, as had become his habit in his role as interpreter for the white men at the agency.

Blue Thunder looked sharply at him and replied, "Your character needs to be approved. It would defeat the purpose of the ceremony to have disbelievers in the audience."

"I am sorry, Blue Thunder." Strong Echo was apologetic. "I did not mean to sound so abrupt. It is just that I do not know much about the Yuwipi ceremony. I would like to attend, if you and the others will let me. I would not want to miss it."

Strong Echo was finding the apology hard to make, and Turtleheart knew this, so he came to his friend's rescue. "Yes, there are so many things which are hard to explain. After my own vision quest, I was supremely at peace. Afterwards, I wondered why Wakan Tanka could not or would not forbid cruelty."

It was Turtleheart who was now in difficulty, and he wished suddenly that he had not said that last sentence. Why did his words come out without thought?

Blue Thunder's face was a mask as he rose and looked at the two men. "I will ask the others if you are to be permitted at the ceremony," he said simply before turning to leave them.

Turtleheart and Strong Echo looked at each other as if to ask if they had offended the old man. After this awkward silence, Strong Echo asked, "Have you thought of becoming one of the Indian police? I brought you this horse, Turtleheart, because the army still needs scouts. I know how you feel about working for the cavalry, but if nothing else, I think you should do it for the sake of the Blue Thunders. You will be given extra food rations for them."

"You are putting me in a position where I cannot reject the offer. I will ride back with you," Turtleheart said reluctantly. "I will have to tell them I am going with you."

"All right. I know that they will be glad to have you go. Do not feel bad about working for the army, Turtleheart. They keep you fed and clothed. Most of the blue coats are not bad men. They just have to obey orders. Sometimes the officer in charge issues cruel or mistaken orders, but the soldiers are a lot like we are."

Turtleheart could not believe it was Strong Echo who was speaking. How could he say such things? Worse yet, how could he believe them? He saw by his friend's face though, that the words were really sincere.

Strong Echo could feel the reluctance his friend had in going to the agency to begin work as a scout. In order to take Turtleheart's mind off of the subject, he managed to ask countless questions about the Yuwipi ceremony.

"Your grandfather was a Yuwipi, wasn't he?"

"Yes."

"Did you ever see the ceremony?"

"No."

"Why not? Didn't you want to?"

"Look, Strong Echo." Turtleheart turned to chastise his companion when he saw the earnest face, and realized his friend was trying to help him. He sighed and said, "Grandfather told me that boys are not permitted to watch the ceremony. One must be a man in years before he can watch the Yuwipi."

"Didn't he ever tell you anything about it? Like what he did or who took part in it?"

"No. Yuwipi men take a vow to not tell of their powers. An old friend of grandfather's told me things that he had seen performed in the ceremony once. Yuwipi means 'all bound up'. At the beginning of the ceremony, the Yuwipi man challenges any of the watchers to tie him with thongs, just as tight as they wish and in any way possible. At the end of the ceremony, the Yuwipi will free himself in just a few breaths."

"I would like to see the performance."

"Maybe we will. Blue Thunder said he would ask if we can watch. I hope he is not too mad at us."

Four days later, Blue Thunder sent word to Turtleheart and Strong Echo at the agency. In whispered tones, the man with the message informed them that the ceremony would be held that same evening at Wounded Knee. They were also informed of the sweat lodge purification which came first.

Arriving at Wounded Knee, they found all activities were centered around the lodge of Blue Thunder. They rode up close to the busy women and handed their horses' reins to a boy.

"Hmm. Like scouts of yesterday, you have returned," said Alice. Without so much as giving either of them a glance, she continued to untie a large leather pouch. Getting it untied, she reached in to pull out a handful of a gray flakes which she promptly added to a kettle of boiling rice.

"What is that, seasoning?" Strong Echo asked.

"Your mind is short. In your early youth you have seen other women do this."

"No, I do not think so." Strong Echo answered slowly.

"You do not remember hide seasoning? What kind of Sioux are you? These fine flakes of seasoning are what we gather from the final scrapings of hides. We do this before we begin to soften the sun-parched skins by beating and twisting them. It is just a final light scraping. Oh, why should I waste my time telling you? You men are all alike, you do not know anything of what we do." She half smiled as she watched Strong Echo's face change color.

"What I just did, was to add Indian flavor to the pale face food."

Regaining his composure, Strong Echo now teased her with, "Interesting, nature girl. Very interesting. Some day you will be a good cook."

It was time to join the other men in the sweat lodge for the purification rites, so Strong Echo and Turtleheart left before Alice could scold them with pointed remarks.

After a supper of Indian flavored rice and wild turnips, Turtleheart and Strong Echo were eager to see for themselves the phenomenal powers possessed by Blue Thunder. When permission was granted to enter the lodge, they were first in line.

The challenge to bind Blue Thunder was accepted by old man Two Sticks, who wrapped the Yuwipi man in buffalo skins and strong rawhide thongs. When he had finished with his efficient task, the only part of Blue Thunder which was exposed was his face. He was then placed in a prone position in the center.

The flickering flame from the altar fire cast wierd shadows on Blue Thunder's features, which by now had been transformed by a mesmeric trance. Small balls of flame leaped and danced from the center of the fire. Suddenly they bounded completely away from the flames and ricocheted around the sides of the tipi.

They careened around the inside, bounced from the ground into the air and skimmed across the heads of the men. Strong Echo was startled and Turtleheart signalled him to remain quiet. They had heard of the dancing fire, but this was beyond belief. It was very surprising to see the balls of fire as they seemed to return to the fire.

As Turtleheart sat cross-legged near the prone figure of Blue Thunder, he felt the fluttering of bird wings as they brushed by his face, his back, his legs.

The chanting, which had begun as the ceremonial fire was lighted, had grown steadily in volume until it was now so loud it made the tipi shake. As if by a silent signal, the chanting began to get lower and lower until it was no longer audible and the drum became silent.

No one whispered. No one moved. All eyes were trained on the horizontal figure of Blue Thunder. The eerie silence was evident all along the Wounded Knee Creek.

Tension mounted, growing and swelling the senses, in waiting for the unkown. Turtleheart closed his eyes and dropped his head slightly. He was searching his own inner soul. The veiled presence of Wakan Tanka was surely there with them. He had felt it in the fluttering wings which had brushed his person.

Very gently, the drummer began to tap the drum. Quickened breaths caused Turtleheart to look at Blue Thunder. The roll of the drum and the movements of the Yuwipi man caused him to move his shoulders. Suddenly the body of Blue Thunder started to rise from the ground. Still horizontal, the bound figure raised in violation of the earth's gravity, to remain suspended above the ground.

Two Sticks led the chanting prayers, which were again filling the tipi with loud incantations. They were asking for the spotted sickness to be lifted from the people. When the fire of the altar had died to glowing coals, the chanting died slowly away until it was but a whisper. Blue Thunder was slowly settling to the ground.

The dim light inside the tipi was almost as if it was nonexistent. The faces of the men seated around the lodge were nothing more than light blobs above the dark blobs which were their bodies.

As they all watched in wide-eyed wonder, the wrappings of buffalo hides rippled as Blue Thunder slid out of them to stand erect. The thongs which had bound him were handed, in a neatly rolled ball, to Two Sticks.

CHAPTER TWENTY-THREE

Crazy Horse Returns

Turtleheart went on many scouting expeditions for the army through the summer of 1877. After each trip he returned to Wounded Knee with a good supply of food. He would rest for a few days before returning on schedule to the cavalry post.

Late in the summer season, Crazy Horse led his band back to the reservation to face the inevitable surrender. With the additional Indians now coming back to the reservation, the food rations were cut even further. Even Turtleheart, who was favored for being a good scout, was given very little meat. The small amount he took to Blue Thunder's family was quickly consumed. None was left for drying.

In the early fall, a council was called at the agency. The government asked the scouts and Crazy Horse to help fight the Nez Perce Indians in the northwest country. The soldier spokesman told them that the blue coats needed them to help defeat Chief Joseph and his warriors.

Turtleheart heard one leader after another object to the government plans for the annihilation of the Nez Perce, who were guilty only of defending their homeland. Besides that, Chief Joseph and his people lived beyond the Blackfeet.

When the council recessed, Turtleheart took advantage of the break to go speak with Crazy Horse. He knew Crazy Horse and his band were back but he had not had an opportunity to see him.

"We stayed away from the reservation life as long as we could," declared Crazy Horse. "Hard times followed us since we left the Greasy Grass after we defeated Yellow Hair. It did not matter where we went, trouble followed us like the wolf. What are you doing now, Turtleheart?"

"I have become a scout for the army, but not because of choice," Turtleheart replied apologetically.

"You are a scout for the blue coats? I would never have believed that." Crazy Horse's face changed to an unsmiling look, his eyes suddenly cold and stony. With no further word, he turned on his heel and joined a group of chiefs. Turtleheart stood where he was in growing humiliation, the anger of injustice stuck in his throat.

"Let Crazy Horse stay on the reservation," he muttered to himself. "Let him see the little ones starve, and he would be a scout too, if he knew he could help others."

When the council resumed, the Indian chiefs took their places, each with his assigned interpreter. A lean, enterprising French-Canadian named Grouard was assigned to Crazy Horse. At the agency he was nicknamed the Grabber, because of his habit of thinking of himself, first, last and always. Turtleheart hoped Grouard would interpret with a straight tongue.

"No," said Crazy Horse, with both hands sweeping across his chest. "We are done with fighting. We wish to live here at peace as you have promised. We do want to go north, not to kill, but to hunt. For years you have been telling us that we must giveup our arms, our land, our way of life. Now that we have done these things, you say we must fight again, in a place many sleeps away, against some people we do not even know."

"We do not understand this kind of 'peace'." He spread his hands in a gesture of perplexity, his cold eyes staring at the white leader. "We have laid down our guns, we gave up our own horses. We have come to talk of peace, and you say we must help the blue coats. Your words leave us no choice, and even though we are tired, we must obey."

Now Crazy Horse turned to speak to the other chiefs. "My heart grieves for what they want us to do. We are conquered, we must obey. I say no, but if the Great White Father wants us to fight, we will fight until no more Nez Perce are left. Three Stars will have his wish." When Crazy Horse gave the sign he was finished, his followers greeted his speech with an appalling silence.

As Crazy Horse took his seat, Grouard rose to translate for the blue coat leaders. "Crazy Horse, here, is long on wind, and all he said was that if he has to he and his warriors will fight. They will fight until General Crook, old Three Stars, is plumb dead and buried,"

There was a look of shocked surprise on the faces of the white men at this announcement, and they immediately had a conference between themselves. The other translators were also surprised at this distortion of Crazy Horse's words. They all wondered what Grabber was after this time.

It was late at night when a messenger rode into the agency with the news that Chief Joseph had surrendered. Turtleheart was still pondering the unusual reactions of the blue coats at Crazy Horse's speech earlier that evening. The news he heard gave him some relief from his uneasiness. Was this the same feeling, he wondered, which made Red Cloud lay down his lance a few years earlier? He felt a little better that night when he rode down the valley of Wounded Knee Creek with salt pork and corn meal resting on his horse's shoulders.

"I have good news," Strong Echo announced to a small gathering in Blue Thunder's lodge the next morning. "They have now selected me as a committee member to go back east and bring back cattle, food, clothing and farm equipment. Perhaps our seasons of hunger are over."

"Good. Your words make my ears glad," Blue Thunder said, a broad grin spreading across his face.

"Father, right now your face looks like that of a mighty hunter who has just killed a whole herd of buffalo." Jim's face resembled that of his father as he smiled.

"I will go tell the others the good news," the old man said. Turning at the lodge entrance, he gave the good sign.

"How many are going? When do you leave?" Turtleheart asked Strong Echo.

"Two days from now. There are two Sioux and six white men going. We are to pick up farm tools from a city they call Chicago, in the territory of the mother lake. Then we go to St. Louis, along the father of waters to get the rest."

"How long do you plan to be gone?" Turtleheart continued to question, curious of these far off places.

"We will be gone two moons, and we will travel part of the way on the iron horse which eats fire."

"That long?" interjected Jim.

"We have a great distance to go, and possibly a great deal of bargaining to do. At least it is a comfort to know that our hard times will be over in two moons."

"Forgive my impatience. It is just that when we are gaunt, everything looks gaunt. It is hard to eat what will be here in two moons when we are hungry now. We can wait when we know it is coming through," added Jim.

"When will they let us leave the reservation? Have you heard any talk of this?" Turtleheart asked, considering this to be a pressing problem.

"I do not know that answer. I fear it will be a long time. There is still a lot of ill feeling toward us for what happened on the Little Big Horn."

CHAPTER TWENTY-FOUR

A Fateful Determination

It had now been four years since Evensigh came east to live in St. Louis. As the years passed she became more and more accustomed to the life of the city. But as the reports of the Indian battles were printed in the newspaper, it became increasingly difficult for Evensigh to put aside her past. She felt a stab of sympathy for the people who had raised her from babyhood.

At first it had been hard to read the newspapers, but as her command of the English language increased, she became more and more conscious of the problems of the Sioux nation. The arrows of loyalty to the people who had been her friends for the first years of her life, pierced at her conscience. She began to ponder the fate of Chiefeagle and his small band, her thoughts being reflected in her increasing restlessness.

She took long walks away from the Callahan home. When she was gone too long, the Callahans worried about her, and they would try to impress upon her it was not proper for such a pretty young woman to be out unescorted. They knew that she was fighting a conflict within herself and they did not wish to interfere with her activities, but it was not to Evensigh's well being to wander too far away.

Their concern for her feelings did cause some of the newspapers to disappear from the house. By sheer accident she found one hidden in the fruit cellar. It gave a report of the battle of the Rosebud. She found another which told of Custer's defeat and which advocated stern measures to defeat the

Sioux. Loyalty to those people burned within her breast, and she knew they were in need of help.

Early one morning in September of 1878, she read a dispatch article which told of a band of Cheyenne under Dull Knife, who were being held as prisoners at Fort Reno in the Oklahoma territory. The paper dropped unnoticed from her hands as she recalled the occasions when she had seen this most respected chief. They had been closely allied to the Teton Sioux and they had often hunted the region between the Big Horns and the Paha Sapa together.

It was not too many years ago when Chiefeagle and his band met Dull Knife and his Cheyennes on the Powder River in the land of the common enemy, the Crow. The buffalo hunt had been very successful and a big celebration was planned. The food was in abundance, there were many sports and games for the men, women and children. There was much dancing and courting. Horses, skins, tools and garments were offered for trade, the bargaining adding a zest to the life of the camp. Of course, there was danger too, as everyone knew the Crow Indians were lurking around the area waiting for a chance to steal horses.

It was agreed by all of the people that they should meet at the same place the next year, during the same moon when the chokecherries were red.

That was the year when Turtleheart began to court her at the social dances and when she was in her grandmother's lodge. There could be no thoughts of good times without including the memories of Turtleheart. As always, when Evensigh thought of her husband, she could feel a strange sense of contact with him. A strange feeling, the thoughts left a warmth in her bosom which she could not explain. After all, Turtleheart could not have survived, so he must be in the land of the great beyond.

When Michael called that evening, she expressed a desire to remain at home so they could talk.

"I came to see you," he said, "so it does not matter if we stay here. Being with you is all that counts." Handing a wrapped gift to Evensigh, he added, "You said you were very interested in the history of this country, so I brought you a book. It is a history of the Thirteen Colonies. I hope you like it."

"Thank you, Michael. You are so wonderful, or have I told you that before?"

"Yes, you have, but please do not stop. It makes me feel important, especially when you say it."

"Michael, let's go out into the garden. I need to talk with you about something which is bothering me. I do not know how to say what is in my heart, but as you know, History is now writing the tragedy of my people, and I feel that I must go back and see them."

"We are your people," he whispered gently.

"You know that is not what I mean, Michael. I want to see my grandfather and grandmother who raised me."

"I know, I understand." He took her hand and looked at her thoughtfully before asking.

"How long will you be gone?"

"Six months. I know that will seem a long while, but it is not so long, really. Don't look so . . ." and she had to laugh at his sad expression. "Oh Michael, when I have seen them and am satisfied, I will return to you."

"Well, I have waited this long for you, darling, so I guess six terribly long months more will not kill my love for you. I just want to hear you say one thing. When you get back will you marry me?"

"Yes, yes, I will. When I get back."

"Even Mr. and Mrs. Callahan will not miss you as much as I."

"Oh, I have not even told them yet, of my fateful determination to return to my childhood home for a visit."

"You must inform them soon, Evensigh."

"I will tonight, but I wanted to talk to you first." She leaned her head on his shoulder and asked him a question. "You wouldn't mind leaving now, would you Michael? I want to have a long talk with Mr. and Mrs. Callahan tonight."

"No, my love. But I shall be over again tomorrow."

After Michael had left, Evensigh lingered awhile in the garden. It was a beautiful evening and Evensigh wanted to think of the proper words to tell of her determination. When she went into the house, the Callahans looked up from their game of checkers to ask where Michael was.

"He has gone home. I asked him if he would, as I would like to talk with you."

"Certainly Evensigh. We are never too busy to listen to our favorite daughter." Mr. Callahan spoke as he moved a chair around for Evensigh to sit on.

"I have just had a long talk with Michael, and he has again asked me to marry him. I told him yes, but that I had to go to my Indian people for a visit first." She was glad the words were out, and she watched their faces anxiously.

Mixed emotions were evident. They were happy that Evensigh had consented to marry Michael, but they were apprehensive about her leaving for the west.

Mr. Callahan rubbed his chin, and said, "We have known for some time that you were upset about the Indian situation, my dear." He smiled at her. "Deep down, I knew this would come up sometime, but I hoped it wouldn't. You would like to marry Mike, but first you feel you must make sure, don't you?"

"Yes, I guess I do. And I want just one more visit with my family back there, then I will be happy to come back here to my family in St. Louis."

"You have made up your mind, so we will not try to stop you." Mrs. Callahan had spoken for the first time.

"Herbert," she continued bravely, "you could take her with you when you go to Fort Smith. I would not worry so much if she went part way with you."

"Splendid. That is a splendid idea. I have to leave in a few days, and we can go to Kansas City. I will arrange for you to get on a stage there. It is on the main road through the Dakota territory. You could be there in two weeks."

"Is Fort Smith very far from Fort Reno?" Evensigh asked, a new plan forming in her mind.

"It must be about two hundred miles, I reckon. Why do you ask?"

"An old friend, Dull Knife, and his Cheyenne band are being held at Fort Reno. I have many good friends there. Maybe I could see them for a last visit too."

"I have some maps. I will go get them, so stay right where you are."

Mrs. Callahan did not want to speak what was in her mind, so she casually asked, "Evensigh, my dear, I have often considered asking you how you made jerky. We were speaking of that just this afternoon."

"Some of the buffalo meat is cut up into chunks about the size of your fist. Then you take a knife and cut almost through only to turn it over and cut almost through on the other side. This is kept up until the meat is spread out in one thin slice ready to hang up on the drying rack. When dried it is stored, and used during the long, cold winter."

"My, that is simple, isn't it? Don't tell anybody, but I would like to try that sometime."

CHAPTER TWENTY-FIVE

DULL KNIFE

The Cheyenne camp was located in a valley of the Canadian River, some distance from Fort Reno in Oklahoma Territory. This 'ghost' land of the Indian Territory was beginning to show the weight of an early autumn. Contrary to the evening practice of the past, there were but few camp fires in front of the tipis. Here and there, among the lodges, were the mothers talking softly to their offspring in the shawl cradles they carried on their backs, as they walked the little ones to sleep.

Most of the people were in the lodges by choice. Even the sounds of the drum were different. These were not the lively tom-toms, but the dull roar of the medicine drum. The only sounds which remained the same were those of the horses as they whinnied and snorted in their paddock.

The entrance of the camp faced Fort Reno, and it was here that the largest lodge stood. It was occupied by Chief Dull Knife, the Cheyenne chief of sixty-eight winters, and what remained of his immediate family; a daughter-in-law, one grandchild and a brother.

As told by the story tellers, the chief's wife, son and daughter were killed by the soldiers when the camp was attacked by the blue coats in the fall of 1876. The band was resting near the North Fork River at the base of the Big Horn Mountains, about one day's travel from the Bozeman Trail.

On this September night of 1878, Dull Knife was holding a secret council with the elders of the band. He was a man of many hard winters, with kind eyes and an excessive amount of wrinkles. His features were now highlighted by the small fire in the center of the lodge. He was leaning forward, nearly over the firepit, and the elders were seated in a close circle about him.

A young boy, assigned to the care of the horses, forgot his manners and thrust his head through the entrance flap to speak excitedly. His words tumbled over each other as he announced that there was a white woman right here in camp. And she was alone.

"She entered through the paddock and is now outside. She acted strangely," he said, "trying to reach our camp by escaping the eyes of the soldier lookouts of the fort!"

"Ah, my boy, you make a fine lookout," Dull Knife said, with a twinkle in his eyes. "Bring this woman in here so we may find out about her, then you return to the horses."

Evensigh stepped into the lodge and instantly recognized the old chief. She was amazed, however, to find him staring at her in complete lack of acknowledgement. Glancing at the other faces, she found them veiled with mistrust.

"Of course," she told herself, "they do not know who I am in these white person's clothes. Quickly she tore off her hat, loosened her long hair, and unbuttoned the tight collar of her dress. Their faces remained stoic, and fearful doubts now began to cross her mind.

"Why-are-you-here?" Dull Knife asked in slow English.

In desperation, Evensigh spoke haltingly in the Tetonwan dialect. "I am Evensigh," she said. "Don't you remember me from Chiefeagle's band?" The old man caught his breath as he began to remember who she was. "I am Turtleheart's wife."

"By the sacredness of the ceremonial pipe! Yes. Now I do remember. It has been many years since we gathered by the Devil's Tower. You were my attendant after the hunt."

"Yes. Yes, you do remember me."

He rose and motioned for her to come to him. He took her in his extended arms and hugged her, then introduced her to the others. He gently clasped her small, white hands in his, and helped her take a seat next to him.

"If you could feel my heart, you would know how happy I am at the sight of you." He acted as if a generation of life had been lifted from his shoulders. "My little girl, my pretty one, I am sorry that I did not know you. Where have you been? Where did you come from? How did you find us this night?"

He laughed, "I am acting like a little boy with his first pony and do not let you answer." Evensigh laughed with him.

"Your husband, Turtleheart, is a good warrior. He is a dependable man and an excellent scout. I am sorry that I did not get to speak to him the last time I saw him." Dull Knife formed one hand into a fist and brushed the knuckles against his lips. "Ah yes, it was two and one-half winters ago, when I saw him come into the village for food and arrows. He left as soon as he came."

Evensigh looked at Dull Knife and said sadly, "Your memory plays tricks on you, for Turtleheart has been dead for these four winters."

The other council members looked at her in surprise. It was evident she did not know he was alive. "I, myself, have seen Turtleheart. He was wandering from band to band, searching . . ." and here the speaker stopped for a moment. "He was looking for you," he continued finally.

These words froze her senses. At each spoken word, her skin glowed with more color, her eyes becoming shiny with the tears. "He lives?" she fairly shouted, as she looked from one to another, seeking confirmation of the news.

The tears now flooded her eyes and she suddenly threw her arms around Dull Knife. She held on to the old man like a little girl. The others were touched by this compassionate scene, and sat with bowed heads in silence.

Slowly her crying stopped and long unused Sioux words poured from her lips. She told her story of believing Turtleheart dead, and again laid her head against Dull Knife's convenient shoulder.

This was a council meeting, and to have a woman interrupt a meeting such as this was unheard of. None the less, much of the early evening was spent in listening to Evensigh give an account of her life during the past four years. She told her entire story, including her capture and her life in St. Louis.

When she concluded there was a long silence. It was a quiet, middle-aged man, Little Wolf, who finally broke the silence. "We have our final plans to make. Perhaps we should get on with them."

Little Wolf had born the heaviest task of the journey to the Oklahoma Territory. By his own choice, he had offered himself to take care of the sick. While on this trip, the blue coats had rejected all of his appeals for rest. Worse yet, they had refused permission to hunt for a group of the children who had wandered away from one of the camps.

One by one, his charges had passed away. For his efforts to delay the procession he was severely whipped and thrown into the guard house as soon as they reached Fort Reno. Little Wolf's wounds were deep.

"I am sorry, Evensigh, but this is a very serious thing which we are to discuss tonight. I only wish to say, you are very lucky to travel home in the fashion of white people."

"I wish you were all going home with me," she said.

"Perhaps we shall see you up there, Evensigh. This meeting is for the purpose of making final plans to go home." Dull Knife confided this information in a low secretive tone.

"How is this to be? How will you manage it?"

"Tonight!" He let this news be assimilated before continuing. "For months we have been carefully laying plans for our escape. And tonight is the night."

"But I thought you were getting along fine here in the Oklahoma Territory. The written words of the newspapers say you are happy here."

"You would have to walk in my moccasins for only one day to see the signs of discontent." Dull Knife's voice sounded very weary. "Long and painful experience has shown that we were not born to be prisoners in this land of sickness."

He looked tired and the corners of his mouth were turned down. "Many things contributed to our defeat when we tried to fight the white man. And after we were beaten, our punishment was to be brought down here where we would slowly fade away into death. We arrived with two hundred and thirty men. Twenty-eight have died. Nearly half of our children have perished of sickness and many women have followed them."

"We cannot live in this ghost land of sickness. Listen, even now you can hear the death chant of the women. It is impossible for us to bear this weight. We do not choose to dic here. We want to go home to die." Dull Knife rose to get a drink of water.

Majestically he stood to make his final statement, "We have made our appeals to the governors for permission to return to our homelands. Each time we were turned down. As a last appeal, I tried to buy our freedom with everything we own, even our ponies. This again fell on deaf ears."

"My mind is pressed with sorrow for you and your people, Dull Knife. I did not know these things." With a pleading expression in her voice, she asked, "May I please go with you? I will do my share. I will not leave you until we see the forested slopes of the Black Hills. Then I will go to find Turtleheart. Do not be deaf, I beg of you."

"I do not know, little one. You have been in the big city and you are not used to our hard life. It will be very hard on you. But I can see your determination, so if you must go with us, you must change your clothes quickly and help the others get ready."

CHAPTER TWENTY-SIX

Running Away

The winds were howling through the camp by the middle of the night. They whistled past the tops of the tipi poles and snapped the entrance flaps. The fine dust swirled into the lodges to settle on the robes of the sub-chiefs, who were receiving their final instructions. The hour of running away had now arrived, and they all sat tense, their nerves keyed to a high pitch. Perhaps each was fighting the battle of his own conscience.

"Even the winds have chosen a kinship to our final plan of escape." The Cheyenne leader spoke with a keen insight. "A moon later, the powers of the wind will have weakened, but by then, winter will be upon the plains of the north."

He cleared his voice with some difficulty and continued, "Our entire welfare depends upon the condition of our horses. Little Wolf, you choose some of the young men who will take care of the extra horses. We have many, but we must use them wisely. The poor animals are not too fat on this sparse grass. They must be handled so they get their share of food and rest. We will have to rest where there is food and water for them."

He looked around, shook the fine dust from his robe, and continued. "When the Blue Coats discover our empty tipis, they will take out after us, but they will not be able to follow us for too long. Their horses are used to grain and stable care, so they will soon tire and become footsore. We must travel at great speed and when our ponies fall from fatigue, we must cut their throats to prevent their capture."

"When this is necessary, be sure to tell Little Wolf and he will see that you get a fresher pony. Now, do we all understand what each must do?"

No word was spoken in answer to the leader's question, but all the men nodded their assent.

Dull Knife measured each man's capabilities in his own mind, then spoke slowly in measured words. "The remaining winters of our lives will not be ones of peace and comfort, as it was in the old days. To keep ourselves from the edge of extinction will call for sacrifices and we will suffer for them. You will have to hunger for freedom enough to be willing to use all of your courage, your wisdom, your knowledge."

"So far, everything has gone according to plan. Now we need only to assemble our personal belongings and leave." Dull Knife looked sharply at each one of them before adding, "I think we all know that none of us may be left to measure the outcome, but it is better to die with courage than to perish slowly and without honor in a strange land, just because of the lack of courage to fight for our way of life."

In the silent way of the Indian, the Cheyennes disappeared with the wind. Only the shell of the camp was left, as they one by one started on the fateful trek to the north. They traveled at top speed as soon as they had put some distance between themselves and the fort.

Dull Knife was leading what was left of his people on a desperate flight, and the responsibility weighed heavily upon him. The only comforting thought he had was the fact there were none of the old or helpless to care for. The few children who were on the trek rode double with their parents or were cradled in the arms of their mothers.

The sun was well above the horizon when they stopped for the first brief rest. The wind had stopped and it was now beginning to get very warm. Evensigh wore her own long, plain muslin dress with a borrowed buckskin shirt over it. A pair of old moccasins were on her feet.

By personal invitation, she was given the privilege of riding next to Dull Knife. She was extremely glad of this, but she had to smile to herself when she thought of the arrangement being solely because she would be under the watchful eye of the old chief.

He feared her incapabilities, and she herself knew the four years of city living had left her woefully inadequate for the rigors of forced travel. A trip such as this would tax even the most strong, and perhaps even they would not survive.

Now that they had stopped, she dismounted from her horse, to stretch the muscles in her legs. Already they felt sore from the unaccustomed movements of the animal. This was only a short rest, and they were soon mounted and going north at a rapid pace.

Determination is a poor substitute for strength and by late afternoon Evensigh was very weary. She hurt from the waist down, and she wondered just how long it had been since she had ridden. It seemed like a hundred years ago.

A scout was riding up to the small group at a fast gallop. "There is a water hole up ahead. It is not far. And there is grass for the horses."

Each jog of the horse as he put his foot down on the ground, jolted her like a knife was inside of her. It would be so good to be able to stand again, and to be able to lay down in the grass.

Dull Knife dispelled any thoughts of rest however, as he gave orders that they would stay only long enough to give the horses a drink. "Let the horses drink their fill, then we must be on our way." While Dull Knife was speaking, he kept looking to the south, along the way they had come.

The brief stop over, they raced westward. The raw pain in Evensigh was becoming unbearable, but she was determined she was stout of body and heart. The sheepskin she sat astride of felt like granite on her tender skin. Then she remembered Dull Knife saying this journey would call for extreme sacrifice and suffering. When she looked around and saw the others, some with babes in their arms, she felt the pain was easier to bear.

They pushed on mercilessly until the second night, when the old chief signalled for a stop. Evensigh was not the only one to slide off a horse and collapse on the ground. They were all bone weary and desperately in need of rest.

Dull Knife covered her with a robe, and she was very thankful for this as she lay there with her eyes closed. He took her horse down to the small water hole and was standing there when Little Wolf approached him.

"Dull Knife, one of the women is sick and near death. I fear she will not see the sun rise." He waited for a response, and when none was forthcoming, he continued, "I assigned Jumping Boy to protect the rear of the band, and he tells me it was almost dark when he noticed her illness."

Still Dull Knife did not answer, and Little Wolf pressed on. "Just before we stopped, the woman fell from her horse. Jumping Boy saw this and ran to help her. It was then that he saw her baby was dead. It must have died this afternoon; the body was quite cold."

"Jumping Boy tried to help her before, but she rejected his offer. He feared injury to the baby, but she told him it was all right."

The expression on Dull Knife's face was unchanged, but his voice was husky with compassion. "My poor people. How can they continue? I have not seen any sign of pursuit, so perhaps we had better move a little slower. How are the rest of the women and children?"

"They are very tired."

"The horses? How are they holding up? How many of them are left in the reserve herd?"

"They are pretty well spent too. Most of them are still with us, but we must destroy a few soon."

"My spirit is on the ground, Little Wolf." Without raising his eyes from the ground, he paused in thought, then said, "You take half of your lookouts and have them stand watch. When the moon has appeared, change lookouts. We must all have some sleep tonight."

With a sudden decision, Dull Knife stopped Little Wolf with a terse comment. "While you sleep, we will move on. When you awaken, you will move on to catch up with us. That is the best way."

Little Wolf did not like this change in decisions, but he nodded and left. He knew that Dull Knife did not always do the right thing; and in this time of trouble, he could make an error. But he also knew the old chief was incapable of doing anything which would harm his own people, if he could prevent it.

The earth was still shadowed with the darkness when Evensigh was aroused from her deep sleep. The reins of the bridle were put in her hand and she leaned on the pony for support. As she stared at the beauty of the star land which stretched far above, she dreamily recalled an old Indian telling her long ago, that up there in the sky there were no cranes flying there to calculate the time for climate changes. The calm and serenity of the stars gave evidence of just one happy and permanent season.

As the dusks followed the dawns, the moon increased and decreased. Evensigh could not remember of days they traveled. The yesterdays were all full of nightmarish events without sequence. She met each dawn with a strong heart, but her body grew weaker and weaker. Eating became a chore. The only reason she choked the food down at all was because she knew that without the daily small rations, she could not go on.

Night and day, the desperate race for freedom went on. The herd had long since been disposed of, slaughtered one by one as the valiant animals dropped from exhaustion. The frantic band raided ranches and farms for food and horses, and if they had to kill those who intercepted their raids, they killed. More and more frequently the soldiers would come up on them, and they fought a delaying action so they could escape again.

The cold was beginning to frost the land, and to make matters worse, more fresh troops were now in pursuit. The scourge of hunger was draining their strength, and rest periods were few. Too many times, the soldiers were lying in wait at water holes, waiting for them. Every day was taking its toll, and each day found fewer and fewer of Dull Knife's people who were still able to ride on.

There was no rest. Daylight, twilight, darkness were all the same. They just pushed ahead until their mounts were plodding slower and slower. Even the elements were against them, and the cold of approaching winter was now a reality. The horses could not be urged to a faster speed for fear the faithful mounts would stumble and fall. A slow horse was better than no horse, and once a horse was down, he had to be disposed of.

Hungry and full of despair, Evensigh sat on her horse very straight as though the bitter cold meant nothing to her. Her companions were just as tired, and did the same. Behind her lips, blue with the cold, she chewed pemmican, the only food that was left. She often thought of how much easier it would have been, to have taken the stagecoach. Such thoughts embarrassed her, and she tried to throw them out of her mind.

The soldiers had not fired upon them for three days now, and it was a welcome relief. The snow which had begun to fall gently, had suddenly turned into a plains' blizzard. Its wrath tore at man and beast alike, as the Indians dismounted to tug gently at the horses to keep them going. It was also warmer to walk than to ride.

As the snow kept building up, the eyelids and nostrils of the horses became crusted with ice. With stiff fingers, the Cheyennes fought to keep the ice from smothering the poor animals. With prayer they kept themselves going.

Finally Dull Knife corralled the band in a circle, with the people huddled inside and the horses were held with their rear quarters to the outside. Shouting above the howl of the wind he urged them to get closer together.

"I can feel a growing hopelessness among you. Do not let the storm destroy your courage." He waited a moment until the wind subsided a little. "You have suffered much on this journey, but take hope. We are close to home and when we reach there we will be taken in with open arms. We will no longer be treated like orphans by harsh and unloving guardians. Do not give up."

"I promise you, we are soon to be among friends. Before this night comes," he encouraged them, "we will be in the sand hills, where we can rest in their shelter for a few days."

"Right now, I want you to think of whether you wish to go with Little Wolf. Yes, that includes the women. Little Wolf will push on from the sand hills after a little rest, to go on to Sitting Bull's camp. When we get to the sand hills, all of you who are going with Little Wolf will help him make preparations. You may choose between the two groups."

The band broke their circle after this brief rest to plod toward the sand hills where they knew they could find wood for warm fires. Reaching the objective, they dug into a small cave in one of the hills for protection from the storm.

Little Wolf gathered those who had decided to go with him to make preparations to move on. Early the next morning they left. It was a sad farewell. Each face mirrored the unspoken thoughts that they would never see each other again.

Nearly half of the group felt they would rather journey to Sitting Bull's camp, and this did not leave very many of the young warriors to stay with Dull Knife. Evensigh remained because the sand hills were not far from her home.

Dull Knife instructed those who stayed with him to wrap their horses' feet in cloths of any kind, so there would be no hoof marks in the snow for soldiers to follow. He hoped the new snow would cover the tracks, but he was leaving nothing to chance. Freedom was too close to throw away now.

What remained of the once powerful Cheyenne band huddled inside the shelter of the small cave to escape the wind. They welcomed the heat and stretched their numb fingers toward the flames. Wood was becoming hard to find though, so all who were able, took turns to search for enough to keep the fires going.

Each member of the band was responsible for his own chores, and Evensigh was tending to hers. She gathered the wet buckskin garments to dry as they were laid down beside her. She tugged at them to remove the ice and snow, then placed them where they would dry.

As the skins became warm, she stretched them by pulling and kneading, a procedure which also prevented them from stiffening. The joints of her fingers ached for relief and the outraged spirit of her mind began to rebel, just as she finished.

Standing, she found her legs were like an old woman's, shaky and weak. They creaked with every movement. Looking up from the fire, she saw a scout coming in to report to Dull Knife. The people soon knew that he had seen a lone horseman approaching on foot, his horse following behind. It was not too long until they saw this man and his horse coming around the hill. He was shielding his eyes from the blowing snow with one hand, and looked grotesque in his bulky, ice encrusted, gray buffalo robe.

"Hau! Hau!" he roared with the voice of a buffalo bull. "May I offer you my bear-like strength and my savage instincts, or should I go help the blue coats find you?"

"Here, let yourself rest close to the fire and thaw out. The wind is so cold it has frozen a smile on your face." Dull Knife was doing the speaking.

"Ho, to see that fire would make even you smile, Dull Knife. To find you in this storm was nothing. I could have tracked you to the base of the Big Horn Mountains, just to sit by the fire."

"Be serious, Jumping Boy. Why did you leave Little Wolf?" Dull Knife's voice showed some concern.

"I had to come back. What good is a band without someone strong to care for it?"

"We are happy to have you back. You can be of great help with your young, strong body. When these winds die down, you can stand on this bank and fan the smoke from the fire so it cannot be seen."

"You would have me do a woman's work? I thought I would be needed for defeating the troops, however I will bow to your demands and do as you ask." They all laughed aloud, and it relieved their tensions.

CHAPTER TWENTY-SEVEN

Dull Knife Surrenders

The storm continued and the band stayed huddled in the shelter of the small cave. The food had been consumed and they were subsisting on horse meat. They butchered the weakest ones first, as the best ponies had to be saved for the rest of the journey. Some of the meat was used to make a thick soup, but much of it was cut into cubes and boiled, then set out to freeze so it could be stored in pouches for later use.

Dull Knife realized that one fire would not warm all of them and that the storm might not diminish for several days. It was cruel to have his people try to warm themselves in shifts, but there was the problem of securing wood. As ordered, the men took turns to get wood, returning half-frozen with scant armloads of twigs. Each time they had to go farther and farther from the cave in their search.

Adding to their difficulties, was the shortage of available grass for their animals. The men scraped at the ice-crusted snow to help the horses clear away the snow so they could graze. The sparse grass did little to appease the horses' hunger.

On the fourth day the snow stopped and the wind died down to a whisper. Dull Knife called the men to council as the skies cleared. "We have been here much longer than could be considered safe. Our food has been barely adequate, but when we travel, that which we have stored will not last long." The rigors of the journey had taken the strong edge from his voice.

"With your permission, and with Jumping Boy's advice, I would like to send a runner to Red Cloud's camp to ask him for help. If they could send us fresh horses, some food and ammunition, we have a chance to outrun the soldiers. I feel certain he and his people will provide shelter for us at his camp."

They all looked at Jumping Boy. It was his word as to whether a messenger could be sent. "I will go. In a few sleeps I will meet you with fresh horses and supplies."

As Jumping Boy prepared for his mercy run, they agreed on a rendezvous six days travel northwest of the cave site. With a wave of his hand and a loud farewell, Jumping Boy mounted the best horse available and set out for Red Cloud's camp.

The next morning, Dull Knife awoke with a severe cold and a high fever. He could hardly speak, and with resignation waved Old Crow and Wild Hog to take command. Evensigh gathered what garments could be spared to bundle the old man against the penetrating cold. He tried to complain, but soon gave up and let her doctor him. He dutifully swallowed the medicine broth and by mid-day was well enough to order their departure. Evensigh rode directly in back of him so she could keep an eye on him.

The strongest horses were put in front to break the trail as they rode in single file. They squinted their eyes against the brightness of the thin rays of sun which glinted from the edges of the tree limbs and the tops of the hills.

On the seventh day, Jumping Boy found them camped at the appointed place. He came in alone, and going to Dull Knife he explained that Red Cloud had sent no help. "He sends you his deepest sympathy, Dull Knife, but he is unable to assist in any way. He says it is futile to fight the whites, and as a favor to your people, to yourself and to him, he asks you to surrender to the soldiers."

Shocked surprise on Dull Knife's face showed the impact of the disappointing words. "Jumping Boy," he finally said. "It took great courage for you to return with this message.

You have done your task well." Tears were in the eyes of the old man and he could not look up.

"Why couldn't he have sent us some food?" demanded Evensigh.

"He had none to spare."

"How could he refuse food for his starving allies? Are you sure you spoke to Red Cloud?"

"Yes, I spoke to Red Cloud. He is a defeated leader of a defeated people. They are also starving."

The unreasoning rage within her racked her whole body until she shook, and the tears streamed down her face. After she had become more quiet, Dull Knife motioned for the others to come close.

"I speak to you with a heavy heart. I have failed you." Dull Knife was searching for something to say to his people. "Evensigh is right in being angry, but it is I whom she should be angry at."

"No," said one of the elders. "This is not all your fault, any more than it is Red Cloud's or ours. We are the ones who helped make the decisions, we were the ones who were willing to gamble on the unknown." His words were supported by the others with their exclamations of incrimination of self.

Dull Knife raised his hand for silence. "Even so, failure must be my burden. Just a little while ago, I was considering the cost of this journey, a journey we all undertook a long time ago, when we were all stronger and showed our true ages. Look at one another. What do you see? You see we are nearly barefoot, our garments nothing but torn rags. Those of us who still live have our hearts on the ground in sorrow. We know we cannot continue long without food or warmth."

Dull Knife was having difficulty in expressing the thoughts in his mind. "Look back and you will see we have stuffed a long season's journey into a much shorter span of time. We have become frail like a summer bird who is left behind to face the long blizzards of winter."

He drew a long, shaking breath before continuing. "It was early last fall when each of you looked to me to show you a way to refresh your sagging spirits. Now, I can only think of how I failed you. We have fallen short of our goal and there is no one to help us."

The old leader had tears running down his weathered cheeks, as he approached the time of telling his people he was ready to bow to the inevitable. "You know the blue coats are camped just a little ways from us. Tomorrow I will go to their camp. I beg of you, do not lose faith even though your hearts weep with sorrow. I will beg for understanding. I will kneel to the blue coats and plead for you, plead for a small piece of land where you can live. Light your fires tonight, and do not fear. The scouts will be watching the movements of the white man, so he will not attack without warning."

His ragged followers were unable to speak as they looked at Dull Knife in disbelief. To surrender meekly, without a fight, seemed the last of many strong blows. Silently they moved away with sick hearts.

The next day, Dull Knife and the elders went to the leader of the soldiers to give up and plead for mercy. This was to be the first visit of many over the next two days, but none of them produced the desired results of the Cheyennes going to the Red Cloud Reservation of the Sioux.

The leader of the soldiers insisted he was going to take Dull Knife to Fort Robinson. The falling snow was heavy during this time, but as the army gave them some supplies, the Cheyennes welcomed the chance to rest.

It was finally decided that Dull Knife and his band were to accompany the cavalry unit to Fort Robinson. Another blizzard was raging as they rode west to face the unknown.

In tattered and worn clothing, their horses stumbling from weakness, they entered Fort Robinson. They sat their mounts erectly, to symbolize the strength which was still in them. They were a proud people, even in surrender.

Dull Knife and his followers were soon marched into a large, two room barracks building, and their meager belongings were dumped in after them. In spite of the brusque treatment they were receiving, they were thankful for being in out of the snowstorm which was raging across the territory.

As the door closed behind them, Dull Knife directed the women and small children to use the larger room. Meanwhile, he was being pestered by Jumping Boy, who whispered, "They did not search our belongings. We still have our guns, some ammunition, bows and arrows."

"Keep your voice down," Dull Knife ordered. "We don't know what the white men are going to do with us yet. We must keep quiet so we do not ruin any chance we may have to take."

Dull Knife signed that he wanted the wooden floor pried up so the weapons could be hidden underneath. The men were busy at this task when Evensigh approached Dull Knife.

"I thought I was the only one with a pistol, but several of the women had guns slung under their dresses with cords. Hide them with the rest."

"Ah, women. You have again shown a natural female distrust of a man's intentions." The smile on his face made the words less caustic. "I am glad you did not intend to surrender completely. We may have use for these guns."

CHAPTER TWENTY-EIGHT

Flight to Death

Days turned into weeks, and the weeks seemed interminable to the occupants of the prison barracks building. Extreme restlessness had now gripped the Cheyenne in spite of the good treatment they had received. The quarters were too small for the many people, and as they grew stronger, they resented the highly overcrowded conditions.

Dull Knife, Old Crow and Wild Hog were the only ones who could leave the building, and then only when they had been sent for by Captain Vroom. After two months of this unsanitary confinement, there were rumors among them that the wrangling was over, that a settlement had been reached. Dull Knife and the representatives from the Departments of War and Interior had met several times, and the patience of the captives was beginning to wear thin.

It was near dusk on a particularly dreary day when Dull Knife and his two aides returned to the barracks. He closed the door behind him, extended his hands for silence, and spoke with controlled calm, although his eyes blazed with extreme anger.

"Pray long," he said, "for what I have to say is not what you wish to hear. We are looked upon as prisoners of war, because in our escape for freedom from Fort Reno we killed some white people. The demands for our punishment are so loud that the Great White Father has commanded that we are to be returned to the Indian Territory."

There was a growing rumble in the people. Dull Knife said further, "Our allies, the Sioux, petitioned the government to grant us permission to stay with them. This was rejected." The old chief sat down, and sobs were heard in the stillness. This grew until the shrill wailings of the women turned into the death chant.

Dull Knife rose to make his way to Evensigh. "I will make arrangements to have you taken to the Sioux Reservation," he told her. "The problem will be small if you uncover your head and let them see you are a white woman. You can talk with them in their language and ask them to let you go home."

"I am afraid of them, Dull Knife, and I do not know what is best to do," she replied. "I was a party to your escape, and if you are guilty, then so am I. If I do as you say and they put me in prison, I will never see Turtleheart. I have been patient for a long time and I must wait a little longer. Maybe a better time will come for us. Let me remain with you for now."

After a long thought, Dull Knife nodded his head and said, "Perhaps you are right in what you say. We will wait and pray to the Holy Mystery to show us the way."

New hope was born the next morning when Dull Knife and his aides were called to headquarters for a meeting. The commander quickly outlined the plans for the Cheyennes' future. The abrupt words killed Dull Knife's hopes for a reprieve. He was appalled to hear the captain announce curtly, "My orders are to take you and your people to Fort Reno immediately. Fort Reno is six hundred miles from here, and as the army does not intend to keep you here, you will have to go. I will be in charge."

"In this weather, my people will die if they are forced to travel," Dull Knife protested.

The captain looked up and said evenly, "You arrived in a snow storm so you can leave in one. You have no choice."

Dull Knife saw the futility of arguing this, and he stated in a flat tone, "If the Great White Father wants us to die, we will die here. We cannot march to Fort Reno in this season. It is too far. We will not leave." He turned and stalked out.

When he rejoined the Cheyennes in the barracks, they knew something was wrong. Dull Knife's face was gray and his hands were nervous.

They want us to leave immediately for Fort Reno under the command of Captain Vessels." This announcement brought new anguish to his audience. Captain Vessels was a notorious Indian hater and they could expect no mercy on the long journey south.

"Old Crow is still at headquarters, but I could hear no more of their talk and left." A sudden coughing spell shook his body, and he fought for breath.

When Dull Knife recovered from this sudden siezure, he managed to continue. "I told them we would not leave. We will stay here in the shelter of this building. It will kill us to march six hundred miles in this weather."

The return of Old Crow interrupted the impassioned speech. "Dull Knife, the interpreter told me to inform you that food and firewood will be withheld until we decide to move peacefully to Fort Reno."

"You tell them," Dull Knife roared, "that I have said the last word. Either they let us go to the Sioux Reservation, or we remain here in this house until death!" These words of defiance were endorsed by every member of the group.

Two days without food or water or fuel, was reflected in the Indians' pinched faces. But their will was strong and no one complained. An interpreter banged on the door late in the afternoon. Jumping Boy admitted him with an insult, but the interpreter disregarded the slur and went to Dull Knife. "Captain Vessels has proposed that you release your children to him so they can be fed and warmed."

"The answer is no! We will not release our children. If we do we will never see them again, and we prefer to die together."

"If that is what you wish. You can expect a sergeant and his detail to come here and search you. They want to make sure you are not planning to leave without authority."

"Let them come. We are at their mercy, and my men will not bother them while they are here."

As soon as the interpreter had left, Dull Knife signed to the men to give any object which could be used as a weapon to the women to conceal under their skirts. The remaining food was hidden and they made sure the loose floor boards were all covered with beds or other bedding.

No sooner had this been done, when a handful of troopers, under the command of a young, bearded sergeant, arrived to make an inspection. A careful inspection was made of the warriors and their few possessions. When the soldiers were satisfied there were no weapons and no possible way to escape, they left.

The January night was clear and bitterly cold. The wind brought its icy touch through the boards of the unheated building. With no fires, the people huddled together for warmth. Death touched the half frozen bodies of two elderly women and a small child before dawn. The mourners cried for their dead, the cries being heard by guards, who made no attempt to enter the cold barracks.

The funeral chants were unnerving, and when relief time came, the guards were only too glad to exchange places. There was undoubtedly sympathy for the cold and starving prisoners, but they did not show it.

After five days of this deprivation, the Cheyenne awoke to see snow falling. It drifted down in its silent way, all day. At dusk the camp was silent as the new fallen snow. The soldiers had fed and stabled their horses for the night, and a cabin of four sentries watched the prisoners' building of confinement.

Darkness closed around the fort, and in the barracks were hushed whispers as Dull Knife passed around the small rations of food. He told Evensigh that the troopers thought the point of surrender had been reached. He then instructed the men to tear up the floor of the barracks and to barricade the windows. They took up the hidden weapons, and warriors were placed at each window.

"Where will we go?" Evensigh asked Dull Knife.

"We plan to head right for the Sioux. Once on their land we can scatter and they will cover for us. On the way there is a ranch where we can get horses. Our first step is to reach the ranch, then to ride north to the reservation."

Before the midnight watch changed, Jumping Boy silently opened a window, and with careful aim, sent an arrow through the throat of a sentry. The only sound was the twang of the bow string. Jumping Boy disappeared into the night to reappear with the sentry's rifle and ammunition belt. It was now necessary to make all haste before the dead soldier was found.

The warriors burst out with drawn knives and pistols and shot down the other sentries, stripping them of their guns and ammunition. The entire band was running across the open when the soldiers came pouring out of their building.

Dull Knife and the men remained where they were to do battle with the sleepy, half dressed soldiers, while the women and children fled. For the first few moments the seasoned men held the upper hand against the numerically superior force of soldiers.

Taken by surprise, the troopers were still groggy, and trying to dress themselves. For every Cheyenne killed, there were three soldiers to fall beside him. Dull Knife shouted to his warriors to use hit and run tactics, and soon the battle was strung across the snowy plains for almost a mile. Whenever a warrior fell, his weapons were seized by a woman or a boy who now took up the battle, often in hand to hand combat.

Dull Knife and Evensigh, along with a dozen or so young warriors raced toward the remuda of cavalry horses. A shot sounded from the corral and an Indian fell. Dull Knife was now realizing that hand to hand combat here was fatal, so he commanded the warriors to crouch down in a firing line, the way the soldiers did. This proved to be a fatal error, as the soldiers' marksmanship was excellent. One by one the warriors were picked off by the soldiers' fire.

Only three braves were left, and they made a hasty retreat for cover behind a haystack. "It is not going well," Dull Knife panted. "Our success in escaping now depends on getting some of the cavalry horses and scattering the rest. If two or three of us could get to the ranch, they would be able to get enough of their horses for all of us."

Looking out over the snow they could see the dark forms of the dead and wounded where they fell. Other forms, however, were moving as rapidly as they could, to the north.

"Come," Dull Knife grabbed Evensigh's hand to drag her over the icy ground. "We must run on foot to the ranch. I see others making their escape." They left to go north in an attempt to catch the fleeing forms.

Evensigh was astonished at the rapid pace set by Dull Knife. It was remarkable that such an old man could keep going at a fast trot mile after mile. "Oh God," Evensigh prayed to the Deity they had taught her about in St. Louis. "Let this escape be a success." Then in sheepish doubt she added a few words for Wakan Tanka.

Her lungs seemed as they were bursting when Dull Knife stopped briefly. Her chest heaved and her throat ached with each breath. But there was no stopping now, so they were soon racing across the snow in renewed flight. Dull Knife's grip on her wrist hurt as he drug her along.

"Please Dull Knife," she gasped. "Leave me, and run for the horses without me. I am only holding you back and you must get away."

"Come," he urged. "I am not leaving you behind." With these words, he circled her waist with his arm and half carried, half dragged her with him.

In the faint light of day they saw the gray shadows of the ranch. Two of the warriors went to the corral for five horses. Dull Knife, Evensigh, and the third brave waited and searched for the sight of any other Cheyennes. There was no sign that anyone else had made it.

"When they return with the horses, you must do as I say. You head for the Sioux, and I will go back. I must go back, as my people are caught in a tragic struggle for survival there."

"No, Dull Knife," Evensigh was panicked.

"I must help my people. Jumping Boy is with them, and he will be waiting for me. I must go back if only to join them in the solace of death."

He was interrupted by the two braves returning with horses. The older of the two warriors turned to Dull Knife when he heard of Dull Knife's plan to return.

"We can understand your wish to go back to the fighting, but death has already blotted out their misery. Time has run out for all of them, Dull Knife. If you return you will probably be the only survivor and they will throw you in prison for the rest of your life. We are here, and we need you. You are also our leader."

Dull Knife never answered but mounted a horse, and without looking back, rode to the north, pointing the way to the Sioux reservation.

CHAPTER TWENTY-NINE

Destiny Follows Many Paths

Weeks went by and rumors carried Strong Echo's return. People of Wounded Knee Valley hopefully looked to the plateau for the happy return. Instead, a delegation of agency men came to see Blue Thunder's scattered village. Most of them were Sioux Indians led by a white man. Through his interpreter, he announced he had brought many good things for the people.

"There will be beef, plenty of trinkets, and some clothing for your band."

"We are grateful to you. If you only knew how much these things mean to us," Blue Thunder said happily.

"We have many things in the wagon which your womenfolk will be glad to get. We will unload them now."

Turtleheart had watched the procession as it came into the village, and now he walked up to see what was happening. "What is the occasion?" he asked.

"We have brought you supplies," the tall, thin leader replied. "I am Jim Randle from the agency. I remember you. I saw you the first day you came in to the agency to register. You are well thought of for your good work."

"But, why are these things brought here?" Turtleheart insisted.

"We have come here to get Blue Thunder and the men under him to give their consent on a piece of paper," he explained through the interpreter.

"Consent to what?" Turtleheart was puzzled.

"For the white people to use the Black Hills."

"Isn't that what they are doing anyway?"

"Well yes, but this paper will make it all legal. According to the last treaty, the white men are in violation of the treaty, so they want three-fourths of the males in the tribe to sign the paper of consent." Randle was becoming irked at Turtleheart.

"Why three-fourths? All of the men should consent to this."

"No. According to the treaty, a thumb mark or a cross made by three-fourths of the adult male population on the paper, makes it all legal."

Turtleheart replied coolly, "Even if most of the people can be fooled into signing this paper, I will never agree."

"Let's wait until we have filled our stomachs, then we will be able to talk better."

Blue Thunder had been listening quietly to the conversation, and he now said, "You have come here to be disappointed. None of my people will agree to signing the paper."

"We can talk better after we stuff ourselves with fresh meat." Randle turned to the interpreter and said, "Somebody break out the whiskey and bring it over here."

Turtleheart took Blue Thunder by the arm and led him away from the others. "Watch this man," he warned. "He has firewater. You drink it and you will be crazy in the head after a few swallows. The next day you will feel bad and not know what you have done. I must be at the agency by sunup, and have to leave now." Turtleheart warned again, "Watch this man."

There were many groups of Indians at the agency headquarters when Turtleheart arrived there. The hour was early and he could not understand why they were there.

"Have you heard the news?" they called to him.

"What news? I have just arrived."

"Crazy Horse has been killed."

Turtleheart looked at them in disbelief. Some of the men were members of Crazy Horse's band, and Loneman was among them. He knew Loneman would tell the truth.

"We are glad to see you, Eyes-of-the-Sioux. This is a bad day for us," greeted Loneman.

"It is true? Tell me, how did this happen?"

"This started some time ago. Nearly every day a family or two has moved away until our band was scattered, split like kindling wood. The government men then sent for Crazy Horse by telling him they wanted to smoke the pipe. He went to the council in good faith, but was seized. When he struggled for freedom one of the agency Indians put a lance through his right side, from the back." Loneman spat on the ground in anger.

"Has his father been told?"

"Wound was at the fort when Crazy Horse came in. He did not see the fight, but his son died in his arms."

"It is a great tragedy for a great chief like Crazy Horse to die from a lance in the back," Turtleheart spoke quietly. "To die by the hand of his own people is an omen of evil."

Sadly they parted, Turtleheart to go sit to think until the coming of the dawn. When his business at the agency had been completed, he rode back to Wounded Knee to inform them of what had happened to Crazy Horse.

He found Blue Thunder with Strong Echo in the midst of a furious argument. "Why did you sell the Black Hills to the government?" Strong Echo was demanding.

"Ask the others. Jim and I did not sign."

"You are leader! You could have prevented them from signing. You, the leader should have told them not to."

"Strong Echo, you above all others, should know that I am no longer a chief. I do not have any power in this band. The agency has convinced them that my power is limited to the giving of advice, if they wish to ask for it."

Strong Echo ceased his shouting. "You could have influenced them. The records show that most all of the men signed away the Black Hills."

"The Black Hills? We have not controlled them for some time now. They control them and they always will, no matter what we say. You know that, Strong Echo."

Strong Echo was now furious at the elder's lack of concern for the Paha Sapa.

"Quit your word fighting," Turtleheart finally broke in. Crazy Horse is dead. Killed by a Sioux."

"Crazy Horse has been killed?" Blue Thunder asked.

"I already knew, Turtleheart." Strong Echo lowered his voice for the first time.

"You knew? You did not say so?" Blue Thunder was astounded.

"I never had a chance to say so, you old ..."

"Yes, I am old, older and far wiser than you," was the retort of Blue Thunder.

"Stop!" was the stern order of Turtleheart. "This battle of the words tears my heart out. If we are to survive, our spirits must be in agreement. You both sound like old women, so it is time to stop and think."

The two other men looked at Turtleheart, their faces beginning to color with shame.

"Now, tell me what has happened here in a straight tongue."

Blue Thunder grimaced as Strong Echo shook his head and started to speak. "Evidently they used the same tactics all over the reservation. They used the firewater to get the men to sign."

He looked at Turtleheart before resuming. "They needed a total of 3,350 signatures or marks to sign away the Black Hills. Do you know how many they received?"

"How many?"

"Two hundred and forty names, the rest being thumb marks and crosses. How many of those were put there by young boys, those who could not vote?" Strong Echo ended on a note of dejection and again shook his head.

"We had that many warriors on the Greasy Grass, and that was but a small part of the Sioux," Turtleheart surmised.

"The government men are nothing but thieves, thieves without honor," Strong Echo spit out the words.

"Strong Echo," said Turtleheart. "I understood the government man to say we would be leasing the Paha Sapa to them."

"The others were told the same thing. All lies."

"Perhaps our people feel like Blue Thunder, that since the Sioux are beginning to disappear, the whites will do as they wish anyway. We are in no position to take them back now."

"Those thoughts would cause some to sign, but not too many. That number would be small in view of the sacred attachments to the Paha Sapa."

Death wails were being heard now, as the news of Crazy Horse became known over the valley. Hearing them, the three men cast aside the problem of the Black Hills for the present.

As if in mourning for Crazy Horse, the wind blew for many days, bringing with it the snow. When it ceased, the land was covered in white stillness.

Turtleheart stepped from the agency building to breathe in the cold air. Glancing at the clear blue sky, he felt glad that the prairie stillness had returned. This was not to last very long however, as he was ordered to accompany other scouts to Fort Robinson. They were to help the soldiers from the fort to capture Dull Knife and the Cheyenne who had escaped.

"Where are the Cheyenne now? Why is it we have to go and help capture them?" Turtleheart asked through an interpreter at Fort Robinson.

"When we last heard, they were making a stand on top of a hill, nearly half a days travel from here. They are scattered and have used much skill in evading capture. Your job will be to keep watch for them. We must end this quickly, so if you have to, kill them."

Turtleheart had trouble in getting sleep to come, as he couldn't get Dull Knife from his mind. "Brother turned against brother." He had heard this many times, and now it had to be applied to him. After sleep came, it was a disturbed slumber.

Fort Robinson was buzzing with excitement at the escape of the Cheyenne. There was a guard chain around the barracks, and they had all been shot down almost simultaneously.

The scouts rode out and soon saw a group of soldiers who were tossing the frozen bodies of the dead Cheyenne into a large hole. The sight turned Turtleheart's insides into a turmoil. What kind of a man had he turned into, pursuing his own friends and brothers?

By mid-day, they came into sight of a small rise to the north where some of Dull Knife's people were entrenched. With troubled mind he fell back, far behind the other scouts, and circled the area.

From a spot on the other side of the hill, he sat on his horse to watch the sporadic action. The gun firing became silent as the sun went down, so he rode closer to the fugitives. In the middle of the night he thought he discerned some shadowy figures crawling down the hill. He watched silently as they crept past him, then reined his horse around to follow them.

When daylight was near, the fleeing Cheyennes stopped atop another hill some miles to the west. They dug into the frozen ground to make places of protection, and Turtleheart saw that their clothing was in tatters. He wondered just how much cold the women and children could stand. Looking down at his own warm cavalry coat, he felt ashamed.

By mid-day the cavalry arrived and the battle resumed. It was light in tempo as the soldiers did not wish to expose themselves to the rifle power of the entrenched Indians. Here and there a soldier fell and once in a while an Indian. The women and children were casualties as often as the men.

Turtleheart searched this small group for a sign of Dull Knife, but he was not among them. He has been killed somewhere. This thought was sad.

A figure wearing a gray robe jumped from behind his earth mound and beckoned for two others to join him. The army guns were trained on them as they slid and dodged down the slope to a dead horse. Quickly they sliced hunks of meat from the carcass and headed back up the hill. Turtleheart sighed a breath of relief when they made it back up the hill.

The night came and again under the cover of darkness he trailed the Cheyenne as they made their silent way far to the west. With daylight, he rode in close to where they were.

"If you have lost all reason for living, just keep coming," a voice called to him.

"I ask only that you hold your weapons until I have spoken," Turtleheart called back.

"I will permit that." It was the gray robed warrior. Turtleheart watched him come down the slope and stop a few yards from where he remained mounted. The Cheyenne stood in his tattered garments with black unfriendly eyes fixed on the scout. The gun barrel was pointed menacingly at Turtleheart.

"It is useless for you to continue this running fight." Turtleheart paused for a reply, but as none came, he began again in softer tones. "I have watched you for some time, and each night there are fewer of you. It is not right that this should be happening. Quit the fight and come in to warm your children."

Turtleheart removed his trooper's coat and, leaning forward, he dropped it in front of the young leader. "Here, take this and give it to a woman."

"We are grateful to you Sioux scouts because we know that each night you could have given the alarm." Turtleheart felt eased because some of the other scouts shared his feeling of sympathy for the Cheyenne.

"We have come too far, and have been hurt too much to quit now. All of the old people are gone. One after another, each has taken his own life. And our children, we have sent the remaining ones to the land beyond. My friend," the Cheyenne brave said, "All we have left is the will to fight, and we prefer to die trying to get home."

"Do you need my horse?"

"No, but we need your ammunition." His voice trailed off as he pointed. "Here they come again."

"Is there anything else I can do for you?" Turtleheart asked as he handed over his small supply of ammunition.

"This is our fight." He gave Turtleheart a strange look and added, "You have what you want." He disappeared up the slope just before the troops wheeled into position. The gun battle continued until almost mid-day.

When the Cheyenne quit firing, Turtleheart guessed that they had used all the ammunition he had given them. Like ants the cavalrymen began to crawl up the hill for the final kill.

Three figures jumped up from behind a snowy breastwork and charged down the hill. A volley of shots brought all three warriors to the ground. Only one rose, a gray buffalo robe clinging to his waist. He took a few short steps forward until more gunfire knocked him down.

None of the figures moved. Turtleheart turned his pony to the north and rode slowly away, knowing he had seen the bravest of men die with honor. Such was destiny.

Not all of the Cheyennes died on this day however. Dull Knife, with the vigor and cunning born of desperation, was leading four survivors of the daring escape north to the haven of the Sioux reservation.

Their destiny followed a different path, to lead them to the lodge of Blue Thunder. On this bitter cold morning, when the dark dye still lingered on the countryside, the barking of dogs roused Blue Thunder from his couch. He wrapped a reservation blanket around himself and stepped out to investigate.

Five weary riders on puffing horses trailed down the hill in single file. The quick vapor puffs of the horses, and the absence of their snorting, told Blue Thunder that they had been traveling at a fast pace. When they drew near, he knew them to be Indians, one a woman.

"Jim. Alice." Blue Thunder called. "We have travelers coming. Wake up." He spoke louder than usual, more to inform the riders that the camp was not all asleep, than to arouse his son and daughter-in-law.

As the riders dismounted, he recognized the features of Dull Knife. He ran to the Cheyenne chief and threw his arms around him. "Dull Knife, my friend from the old days. How did you get here? The sun will be bright today. Come in, come in and warm yourselves. Alice will prepare some hot broth."

As soon as all identities were known, Blue Thunder informed Evensigh that Turtleheart lived with he and his family. "He is gone on a scouting mission now, but will be back soon."

"I have waited to see him for so long now, I do not know whether I can wait longer." she exclaimed. "I will go to the agency and wait for him there."

"No, he might not go to the agency, but come here first," Blue Thunder explained. This convinced her to remain.

Turtleheart was just inside the agency gates when the army loafers crowded about to question about the chase. The end of Dull Knife and his band plagued Turtleheart so deeply, their inquisitive words gave him a headache.

He was greatly relieved to see Strong Echo walking toward him. "Come on, Turtleheart, I have your food rations with me. Let's go home."

On the ride to Wounded Knee, Strong Echo's mind was filled with questions he wished to ask about the Cheyennes, but the scowl on Turtleheart's face prompted him to hold his tongue. When they reached the wagon trail going down the slope into Wounded Knee Creek, he was glad to be able to break the silence.

"Strangers are in the camp. Do you see the horses staked out by Blue Thunder's lodge?"

"Yes, I see them," answered Turtleheart. "I wonder."

"They do not look like Indian ponies," Strong Echo added. "Hey, your horse is beginning to limp, Turtleheart."

"Yes, but we are nearly there." He kept his eyes trained on the persons who just made an exit from the lodge. He unconsciously patted the neck of his horse. No, he did not recognize them.

Turtleheart flung himself from his horse and dropped to one knee to attend to the horse's lame foot. "I wonder who they are," he mused, as someone came to the entrance of the lodge.

He thrust his knife into the ground and rose. Had he seen a dream? The way the girl's head tilted to one side, her eyes, the way she looked at him?

He blinked to clear his vision and looked again, but directly. With trembling hands he touched her thin face, then cried, "Evensigh! Evensigh!"

With tears and sobs of joy, they embraced, to hug each other tightly and to kiss, and to kiss again and again.

CHAPTER THIRTY

The New Way of Life

The Sioux Indian Reservation in 1883, showed but few changes, except that now nearly all families owned a wagon and a team of horses. Food regulations and distributions were as always, a dismal failure.

Civilization, which was to be brought to the Indians by the "Great White Father", in exchange for the land and freedom of the people, now appeared to be merely courtship promises which never were intended to be kept.

By treaty and by sale, the territory of the Teton Sioux had dwindled from two thousand acres per person in 1851, to around two hundred acres in 1883. The most valuable treasures of gold, other minerals and timber, were gone.

For two years, Turtleheart and Evensigh lived along White Clay Creek on their allotted land. The three hundred twenty acres of rocky, uneven ground, narrowed by small hills, lay five miles north of the agency. Turtleheart's canvas tipi was staked a few paces from the curve of the creek, with a giant cottonwood tree nearby to provide shade.

On clear days such as this one, Turtleheart could view the Black Hills from the tipi. When Evensigh saw him standing there with a wistful expression on his face as he looked at the familiar vista, she knew what was on his mind. She went to him, and said, "I am glad we are going to be farmers."

Turtleheart turned to her and grasped her with a playful hug. After a thoughtful pause, he questioned, "Do you still like it here?"

"Yes, this is our land, yours and mine. Here we are our own leaders. We don't have to conceal our ways from anyone. We do not even have to conceal our thoughts from each other." She snuggled closer to him and grinned. "And besides, you're here."

"You don't mind living on dried foods, eating leaves and wild roots and perhaps a prairie dog or rabbit?"

"No. How many times must you ask me that? I have told you before that food keeps me alive so I can be next to you. When I am with you, I am happy. What more is there to ask?"

"Your words are comforting." Turtleheart smiled at her. "I am getting attached to our land too, but I wish it would grow something besides dust."

"Turtleheart, I hated to leave Wounded Knee. I felt warm toward it, because that is where we were reunited. It was there that my happiness came back."

He gave Evensigh a playful slap on the backside and said, "Of course the meat was plentiful too." They both remembered the small herds of cattle which had been brought into Wounded Knee for butchering. But they were both thinking back when the cattle no longer came.

In the midst of a great feast, the Indian Agent told them that the cattle would no longer come. The commodities were to consist mainly of beans and flour; but there would be seed for farming for those who wished to make the effort to make adjustments to the white man's manner of living.

Many lean months followed that day, and only families with children were given any extra commodities. By necessity, the Indians started to make awkward use of the plows which had been lying around unused for three years.

Turtleheart lived in a world of disheartening confusion. For months he and Evensigh were on the ragged edge of starvation. He also wondered why Strong Echo never came to visit them. He wondered about many things, until one night he came face to face with the brutal facts of life. The government was trying to force the Indian to subsist on his labors in a foreign world of farming.

They were not allowed to leave the reservation, and the buffalo had all been killed off long ago. They were not given the meat rations promised in the treaties, and the tasteless beans and flour issued to them was the alternative to starving.

When the government issued plows to men used to riding all day on a wiry pony or driving an arrow through a charging bull buffalo, he left out one important detail. No one told them how to be a farmer. As a result, it was not long before the will to wrest a living from the soil had gone.

Turtleheart put part of the blame on Strong Echo, as he had failed to keep his friend informed of how to enter into this strange program. He had wasted no time in hunting out Strong Echo, who was now corpulent with inactivity, at the agency.

Turtleheart had called him the Great Wide Father, the lazy Indian with a white man's body. They argued in cutting words, and Turtleheart was angry at himself for this situation, but pride kept him from retracing his steps to apologize to Strong Echo for many months.

The day of the apology, Turtleheart blamed his temper as a step toward the white way of life, and they made up. In fact his good friend, Strong Echo, helped Turtleheart make out his application for a piece of land.

After Turtleheart and Evensigh moved to White Clay Creek, they waited for months for their farm equipment to come in. A plow and a cultivator finally arrived and this encouraged him to make frequent trips to the agency with inquiries as to when he would receive seed. On each trip he took the opportunity to stop at the farm agent's building for information as to the best method to plant and cultivate.

When spring softened the ground, he spent many days practicing with his plow and cultivator. He worked hard at tilling the soil, clearing out the rocks, and finally planting the seed. It was a keen disappointment when a few sprouts appeared, only to wither and burn in the hot summer sun.

The disappointment stayed keen in his mind and he blamed himself, until Strong Echo told him one day that even the good farmers outside of the reservation had no crops. The extremely dry weather was to blame. So again they existed on rations and an occasional jack rabbit or grouse.

This spring, Turtleheart had renewed hopes and again he was laboriously working his fields. Bringing his mind back to the present, Turtleheart wondered just what time it was. He had been out there all morning and Evensigh came out at mid-day to find him dreaming instead of working. Realizing he had been caught dreaming he was a little angry.

"Turtleheart," her words interrupted his thoughts. "Please let me do this."

"No," he replied sharply.

"Won't you even let me help you?"

"No, I think not. I must do this alone." The look of anger melted into a smile. "Forgive me, but our old ways are gone forever, and this is what I must do. Don't you understand? This is a man's job, and only I can do it."

Evensigh left and Turtleheart continued at his task until almost dark, hoping that the activity of his body would conquer the soil. He plowed the lower slopes, holding the plow handles and the horse's reins around his shoulders. With his back straining, his feet stumbling over the clods of earth, he forced the metal point deep into the soil.

When he went back to his tipi for a meal of beans and salt pork, Evensigh had encouraging words for him, but she had been thinking of the sadness of Dull Knife. Day after day he took his robe to the top of a small rise, to sit like a statue, cursing the fate that left him to die alone. In the past, Evensigh had tried to cheer him by going to visit and talk. He was always polite, but silent. His heart carried a heavy load and he preferred to be alone, so she no longer went to his lodge. Perhaps he was right when he said an Indian belonged on the open prairies, not tied to a plow like a beast of burden.

As Turtleheart hobbled his horse the next evening, a sound of laughter came from his tipi. A stranger's voice was singing, "A rabbit got jealous and kicked his tail off. That is why it lives in humiliation." The song of the stranger was lost in the sound of laughter.

As Turtleheart listened to the sounds of merriment, he forgot his aching body. It had been a long time since he had heard Evensigh laugh like that. His curiosity aroused, he hurried to join those in his tipi.

"Ah, Turtleheart," welcomed Strong Echo. "I want you to meet Silas Fast Horse. He is a heyoka, a clown looking for a temporary shelter."

"Hau, Turtleheart," Silas greeted. The heyoka sprang to his feet to grasp Turtleheart's hand with both of his.

"Hau, Silas. We will be glad to have you here, to enjoy our food and lodging." He was remembering how unselfish Blue Thunder had been in taking him in.

"I am glad for all of you," Strong Echo said, with a broad smile on his face. "I am sure you and Evensigh could use him and his wit around here. He can chop your wood, haul water, hunt the prairie food, cheer you up. In fact, this heyoka will grow on you." He finished by slapping Silas on the knee.

"Where are you from, Silas?" Turtleheart asked.

"Originally, I came from the Iron Shield band. Then I chose to pick up the lance with Sitting Bull. We lived in the north until he decided to flee the land of the Red Coats. I have been staked to the Standing Rock Reservation north of here ever since. It took me eighteen moons to finally grip a transfer down here."

"Sitting Bull," mused Turtleheart. "How is he and Gall getting on?"

"You know Sitting Bull. He is still a pompous old man, and he always seems to have the government guessing about his conduct. As for Gall, he appears to be always mourning. He does not do too much, and hardly speaks at all. He is far different than old talks-too-much."

Turtleheart let his mind dwell on his Hunka relative, and understanding why he wore a wet blanket.

When Silas stepped outside to bring Strong Echo's horse, Strong Echo whispered in a guarded tone. He told Turtleheart and Evensigh that Silas' wife had been killed in a fall from her horse ten winters ago. His mother and father and two children were killed by the soldiers as they were returning from the Little Big Horn with Iron Shield's band.

"That is when I lost my grandmother," recalled Turtleheart.

"And yet, he likes to make other people laugh," Evensigh spoke admiringly.

"I think that he does this to hide himself," Strong Echo spoke rapidly as the humorous song came out of the darkness. "A rabbit got jealous and kicked off his tail. That is why it lives in humiliation."

The next day the dust lay heavy over the tilled land along Clay Creek. Turtleheart spent the morning around the tipi. When the wind did not let up by noon, he became frightened and sat against the huge cottonwood trunk to watch the soil blow away.

Evensigh came out wearing an ankle length calico dress. "How do you like the dress Strong Echo brought me?"

"I like it, but I wish it was green instead of yellow." He didn't know why he said that.

Evensigh knew however. "Turtleheart, you have had nothing but the color of green on your mind for a month. I'll forgive you." She spoke with happy light in her eyes. Looking at Turtleheart, her mood was quick to change. "You are thinking of that awful wind, aren't you? I wish I could be of more help to you," Evensigh said pensively. "The training I received in St. Louis was so different that it is useless." Suddenly she laughed, "I wonder what Michael would think of me now?"

"You are of more help than you realize," Turtleheart said affectionately.

Day after day the hot wind blew. The days of drought stretched into weeks, and when nothing sprouted in the scorched soil, Turtleheart's hopes vanished. His mind in darkness, his hands in the light, he dug into the earth only to find the hard pellets of corn and beans and squash seeds. Even the potatoes shriveled to dried hunks of nothing.

Even Silas had his job cut out for him to keep Turtleheart smiling. However, this second failure was too great for the would-be farmer. His hopes had shriveled with the seed, and his spirit was washed away by the one cloudburst of the summer. For days he was nervous and irritable, baffling even his good friend, Strong Echo.

The following spring, Turtleheart waited to see how nature dealt with the white farmers. He neither plowed nor planted, and by early summer he was glad he had not wasted his time and his strength. The drought clung to the earth for miles around, and the relentless winds blew across the Dakota Territory.

When the next planting season opened the face of the earth, Turtleheart had given up all hope or thought of farming. By now he had become a regular recipient of dried commodities. His plow lay idle and rusting against the huge cottonwood.

CHAPTER THIRTY-ONE

The Black Robe

In the fall of 1886, a Blackrobe came to the reservation, and tirelessly preached a new doctrine. His knowledge of the Sioux language was astonishing, even though his words were of the Santee dialect.

In a small, open buggy, heaped with camping supplies, he traveled the autumnal season over the reservation. He consoled the sad, quieted the children, shared his food. He also gave away many clothes and small gifts with no sign of expecting anything in return.

He never volunteered information about himself, and the Sioux would not ask, so no one knew where he came from. He proved to be a figure of considerable interest, this stout man clothed in flowing black robes. The Indians did not look upon him as being a white man and considered him a strange one, one who somehow had the spirit of Wakan Tanka in him.

Slowly, he won their trust, and they listened as he spoke of his doctrine. With signs and diagrams, he told them many times that he was sent to teach them of The One Above.

Before the snows of winter came to cover the ground, the tent of the Blackrobe was set up on White Clay Creek just one mile from Turtleheart and Evensigh. It was not long after this that the gray clouds of the first storm hovered over the earth to chill everything. It snowed off and on for nearly a month, the northern winds stopping only in the darkness of night. The snow would stop as if in collaboration with the coyotes who could be heard howling in the sudden stillness. When the storm moved on, many of the trees were collapsed in defeat.

All during this blizzard, Turtleheart, Evensigh and Silas stayed close to the lodge. Not having much food, they ate very sparingly while waiting for the snow to cease. On the first day of brilliant sunshine, they heard the dog barking.

Silas was the first to peer through the tipi entrance. "It is Strong Echo. Blue Thunder and the Blackrobe are with him," he exclaimed. They stepped out to greet the visitors, but as it was very cold, they sought the warmth of the lodge.

"We brought meat and rice, Evensigh." Strong Echo handed her a burlap bag. This food would be a welcome change for everyone, so she busied herself by preparing a noon meal.

The entire meal was eaten in silence, and it was only after Evensigh had scraped the remaining rice into a hide bowl that she spoke. "It is good to see you again, Blue Thunder, but a man of your age should not be on the trail in this weather. The paths are still hidden and hazardous."

"It was not this way when I started," he answered. "The climate of the hunt was upon me when I left Wounded Knee. I was on my way here when the storm forced me to go to the agency. They have been holding me as prisoner until yesterday." His face was very serious as he said this, but he had to laugh out loud when he saw the expression on Turtleheart's face.

"They treated me as a child in the infirmary. Every day some one came to hear me breathe, to feed me hot broth, to put many blankets on me. I am not used to such treatment and I had to wait for a chance to escape." They all laughed in appreciation of his wry humor.

Strong Echo concluded Blue Thunder's tale. "When he came to my office, he sneaked in as if an enemy war party were about to discover him. He rushed to me and asked me to get him out of there." Strong Echo roared with glee.

"I did not have the coughing sickness," interjected Blue Thunder, "nor am I a child, and to be kept in that crazy sick house was not my idea."

The Blackrobe now took up the story. "When they passed my humble camp, I asked them where they were going. When they said here, I came along." He spoke softly, but all were surprised his voice carried so well. "Does it snow like this often?"

"No," Blackrobe. This is very heavy for being so early," Turtleheart explained.

"I pray God has protected all of his children of the bow and arrow," the Blackrobe spoke slowly, but with concern.

"Do not worry," Strong Echo assured, "we sent riders from camp to camp to check. I am sure everyone is all right. They even reported seeing smoke come from your tent."

"Why didn't they come in?"

"Our people like and respect you, but they do not understand you yet," Strong Echo told him. "Do you get lonesome out here by yourself?" he suddenly asked.

"At first perhaps, as I missed the trees and the green of the meadows, but this is now my home and you are my brothers." He stopped before asking, "Do you believe in a Supreme Being?"

"In Wakan Tanka? Yes, we believe as the Santee. He is the one who created everything," Strong Echo answered.

"Then your religion is based partly on mythology, partly legend; your rituals must bear this out?"

Strong Echo turned to Blue Thunder for assistance, but the Yuwipi man had his head bowed and did not answer. When it was evident he was not going to speak, Strong Echo endeavored to carry on the conversation.

"Yes, our rituals are all given for Wakan Tanka. One of our highest ceremonies is the sun dance, and it is given to the sun as the sun is the greatest power of the Holy Mystery."

"You do not pray directly to the sun?"

"No, the sun is just a symbol of His power. Nagi Tanka, the name of the sun, means great power or great symbol, and that is all. The sun is not a deity."

"Strong Echo, you have just told me something I have been searching for."

"I am only a brave. You should be talking to a Yuwipi man like Blue Thunder. He knows of the mysteries."

"Ah, I did not know that, Blue Thunder. I do not want to offend you, but could you tell me a little of the Yuwipi?"

"Blackrobe," cautioned Blue Thunder. "I have taken a vow to not reveal my knowledge. All I can tell you is what everyone already knows." He did not look at anyone when he spoke. "The giver of the good life is Wakan Tanka and we do not express our gratitude in any special way other than the offering of the pipe. There are many ways our people worship the Great One."

"Many ways?"

"To the Sioux, all of the ways are good. We teach our children that the way is not as important as the belief. Only Wakan Tanka himself knows which form is the most pleasing to him; it is not for us to know, but we must believe in the hereafter."

"I believe that Strong Echo said the sun dance was your highest ceremony."

"Yes, it is. One of the rewards of performing the sun dance is the gaining of a better knowledge of our spiritual beliefs. During the vision quest or the sweat bath or the dance one learns that nature is the substance of our knowledge."

"What is gained from our inner nature is exact knowledge, which gives us a far-reaching outlook over the earth. The many powers of inner nature are hidden in everyone, and these are identified with Wakan Tanka."

"Forgive me, Blue Thunder," Turtleheart interrupted, "but I must say this. The greatest obstacle to the internal nature is the mind. If it relies on logic such as the white man's mind, the domain of the inner nature is not accessible. The simple fact is a man does not challenge the wisdom of the Holy Mystery."

"Very interesting," commented the Blackrobe. "I would like to stay and learn more, but I must go." Turning to Silas he asked, "Silas, could you help me at my camp?"

"If I can be of any help, yes."

"Good for you Silas. Do not forget to come and visit us," Turtleheart reminded.

As the two men started to walk up the snowy path, those in the lodge could hear the familiar, "A rabbit got jealous and kicked off his tail . . ."

CHAPTER THIRTY-TWO

A NEW RELIGION

In the late summer of 1890, Evensigh was helping at the mission school. On this particular day, Turtleheart had spread a blanket in the shade and was playing with his eight-month old son. This was Evensigh's day to be at the school, and Turtleheart frequently looked up the road to see if she was coming.

When Evensigh first began helping the Blackrobe, she would walk home in the evening, declining the offer of the priest's buggy. Later she realized she should accept the offer, as these occasions were the only opportunities the Blackrobe had to visit Turtleheart.

Her husband helped Silas around the school two mornings a week, but the Blackrobe was always so busy with his schedule, he didn't have time to visit. The school had grown into a full mission now, and the only time the two men talked was when Evensigh came home in the buggy.

He could hear them coming before he saw them. Evensigh was holding the reins and the Blackrobe relaxed to listen to the noise of the wheels and to enjoy the countryside.

The trees were already turning color. It was going to be an early fall and there were more mouths to feed this winter with less food. Perhaps next year, he dreamed, he could do more.

As Turtleheart watched the priest get out of the buggy, the late sun made the round face appear redder than usual. The same eager smile was still present however.

"Turtleheart, what can be done about falling hair? Don't you people have a strong medicine for that?"

"It is that little cap you wear," Turtleheart teased as the priest bared his balding head. "There is no medicine for that. Anyway, you can't grow any taller, so you are spreading in the middle."

"That is a little different from what Silas tells me," the Blackrobe spoke with a flash of humor. "He says the Sioux are sneaky enough to be scalping me, and I have been too busy converting them and haven't noticed."

When the sounds of laughter died away, the Blackrobe asked, "How old are you now? I have been meaning to ask you."

Turtleheart did not answer. He went into the tipi and came out with his winter count. "Here is my calendar; count each symbol."

"Well now, there are . . . thirty-six of them. You are thirty-six years old."

"Thirty-seven," corrected Turtleheart. "I have not added this winter's symbol yet."

"Turtleheart, here, take the baby." It was Evensigh as she approached with the boy.

"How is this little one?" Blackrobe asked as he chucked the baby under the chin.

"He is so quiet that I am afraid one of these days he will be playing with a snake and I won't know it. I always have to check on him," Evensigh said as she blew against Little Sun's neck. Little Sun giggled with the ticklish sensation.

"He is a typical man-child," Blackrobe smiled. "And so is Silas. He is a remarkable gardener. He knows and understands the earth and he plays with it as though he had a secret way." Blackrobe looked intently at Turtleheart and continued, "Silas has kept his head and does not feel despair. He does not yearn for the past."

The sound of a horse at the trot caused all to turn toward the creek. "Hau!" greeted Strong Echo.

"Hello. I am glad you came. I was just going to ask our friend to robe himself with the Christian faith."

"Having any luck?"

"Blackrobe, my old Sioux faith is all I have left of the old way." Turtleheart spoke with an air of finality. "You have baptized my wife and my son, and you have given us food and clothing, but I am not ready. When the white men have learned to live as you say, I will look at your way again."

"You must remember Blackrobe, that Turtleheart is an earthman. An Indian such as he can stand at the mouth of two mighty rivers, and all he can see is a promising school of fish or a beautiful stream to float his canoe."

With a sweeping motion of his hand, Strong Echo continued, "He sees buffalo on the prairie and thinks only of food and robes, he sees the mountains and thinks of turkey and deer. The white man sees the same things but he sees cities, gold, silver, cattle."

Evensigh could sense a great oratory coming and wishing to change the subject, she put her arms around Turtleheart before saying, "Next time you see Silas, ask him to show you what he is making out of a large log."

"You must," interjected the Blackrobe. "He is carving a statue of the Blessed Mother for our school. It is astounding what that heyoka can do with his hands. Evensigh has already named the statue 'The Lady of the Teton'. It is beautiful."

"Even her eyes are proud," exclaimed Evensigh. "Silas is rubbing it with a stone to polish it. Both of you must see it."

"It is getting late and I must get back to the school. Which way are you headed Strong Echo?"

"I was heading that way, Blackrobe."

"Good. Tie your horse onto the buggy and ride with me."

"If you wish. Goodbye everyone. I will be back soon."

As the buggy jolted across the rutted road, Blackrobe asked, "Strong Echo, can you tell me about this ghost dance religion?"

"There is not much to tell, except they all wear long sack-like shirts of muslin. They are painted with certain symbols and are supposed to ward off bullets."

"What do they do, dance?"

"The dance is the important part. They start the dance in the ancient way by sidestepping, then as the dance progresses, the momentum speeds up gradually until the dancers are in small circle groups. The fast pace makes them frenzied and one by one they collapse to the ground."

"Interesting, but they are foolish to believe in this." Blackrobe's voice sounded perturbed.

"You certainly found many things to pray for when you came here to this land."

"This is the land of sorrow, but then there are other lands of sorrow too. You find them all over. Tell me, is it true that the government is going to reduce the food rations again?"

"I wish it were not true, but yes, they are. The men in Washington have chosen a bad time to make the Indians independent of the government."

"Don't they know that we have had drought in the area for the past several years?"

"I suppose they know, but they do not care what happens away from where they live. It makes me sad when I see Turtleheart. He used to smile, but now he is grim and just sits at home. He is lost within himself, like the others, as they do not know what to do. They have no jobs, no education and without them they have no future."

"No wonder my people grasp at the last ray of hope the ghost dance religion promises. This is their last stand."

"They are putting their faith in the supernatural because they think there is nothing else for them to believe in. My job is to convince them they must put their faith in God, and I must hurry. Look up ahead, those people are at the mission because they do believe."

The usual gathering was at the mission kitchen. They had traveled a long ways to see their children and were now waiting for the Blackrobe to feed them in accordance with custom. The priest counted them while mentally picturing his food cellar with its dwindling supplies.

"Food is a precious commodity here, and every time I see these people waiting at the kitchen, I cannot but help think that Christ was speaking of people such as these when He told the parable of the Good Samaritan."

When the buggy stopped, the Blackrobe reached into the folds of his robe and pulled out a handful of candy. He tossed the candy to the young boys who scrambled up to the buggy.

CHAPTER THIRTY-THREE

Apprehension

It was early autumn and the wild rumors about the ghost dance religion grew and multiplied. As a result of the dance performances, the military sent fresh troops into the area, and this action brought panic to the Sioux. Fearing the soldiers had come to kill them because of their ghost dancing, the religious practitioners fled their homes and went to the badlands. There, they felt they could practice their cult while anticipating their deliverance.

Rumors were spreading like fire now, and the police were sent to arrest Sitting Bull, as they feared what he might do. The Indian police entered his log house and brought him out, despite his vehement objections.

Sitting Bull's band pressed close around them, and his cries of Crazy Horse's fate soon triggered a pitched battle between his followers and the police. The Hunkpapa medicine man went down with a yell of defiance.

At news of Sitting Bull's death, even the friendly Indians who were not participants in the ghost dance movement, fled in fear of the soldiers. In consequence, the death of the Hunkpapa leader began a mass movement into the badlands.

Other Indians, especially those with children attending the mission school, moved closer to the mission for refuge. Turtleheart and Evensigh were among the first to move onto the mission grounds where he offered his services to Blackrobe.

Days of fear and unrest followed this influx of people, and the Blackrobe's face was creased with worry as he and the four 'holy women' struggled to help the refugees. Working from dawn until far after dark, they could not stretch the days long enough.

Turtleheart's offer to assist was gratefully accepted, and he was assigned to the task of caring for the needs of the camped Indians. He now had something besides himself to worry about, and the responsibility felt good.

One morning, as Turtleheart was assigning the daily camp chores to the people, Blackrobe silently strode up to him and whispered, "If you wish to use only a part of the name of the school use the first and not the last."

"I am sorry," Turtleheart said. "From now on I will call it as you do, 'Holy Rosary'."

"You visited the church?"

"Yes."

"What took you there? Did you like it?"

"It is mysterious and quiet."

"Turtleheart, have you ever thought that this all means as much to me as your Black Hills do to you?"

"I was thinking that just last night. Two days ago I went into your church, and yesterday, Evensigh, my son and I went. She explained many things to me, but I do not understand yet."

Turtleheart raised one hand as Blackrobe started to speak. "No, do not try to explain any more. I know our ideals are the same, but the paths are different."

"As a Sioux, I consider myself as the highest form of life under Wakan Tanka. When I turn to a higher power, I turn to the Holy Mystery. I pray to Him through the four winds, the trees, the other things He has put on this earth."

When Turtleheart detected a flicker of understanding in the Blackrobe's eyes, he added, "In time to come, I may discover that your trail is the right trail. If that time comes, I will kneel in front of you for the Christian totem."

"Hau Kola." It was Strong Echo who interrupted them by walking around the tipi they were standing in front of. "Don't you ever do anything but talk? Every time I see you two together you are talking the council fire to a high heat." A hearty laugh brought smiles to Turtleheart and the Blackrobe.

"I am hard about my business of saving souls, Strong Echo. I was about to tell Turtleheart that man is dependent upon man for many things, and that all men are dependent upon God for salvation. God will rightfully fix the blame for wrongs on those who refuse justice for others." Blackrobe bowed his head in prayer.

After a moment of silence, Turtleheart asked, "Strong Echo, how do things look to you? They are not looking good to me."

"No, Turtleheart. I am afraid of what might happen. That is why I came to see you. There are many groups from other reservations going to the badlands."

"Other reservations?"

"Yes. Short Bull and Kicking Bear are the leaders, and I have been told that they are holding a tight rein. Anyway there have not been any demonstrations of war yet."

"What are they doing?"

"The agency is getting many reports of cattle stealing and destruction of property, but there has been no report of violence to the settlers," Strong Echo shrugged his shoulders.

"You think they will send soldiers to the field?"

"That is what it is all leading up to, and you know what can happen if that is done?"

"It is not good," exclaimed Turtleheart vehemently.

"I have also heard that Big Foot and his band have decided to come into the agency to surrender."

The Blackrobe broke into the conversation with, "When did you get this information, Strong Echo?"

"Just last night. A runner brought in the information that Big Foot is seriously ill with pneumonia sickness, and that the band has no leader who is able, so they wish to surrender."

"Big Foot has been one of the last to come in, so this is a good sign. Which way are they coming?" Turtleheart queried.

"From the north."

"What if they contact Short Bull or Kicking Bear?"

"You know the answer to that Turtleheart. They could join the ghost dancers and decide not to come in."

"Strong Echo. Would it be best if I rode north to intercept them before they are contacted?"

"Yes, by all means." Blackrobe's voice was firm. "You must go to them and bring them here. Does the military have the information on Big Foot?"

"I do not think so," Strong Echo shook his head. "But they are planning to go with a civilian delegation to see Short Bull and Kicking Bear for a parley."

"Civilians taking troops with them to the badlands could create a crisis. What will the Indians think, and what will be their reaction to the soldiers?" Blackrobe mused this question over for a moment, then suddenly raised his hand.

"I am sure that bloodshed can be avoided by reason, so I must go to Short Bull and Kicking Bear to help them. Turtleheart, you take the best horse in the corral. Find Silas and ask him to get my buggy ready for a fast trip." Blackrobe now turned abruptly and headed for his room in the mission. A worried frown creased his forehead and he muttered to himself.

CHAPTER THIRTY-FOUR

THE LAST BATTLE

A few days later, Turtleheart was leading Big Foot's band through the southern flanks of the badlands. He was exhausted but happy. Wasn't this like he used to live? To put physical strength to the test when conditions demanded was the good life.

Turtleheart rode alongside the wagon which carried Big Foot, but the sick leader had little to say. It seemed that he had given up his leadership, so he just lay there in the wagon box. Occasionally an attendant would lift his head to give him a mouthful of water.

About the time the sun was at its highest, the small caravan was met by a group of troopers. At the first appearance of the cavalry, Big Foot commanded the raising of the white flag. A short talk ensued, and afterwards an interpreter informed Turtleheart that Major Whiteside demanded an unconditional surrender. Big Foot's request for negotiations on better treatment was rejected.

The soldiers took command of the Indian procession and set out for the agency. When they reached Wounded Knee Creek, the major ordered camp to be set up, even though it was still early in the day.

Turtleheart puzzled, "Why camp here when it is only seventeen miles to the agency? We could reach it before dark."

After the women had started the cooking fires, Turtleheart walked down the creek. Dropping to one knee, he scooped a handful of water and splashed it on his face. Refreshed, he stood up to look around. If Evensigh was along, they could go but a short way to visit the graves of their parents.

Soldiers appearing on top of a small hill drew Turtleheart's attention. They were pushing four cannon and facing them toward the encampment. His throat tightened and his heart raced as he knelt again to stare at the ground.

Big Foot must be warned. With quick steps, Turtleheart headed for Big Foot's tipi, hoping against hope that what he now suspected was not true.

Arriving at the camp he stepped into Big Foot's tipi without hesitation and announced what he had seen.

"Do not be alarmed, my relation." Big Foot spoke weakly from his propped position with a curious calm. "Our mistrusting captors are afraid, but they have nothing to fear, as I have given my word of surrender."

Big Foot held his weak words for a moment to regain his breath. "Their activities are an insult to my words, but the lake of calm will return to you if you glance outside and see the white flag staked near my wagon."

"I saw the flag. But I am not feeling easy about this." Turtleheart answered in a low voice.

"I do not like it either, but what can we do. They have four soldiers to every warrior of ours. Besides, where would we go? Turtleheart, I am an old man now, but there was a time when I had the strength of two warriors. Now I cannot fight any more, and I want to finish my days in peace." Big Foot was completely exhausted from his efforts to talk and he closed his eyes.

As Turtleheart stepped from the tipi, there was a sudden cold wind from the north. "The north wind is an ill omen at this time." He shivered from the cold and from the thoughts he had in his mind. Going back into the tipi he wondered how the Blackrobe was doing with Short Bull and Kicking Bear.

Blackrobe had been instrumental in bringing the consolidated bands into the agency. For two days he remained at the agency, impatiently awaiting for news of Turtleheart.

Late on the third day, Strong Echo rode into the Holy Rosary Mission and rushed into the Blackrobe's office. Evensigh saw him, and she immediately blanketed Little Sun over her back. A cold wind had now come up so she lost little time in getting to Blackrobe. She was only halfway, when Strong Echo ran out to his horse, to mount and ride away at a gallop.

Her heart was in her mouth as she anxiously asked of news of Turtleheart.

"Yes, my dear girl. Turtleheart is with Big Foot's band and they are camped up on the Wounded Knee. They will arrive here tomorrow, so do not worry. Strong Echo told me the news."

"I am so relieved, Father," Evensigh spoke with a deep sigh, the tightness gone from her chest. "I must worry about Turtleheart, he and his son mean so much to me."

"How is the little one?" asked Blackrobe.

"I can see he is asleep already," she laughed.

Blackrobe peered beneath the blankets to see the baby, then patted the covers very gently.

"Do you know any more about the ghost dancers?" she asked.

"No, but my eyes and ears give me quick understanding. The ghost dance is nothing more than a curious doctrine touched with Christianity. It is superstitious, but inviting to hungry and desperate people."

"It is pitiful to see the hungry bodies, but it is also pitiful to think of their starving souls. They are trying to reach the unknown, so they cannot be condemned, but someday they will have to pay for their sins." The Blackrobe lowered his head and gave a short prayer.

"I must leave, Father. Little Sun is getting heavy and the wind is turning cold. Thank you for your kind words. I will sleep better tonight because of them."

"I have more good news, Evensigh. Strong Echo is going to join the Christian faith."

"Today has been good to us. May tomorrow be just as kind. Goodnight." As Evensigh went outside she looked at the sky and shivered. The north wind and the ominous clouds to the north seemed foreboding. Their prophecy was of no comfort.

As she walked away, she hummed Silas' rabbit song. The thought of the words made her spirits rise and she felt better.

In the darkness of the night, Evensigh heard a scratching noise which aroused her from a light sleep. "Who is there?"

"Strong Echo," a voice answered.

"What is wrong?" Her heart told her all was not well. "Get dressed. I have something to tell you. This is very important."

"Yes, yes. Just a moment."

"Evensigh?"

"Yes, Strong Echo, I am hurrying."

"I can talk to you while you are getting dressed. A scout returned to the agency from Wounded Knee. He slipped away to tell me that Custer's old cavalry command arrived at Wounded Knee with Big Foot and his band. Colonel Forsythe is the commander, and in the morning he is going to demand the Indians to give up all their guns and other weapons." Strong Echo was now shivering in the mounting cold.

Evensigh let Strong Echo into the tipi and stared at him with frightened eyes. "You fear trouble," she stated flatly.

"The words of the scout trouble me, as I know some of the warriors will accept this order as a challenge. Big Foot's band has come a long way to surrender of their own free will, and to have this happen could be disastrous. They will not give up their weapons until the peace talks are over."

"What can I do to help? I fear for the safety of Turtleheart if there is trouble." Evensigh could hardly breathe, her throat was so constricted.

"If there is any trouble, Evensigh, Turtleheart must not be involved. After being with him for thirteen years, I know he will stick with his own people. We must get him away from Wounded Knee."

"How, Strong Echo? Do you have a plan?"

Leaning closer to her so as not to disturb the others who were still sleeping, he whispered, "I have a wagon with a pair of fast horses hidden." He motioned with his hand toward the foot of the low hills.

"You pick up Little Sun, take the wagon and go straight to Wounded Knee Creek. Follow it upstream until you are near the encampment. It will be daylight by then and you will see it. Hide Little Sun and go straight to the lodge."

"How will I know which lodge he is in?" she asked.

"I do not know. You will have to ask, but when you find him, tell him you and Little Sun have come after him. I am sure Turtleheart will go with you when you tell him Little Sun is down by the creek, and you left him there because you fear the trouble which may come."

"Yes, I will do anything to get Turtleheart away from there."

"Good. Do you understand all that I have told you?"

"Yes." She nodded assent.

"Take my coat with you. The north wind has snow in it, and Turtleheart is not dressed for this cold weather."

"What will you do, Strong Echo?"

"I am going back to the agency to find out more, then I will ride to Wounded Knee. Now hurry, but be very careful."

The night seemed to last an eternity to Evensigh as she made her way to Wounded Knee. The gray light of dawn was beginning to be seen when she rounded a turn of the creek and saw the dim shapes of the tipis in the distance. With all haste, she did as Strong Echo directed her, and walked to the village to find Turtleheart.

The soldiers paid little attention to her as she inquired as to the whereabouts of Turtleheart. Finding out where he was, she entered the lodge quickly.

"Evensigh! What are you doing here?" was his greeting.

"Please Turtleheart, do not be angry with me, but listen to what I have to say." She quietly told him why she was there.

"You go to the wagon, and I will join you as soon as I can. We cannot leave Little Sun alone," Turtleheart commanded.

A little later, the command for the people of Big Foot's band to assemble was heard. It was just eight o'clock in the morning when he stepped out of the lodge.

"Hau, my friend." The voice startled him.

"Strong Echo!"

Breaking the clasp of hands, Strong Echo feigned surprise as he asked. "How long has Evensigh been with you?"

"Not long. How did you know?"

"She is waiting for you in the wagon, and is waving for you to join her. What are you waiting for?" Strong Echo was insistent.

Turtleheart turned to walk away when he was stopped by a soldier. Strong Echo stepped up quickly and said, "He has been a good soldier scout, and that woman is his school teacher wife."

The soldier looked skeptical and said, "She don't look like a school teacher to me. Say, is she a white woman?"

"Yes. She has lived in St. Louis," hastily replied Strong Echo. "Come on, you can see for yourself." They had started for the wagon when Blue Thunder arrived at the wagon and attached a white flag to the near back corner of the box.

The soldier made his examination and walked back to the camp. Blue Thunder and Turtleheart urged the horses to move. "Where is the boy?" asked her husband.

"Do you see that tall cottonwood over on the other side of the creek? He is just below them in some plum bushes."

"Here, Strong Echo wants you to have his coat. He knew you did not have one."

"Hah, a cavalry coat. That is good." Turtleheart turned to see where Strong Echo was. "Aren't you coming with us?"

"No, Turtleheart," replied his old friend. "I will stay here for now. I will be over tomorrow night." He was already taking long strides toward the encampment.

As the wagon jolted across the rough ground, Evensigh was about to speak to Blue Thunder when they all heard a single gun shot. This was followed almost immediately by a volley of many guns and much shouting.

Shouting to the horses and snapping the reins with force, the rattling wheels echoed the faster pace. Crossing the creek without slackening the pace, Turtleheart headed the horses for the tall cottonwood tree.

Chancing a quick glance over his shoulder, he was just in time to see the bursts of shells exploding in the midst of the Indians. Strong Echo was there with them. His face was a mask of rage as he beat the horses into a faster run.

Jerking on the reins as he neared the tree, he slowed the horses; he searched for the blanketed form of Little Sun. Evensigh and Blue Thunder were raising themselves from their prone positions in the wagon box when it happened.

There was a terrific explosion and a blinding flash. The wagon was lifted and shattered, its occupants thrown into the air. The horses were no longer attached to the wagon, and they ran in terror down the creek bank.

Turtleheart found himself lying on the ground, his left arm numb and oozing with blood. Raising himself with all the strength he had, he looked for Evensigh and Blue Thunder. The realization that they had been hit by a shell from one of the cannons on the hill, filled his mind with complete and utter hatred.

Evensigh lay some distance from the remains of the wagon, so staggering to his feet, he half ran, half crawled to her side. He touched her eyes, her cheeks, her lips in shocked disbelief. His child did not have a mother.

Blue Thunder lay in a grotesque fashion and Turtleheart knew he was also beyond help. Ignoring the pain in his shoulder, the grieved Turtleheart ran erratically from bush to bush in a desperate search for his son.

Blood was running down his arm and dripping from his fingers, his head whirled, but he knew he had to find Little

Sun. He finally did see the blanket. Falling to his knees he crawled to the boy, where he crouched and fought for breath.

Javelins of pain were shooting through his arm and shoulder and his vision blurred. The sounds of battle had ceased and only the wind was heard as it moaned a funeral dirge for the dead and dying. Looking up through the limbs of the bush, Turtleheart watched the swirling flakes as if hypnotized.

Regaining his senses, he automatically felt of his shoulder. Sitting up to unbutton Strong Echo's coat, he exposed the wound. It was bleeding profusely, but here were some dead leaves under the bush. Crushing them with his good hand he put them on the wound until the bleeding stopped.

Sounds of soldiers in the area were of apprehension to Turtleheart, so he and the boy remained hidden until the darkness of night had settled around them. There was only one haven he could think of, the Blackrobe. He must get to the mission.

Desperately and without even knowing how he did it, he tore one blanket and made a sling for his arm. Reaching beneath his shirt, he took out his winter count and formed a shield for Little Sun's face. All of his preparations done, he picked up the baby and cradled it in the sling on his arm.

He crawled from the thicket on his knees and rose to examine the terrain. With his back to the storm, he started on the long trek to the mission. His own warm breath would break the freeze for Little Sun and the sling offered support for his useless left arm which throbbed with pain.

Turtleheart walked until his body screamed for rest. The weight of Little Sun increased with every step, but he refused to sit down. It was many hours later when he noticed that it was not snowing, and it was getting much colder. The mounting cold shocked him as it seemed as though all of the elements of nature had turned upon him.

Even more distressing to Turtleheart was the absence of pain. In its place was a warm glow, which spread over his entire body. The freeze was starting to claim him. Struggling forward, he offered prayer after prayer to Wakan Tanka. Like a never ending nightmare, he pushed his heavy feet, one in front of the other.

He had reached the point of being halfway between self and unconsciousness, and memories of his life wound in and out of his mind. The vision quest, the sun dance, Evensigh's voice, the warm glow of the fire in the lodge, all appeared briefly in his mind's eye.

Eventually, Little Sun's cries brought him back to his senses. His mind began to clear, and he was able to see a dim shadow in the early morning light. Was this another vision or was that the mission? Blinking his frosted eyes, he prayed.

"Blackrobe, take my son. Take my son and give him protection, your kind protection. Blackrobe, take my son."

The Blackrobe was in the kitchen reciting his daily office. He frequently looked out through the frosted glass to see the dim figure of the Lady of the Teton. The murmuring voices from the early Mass soothed his troubled thoughts.

Approaching the mission with lurches, Turtleheart was falling time and again only to rise again with the unknown strength of desperation. Blackrobe stopped. Was that a human being out by the statue? Rubbing the frost from the glass, he stared intently in that direction.

"Sister!" he cried. "Sister, Sister, come quickly. There is someone out in the storm. Hurry!" He flung the door open and ran toward the now kneeling figure at the foot of the Lady of the Teton. A light-footed nun was right behind him.

Reaching Turtleheart, he heard the cry of a baby. With deft movements he brushed away the snow and removed the child from the sling. "It is Little Sun," he cried in astonishment. "Quick! Take him inside, he is half frozen."

Looking closely at the blue face of Turtleheart, he gasped and quickly he signed over the kneeling figure. The lips of the near-frozen hero moved, but there was no sound except a hoarse, indistinguishable word. They formed the word Blackrobe, and the priest knew what he was trying to say.

Gently the Blackrobe put his hand on the frosted head and administered the Christian totem. Turtleheart felt this touch and his tired mind knew that his prayers had been answered. The light faded from his eyes, his labored breathing faltered and stopped, and a small smile of thankfulness appeared as the frozen form fell forward in the snow. His spirit had gone to join his ancestors.